Devil's Heart

Native American Lore and Modern Police Work

Ron Walden

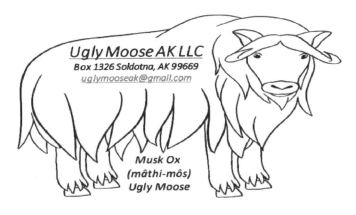

Musk Ox
(mâthi-môs)
Ugly Moose

ISBN 978-1-95-726303-8
eBook 978-1-95-726304-5
Library of Congress Catalog Card Number: 2009930221

Copyright by Ron Walden

2009 - First Edition
2022 - Second Edition

All rights reserved, including the right of reproduction in any form, or by any mechanical or electronic means including photocopying or recording, or by any information storage or retrieval system, in whole or in part in any form, and in any case not without the written permission of the author and publisher.

Manufactured in the United States of America.

Dedication

In memory of my dear friend,
Clarence "Etoncha" Longie

Acknowledgements

It is with great pleasure that I thank the many wonderful people who contributed to this book. When writing on any subject, it is necessary to glean information from every source possible. It is my objective to thank a few of those people now. Since I have little personal knowledge of Native American life, especially of life on the reservation, I traveled to North Dakota where I spent some time on the Fort Totten Reservation. I thank all the people there who made me feel at home. I hope I have done justice to the information you have given me.

I give special thanks to Fred and Helen Jacobs for allowing me to stay with them while researching this book. Helen, along with her associates in the library at the Four Winds School, gave me access to valuable information I could have learned no other way. I will always remember your hospitality and assistance.

My good friends, Clarence and Cathy Longie, loaned me many reference books and provided personal insights for me into life on the reservation. He has pointed out the error of which schools would have been attended during the period of time the characters would have been there. I have not corrected this only to simplify the reading for those outside the reservation. There would have been many other laughable errors in this text if not for the help of this good friend and his family.

Many of the legends and traditions quoted in this book were learned from Lenore White Lightning. She was an invaluable source during my research. These residents of the reservation, each and every one, were my sources in developing the personality for the main character in this book. I hope all of their personalities is reflected here, for each of them is a part of this book.

Special thanks must be paid to Dr. Paul Turner who helped me to develop the background and the personality of the villain portrayed in this text. As a psychologist he was able to give me a believable profile for the bad guy. With his help I hope I was able to represent this characters' proclivities without condoning or condemning his lifestyle.

This book was written on a new computer which I had no idea about operating. Thanks to patient tutoring by my friend Jason Elson I fumbled through. I thank him for finding all the lost chapter hidden inside this machine. Without you I might have been lost, along with the test, inside this electronic marvel.

Credit must be given to Marthy Johnson for editing this book and making it a readable work. She made me look good. And I thank Tom Willard for taking time from his Silver Salmon fishing to do the artwork on the cover. These two friends made this a professional literary work.

Most of all I thank my wife for basic editing and constructive criticism during the writing of this volume. She is my severest critic and my greatest inspiration. Without her I am not sure the book would have been finished

Finally I thank all my friends who encouraged me to write another book If you read this and are entertained, I accomplished my goal. I thank you all for your support.

CHAPTER 1

Only a few puffy white clouds were visible above the mountaintops, though the man on the radio had predicted rain. When rain came, in western Washington in mid-July, it usually meant light showers, and those came only here, at the base of the mountains.

Sheriff's Deputy Jodi Eagle had received the message when he reported into the office. Miss Emma, the secretary, had told him of a reported body, no other details. A Department of Highways foreman was on the scene with further information. The site was a few miles east of North Bend at exit 38. Jodi knew the area well; it was in his assigned patrol area, on U. S. Interstate 90 at the foot of Snoqualmie Pass.

Blue and gold stripes and red and blue lights buried in the grille, along with those in the rear window, identified the white Chevrolet as belonging to a King County Police official. Traffic was light this morning with only an occasional truck moving east over the pass. With three lanes going east and three lanes west and the lanes divided by a large median and in some places a huge vertical separation, there was no need for the siren.

Jodi saw the Department of Highways pickup parked on the side of the road as he turned down the ramp at Exit 38. Lenny Packwood stepped from the truck as Jodi pulled to a stop.

"What ya got, Lenny?"

"I didn't want to put any information on the open Highways channel, Jodi." His voice was weak, his shoulders sagged and his weathered face showed deep furrows from his obvious stress. "It's another kid." His eyebrows rose nearly to his hairline when he spoke, but from the sadness in his eyes you could see just how deeply he felt this. "He's down the old highway about a mile; in the rocks above the bridge. I didn't touch anything, except to climb up there and check to see if he was alive." Tears were in his eyes now. "God, Jodi. I've never seen a dead child like this. I'm sorry."

"I understand, Lenny. Come on, let's take a look." Jodi pointed down the road.

With the road foreman's truck in the lead they drove to the site. The foliage here in this deep canyon was lush and green. Because of the dense growth, visibility was limited to the road and the creek bed. A short, moss-covered concrete bridge spanned the small stream. The slope of the hill made it more a waterfall than a stream. Jodi noticed an old cedar stump with spring board notches. Loggers had cut the tree in the early 1900s. A green cedar tree with a base nearly as large as the old stump grew out of the old stump. *Life resurrected*, Jodi thought to himself.

Jodi walked to the orange pickup, and Lenny rolled down the window. "Wait here until I get back. I have to check. I'll be only a couple of minutes."

This was the third one in five weeks. As he walked to the guardrail he could see faint tire tracks and some scuff marks on the ground. He deliberately walked a wide path around the marks before stepping over the steel railing. The boulders, used to protect the creek bank, were large but about the right size to easily step from one to the next. He could see the body lying face down on a large, flat rock. The clothing was neatly folded and placed on the rock by the left arm of the victim. It was pointless, but he felt for a pulse … there was none. He could feel Lenny's sadness as he turned to climb down to the old U. S. Highway 10.

Jodi walked slowly back to his car, attempting to compose himself before using the radio.

"Dispatch, C-1."

"Go ahead C-1."

"Call the sheriff and tell him I need the Major Crimes Unit immediately. And see if you can locate C-11. Tell him to get up here NOW. I confirm we have a 10-79."

"Ten-four, C-1. Do you request any other assistance at this time?"

"No, but get those people moving. I want to do this before we get a crowd."

"Lenny." Jodi called to get the highway foreman's attention.

"Yeah. What do you need?"

"I'll park my car across the road to block traffic. Would you go back and barricade the other end for me?" He asked. "Let's try to keep people out of here."

"Sure thing. I'll be back in a few minutes."

After blocking the road, the deputy opened the trunk of his patrol car and removed a stack of red traffic cones. He walked back to where he had seen the scuff marks in the dirt and placed the cones in a semi-circle around the spot to prevent anyone from inadvertently walking through the area. He could have begun the gathering of evidence, but opted to wait for the Major Crimes Unit; a large motor home style vehicle with a built-in forensics laboratory.

The deputy was still having trouble controlling his emotions when the Highways pickup returned. He tossed his notebook on the hood of the orange truck. "A hell of a way to start a day," he said.

"Both the last two kids we found were classmates of my own kids. Did you recognize this one, Lenny?"

"No, but I don't have any kids in school anymore so I don't know many youngsters this age." He took a deep breath and let out a long sigh. "What kind of person could hurt little kids like that? I hope when you catch this guy, you hurt him real bad before you hang him. Do you have any idea who he might be?"

"Don't tell anyone I said this, but we don't have squat for evidence. The other scenes looked just like this one, just some smudges for tire tracks, and footprints only good enough to get an approximate shoe size. We don't have a tire tread mark or a shoe print good enough to take a cast from. The only positive thing we have is a witness who saw a Toyota pickup driving away from where the first body was found. We don't have anything to connect the truck with the killing, but the driver may have seen something. Like I said, we don't have much to go on."

Lenny still had the sad look on his face. "The clouds are building up, it's probably going to rain this afternoon. Do you think you'll be done before it rains?"

"Once the Major Crimes guys get here it won't take long. The coroner should be here about the same time, and unless things are different here from the last two, we should finish in less than an hour." Jodi opened his trunk lid again, took out a 35mm Minolta camera. "Listen for my radio, will you Lenny? I have to get some pictures before the area gets changed."

"Sure thing. I have a thermos of black coffee. When you're done we'll have a cup."

It took quite some time to take all the pictures and record each one in his notebook. He had taken almost a hundred photos. There would be other pictures, as well as videotapes, of the scene when the others arrived. But for now he wanted a record of the scene before anyone else arrived.

This piece of old Highway 10 was between two freeway exits, both marked Exit 38. The scene was out of view of the freeway, which made traffic control almost unnecessary. Spectators were always a problem at these scenes. It also meant it was unlikely there would be any witnesses. The deputy made a note to check the State Fire Training Academy on the other side of the freeway. Someone might have seen something.

Jodi had just dropped the camera case back into his trunk and closed the lid when his partner, Brice Roman, turned off the Interstate and edged his car past the nose of the white Chevy blocking the road.

Jodi respected Brice's ability. Brice had his faults, but he was a good cop. He was aggressive, with incredible natural instincts.

"The Major Crimes Unit will be here in about ten minutes. They were in Bellevue this morning when you called. The coroner will be a little longer." Brice reported as he stepped from his own vehicle. "Have you looked at the body? Is it the same as the others?"

"Looks like it, but I didn't want to move anything. We have some possible footprints and tire tracks, but they look like the others, too faint for casts. I coned that area off just in case. Do we have any missing kids in town?"

"Yeah, we do. That's why I asked if this looked the same. The missing kid is a girl this time, and older." Brice ran his fingers through his blonde hair and opened his notebook. "The missing girl is almost fifteen years old, but she is small and has short black hair. When she left the house she was wearing a plaid cotton shirt and blue jeans with white tennis shoes and white socks. Another thing different this time is that she came up missing last evening. She was going to stay with a girlfriend but never got to the girlfriend's house. The parents didn't know she was missing until this morning. The girlfriend called to see why she hadn't spent the night. The missing girl's name is Shirley Ng; her folks are Vietnamese. The father is a computer whiz for Boeing."

"You've been busy this morning."

Brice couldn't bring himself to admit the information had been handed to him when he got to the office. Instead he said, "A good officer does his groundwork." Then added, "One other thing though, Jodi. This family lives only three blocks from your place. We have to catch this guy. He's getting too close to home."

"Neither Lenny nor I turned the body over. I didn't know it was a girl. If she was dressed like you say, then it's possible that whoever picked her up didn't know it either. What kind of a sick damn world are we living in?" Jodi wondered if his own children knew this latest victim. In a community this small it seemed all the children of the same approximate age were acquainted.

The sky above the narrow canyon was becoming more threatening. The Major Crimes Unit approached slowly down the old highway. The driver gave a gentle tap on the air horn and waved to the two sheriff's deputies as they turned to see who was arriving. Both deputies waved in recognition as the 36-foot-long, blue and white mobile crime lab stopped on the shoulder of the old road. The side door opened and a deputy, dressed in black coveralls, stepped from the van carrying a roll of yellow plastic ribbon printed with the continuing message, "POLICE—DO NOT CROSS". While he marked off the area most likely to contain evidence, three other officers emerged from the van carrying an assortment of cameras, notebooks, paper and plastic bags. They began the job of gathering the evidence that, each hoped, would catch and convict the person responsible for this crime. Every man on this team had seen hundreds of crime scenes and dozens of bodies, but each one had to stop and regain control of his emotions as he viewed the tiny, frail nude body on the rocks above. When the victims were children it was difficult to maintain one's objectivity--it became personal.

CHAPTER 2

Deputy Jodi Eagle was looking at his watch and writing the time in his notebook as the leader of the lab team approached. They had worked together many times, but this was the third time in just over a month the two had met at a crime scene like this one.

Team leader Lewis Cornetti looked like the class nerd. He was skinny, wore wire rim glasses and met you with a lopsided smile on his pockmarked face. In spite of all that he was instantly likable with the strangest sense of humor on record. His usual jokes were absent now and he was all business.

"Hi, Jodi. Do you have anything?"

"Sorry, Lew. It looks about like the other two. I coned off the spot where I thought the vehicle was parked. I saw some scuff marks there," he pointed, "where he might have taken the body out of the back of the truck. They're pretty faint though. When I was taking pictures I saw a spot behind that guardrail," again he indicated the place he meant, "where he might have slipped on the loose gravel. It could have been going in or coming back, but it's close to the steel railing. He may have grabbed it to balance himself."

"We'll check it out. Anything else?"

"I'm going to wait around for a while. I would appreciate it if you could deal with the body as quickly as possible. We haven't determined the sex of this victim yet and we have a missing girl in town. I need to know if this could be her so we can talk to the parents."

"Sure thing, Jodi. I'll get the crew on it right away and I'll personally check out those marks by the guardrail."

Deputy Eagle stepped to the passenger side of the Department of Highways truck. He looked at his watch. "The coroner should be here in about twenty minutes," he thought as he parked himself in the seat next to Lenny.

"I'll take that cup of coffee now."

As he silently drank the coffee, he thought how different this part of the country was from the Fort Totten Indian Reservation where he was born and spent his young life. His earliest recollection was of the day when, he must have been about four years old, his grandfather took him for the first time to the top of the Devil's Heart.

"You must come here often," his grandfather had said, "to pray to each of the four winds. To ask the Great Wakan to make you strong and wise." What he had not said was that this was the highest point on the reservation, and by coming here and studying each of the four directions he would never lose his way while traveling anywhere on the reservation. Over the years he had climbed to the top of that butte many times to speak with the Great Wakan.

He was brought back by Lewis Cornetti's voice. "I don't know if it's good news or bad, but the body is female and oriental. Looks to be strangled like the others. The clothing was folded neatly, just like the others. I'd say it was the same guy. I have some good news, though. That spot on the guardrail does have a print. I haven't lifted it yet, but we can see four fingers, the thumb, and a partial palm, left hand."

He turned to the highway foreman, "Hello, I'm Lewis Cornetti. I'd like to remove that piece of guardrail, if that's possible."

"I guess I can do that if you think you need it. I have the tools in the back of my truck." Lenny reached into his pocket for the key to the toolbox as he stepped from the truck.

"I'll have a couple of my men give you a hand. We need to get this rail inside before it rains. It's going to take some time to lift the prints from it. We can do it later if we can put it inside out of the rain."

Brice walked back from the crime scene van to meet Jodi at his patrol car. "I just had a look at the clothing. They match the description of those worn by the Ng girl."

Traffic was picking up on the Interstate now. A blue station wagon with small white lettering on the door which read **King County Coroner**, slowed and eased up to the area as Jodi moved his car to allow him through.

"I'm going into town. I'll stop at the office, then go to the Ng home," Jodi told Brice, speaking through the open window of his car. "You stay here until everyone is clear. Have Lenny stop by the office and give us a written statement. I'll see you at the office this afternoon."

"See you at the office. I hope we can finish early today. The Mariners are playing at home and I have tickets."

Jodi could only shake his head as he drove away. "I wonder if the Mariners have cheerleaders. If they do, he probably has a date with one of them." He had to drive a mile east before he could cross to the westbound lane.

The North Bend city police department had been disbanded in 1973. Since that time the duties of enforcing the law had been left to the King County Sheriff's Department. The office had once belonged to the North Bend Police. Jodi occupied a small office a few doors down the hall from the administrative office of Sergeant Pete Kaufman.

Jodi was checking the file for the address of the Ng family when Pete stepped into his office carrying a handful of daily reports. "Have you seen the missing person report on the Ng girl?"

"Not yet. I just got in from the scene. I'm sure she's our victim. The scene was just like the others, looks like the same guy. I was just going to the girl's house to talk with the parents. I would guess the father is at work, I'll call and let you know. If he is, would you call downtown and have someone go out to Boeing and contact the father? It would probably be a good idea to have a deputy drive him home."

"Good idea. You've sure had your share of these notifications lately. Want me to send someone else to do this?"

"Thanks, Pete." Jodi said in a tired voice. "I can handle it. I have to talk to the parents sometime. They may as well meet me now. I would like to take Connie with me if you don't mind. This is going to be emotional, and it might be a good thing to have a female officer there."

"This is number three, and all kids. The news media are going to start calling them serial killings. We need to nail this guy, and quick. The town is already in a panic over the dead kids and they don't even have the news about this one yet. I can handle the media. I want you to know that any resource we have is at your disposal. I've talked with the sheriff. He has given you the green light to use whatever you need. If you want additional personnel, he will assign some people from downtown. He just wants this cleaned up before we have any more missing kids."

"I appreciate that Pete. The truth is we just don't have evidence or leads to warrant sending out any more people. I may change my mind when Cornetti finishes today, but the way it stands now it would be a waste of manpower. I have Brice and if you let me use Connie I think we can cover it for now."

"Okay, just don't let anything get ahead of you. I'll assign Connie to you temporarily." He shuffled through the stack of papers in his left hand, pulled out a manila folder and laid it on Jodi's desk. "Here's the report on the missing Ng girl. I'll have a deputy from Renton notify the father and drive him home. Keep me informed." He turned to walk away, then turned back into the small office again. "Keep Brice away from the news people. Tell him I want all, and I do mean all, media coverage to go directly through my office. No impromptu news conferences. Got it?"

"Got it, boss."

It had been only a few minutes but it seemed like an hour since the sergeant had dropped the missing person report on his desk. Jodi was certain the victim was the missing Ng girl. Connie Lupine was standing in the office doorway when he looked up from his notebook. She said nothing. Pete had given her a short briefing. Deputy Connie lupine was a five-year veteran with the department. She had a reputation for no-nonsense police work. Jodi had asked for her because she was good with people.

"You ready?" Jodi asked.

"I think so. You can fill me in on the latest on the way."

It was less than five minutes to the Ng home. Not a large house, but well kept. An older, bungalow style home on a north/south avenue. The street was lined with large locust trees. Lilac bushes stood at either corner of the front porch. This time of year there were no blossoms on them. As a young man, John Ng had emigrated from Vietnam with his family. The family had settled in southern California. John's father had become a farm laborer and his mother a school custodian. They managed to save enough to send their son to UCLA where he graduated with a Master's Degree in design engineering. He had met his wife, Ruth, when he first went to work for Boeing. She, too, was Vietnamese. When Ruth became pregnant with Shirley they decided to move out of the urban area to a place with a safer atmosphere in which to raise a child.

Jodi parked his car at the curb, under the huge locust tree directly in front of the Ng house. "I live two blocks up and one block left." He told Deputy Lupine as they stood on the sidewalk. He saw an occasional raindrop making its mark on the dry street as they stepped over the curb and began the sad walk to the neatly painted white house with the green trim. A wooden bench on the front porch held a pair of white tennis shoes and a class sweater; the date on the sleeve identified it as the property of one of this year's freshman class. Jodi took a deep breath, nodded to Connie, then tapped gently on the door.

Ruth Ng stood barely five feet tall and, Jodi guessed, weighed less than ninety pounds. She was a beautiful woman, but the strain of her missing daughter made her appear frail and weak. She stiffened when she saw the two deputies standing at her door. Though she presented a picture of composure, her red eyes told of her emotional stress.

"May we come in, Mrs. Ng?" Jodi asked.

The deputies had been with Ruth Ng for nearly an hour when the sheriff's car brought John Ng to the house. Mrs. Ng met her husband at the door, crying uncontrollably. Connie Lupine had attempted in vain to console the distraught mother but it was impossible. The father had many questions which the deputy tried to answer as completely as possible without adding to the trauma they had already suffered. The Ng's had seen much death in their lifetime, but they had not expected it to come to their own child here in America.

Connie Lupine had gone next door to ask Mary Lafferty to come sit with the grieving parents. When she arrived the two deputies excused themselves and returned to the office.

CHAPTER 3

Melvin Eagle, Jodi's father, had been a troubled young man. He drank as much beer as he could buy. Melvin's father used to say that he nurtured the bad seed inside him with his drinking. "Everyone has bad seeds within them," Jodi's grandfather had said, "If you feed it with evil it will eventually consume your spirit. The Wakan gave us choices, not responsibilities. Each man must choose his own future and care for his own spirit."

Melvin had met Heather, Jodi's mother, when they were just children. Their families lived on adjoining parcels of land east of Fort Totten. They had grown up together and both attended the mission school at the Fort. The army had long since left and the Catholic Church used the buildings for a mission and school. The two had married soon after graduating from high school. Melvin went to work for his father farming on tribal land. They grew wheat, corn and oats. They also had a few cows and several horses.

Melvin was never happy as a farmer and rancher. He wanted more from his life. He drank more and worked less. His father complained, but Melvin wouldn't listen. He settled down for a few months after Jodi was born, but soon went back to his old ways. He began to stay away from home more and more. When Jodi was three years old, his father took a job as a long-haul truck driver. After that Jodi only saw him about once a year and later not at all. From the time Jodi was four years old, the only male guidance he had had came from his grandfather, who tried to teach him the life values of the Native American Dakota culture. His grandfather had repeatedly warned him of the dangers of feeding his bad seed. He had also taught him other values. "Always be honest," he had said, "but be careful not to hurt others with your honesty." Jodi had found this to be a difficult lesson.

There were many lessons to be learned over the next several years. The most difficult was the lesson of loss. Heather Eagle died at the age of twenty-eight, of a broken heart, her father-in-law had said. Jodi was nine at the time. His grandfather's house was filled with relatives and friends. There was crying and laughter and stories and, for Jodi, confusion. He left the house and walked to the top of the Devil's Heart to talk with the Wakan.

"You're awfully quiet, Jodi."

The patrol car had just turned onto North Bend Way. The lunch crowd had left the Mar T Cafe more than an hour ago. "Just thinking," Jodi said, "How would you like a cup of coffee before we go back to the office?"

"I'd like that, but I have to warn you, I don't like Espresso."

"That makes two of us," Jodi commented as he parked the car on the nearly vacant main street. The rain had stopped and the clouds were dissipating. Up the canyon, toward Snoqualmie Pass, he could see a perfect rainbow. The Wakan has come for the child, he reflected. The television series Twin Peaks had made the Mar T Cafe famous for its pie. Looking from the front window of the cafe he was able to see the mountain, Mount Si, for which the television show had been named. Jodi sat in the booth looking through the front window. He loved that old mountain. It wasn't the Devil's heart, but he thought the Great Wakan would like it too.

Ester Parks brought coffee for the two deputies, good coffee, not Espresso. "I think this killing was done by the same guy who did the other two," Jodi told Connie between sips of hot coffee. "We can't be sure, but there's a good chance this is a pedophile or a homosexual and he's abducting and killing little boys. I think he made a mistake with this one. I saw the body and, until Brice told me it was a girl, I thought it was a boy about ten years old. She was built small, short and had short dark hair combed straight back. What I can't figure though, is why. Why is he operating here in North Bend? All three victims were picked up within three blocks of the elementary school. Two of them were students there. Each one was alone on the street, as near as we can determine. I've talked with the parents of each of these kids and they all say their kid knew better than to get into a car with a stranger." He gave a long sigh, "It just doesn't make sense. The risk of discovery would be a lot less in the more populated areas of Seattle or Bellevue. The only reason I can think of is he lives here, but I can't think of anyone who fits the profile. We have to get him before he hurts another little kid."

"It's getting personal with you, isn't it?" Connie asked. "The sergeant assigned me to you temporarily, but I would like to stay on this with you until

Chapter 3

it's finished. That's if you don't mind. It would give me a chance to learn something about investigations from you and perhaps I can contribute something along the way. Would you ask him for me?"

"Sure. I could use the help. Besides, you're such a good listener, I can bounce my ideas off you. In fact, you can do something for me this afternoon. Up there at the second exit is the fire training academy. They're to the left, off the freeway, about three or four miles. Just follow the signs. They run classes up there and a lot of the cadets go out walking and hiking. It's a remote possibility, but maybe someone saw something early this morning. I would appreciate it if you would do the interviews today, before any of those cadets ship out."

They slipped out of the booth; Jodi dropped a five-dollar bill on the table.

"My car is at the office. I'll go do the interviews right away. Anything special I should ask?"

"No, just use your instincts. Like I said, the chances of anyone seeing anything at all are remote. The director of the academy is a nice guy, I know him slightly, and his name is Smith. Use my name to introduce yourself. He'll help you."

Connie Lupine walked directly from his car to her own. Jodi stood on the walk and watched as she drove away. When she rounded the corner, turning left, he walked into the office. The offices of the King County Police Department, North Bend, were too small to be kept tidy, especially when there was as much activity as was now in progress. Emma Garson, a pleasant middle-aged woman who kept track of each and every slip of paper passing through the office, looked up. She had been here since before the sheriff's department took over policing the city and surrounding area.

"Brice is on his way in now and the Major Crimes Unit will be here in about a half hour. Officer Cornetti left a message that he wants to see you," she reported. "And Sergeant Kaufman would like to see you." She thought a moment, then asked, "How are the Ng's doing?"

"About as well as you could expect, under the circumstances. Connie had a neighbor come so the family wouldn't be alone."

"That would be Mary Lafferty, she is such a nice person. Her son graduated Valedictorian here in 1968. He's a stock broker now, in Boston I think." There were about thirty five hundred people in North Bend, and Miss Emma knew them all.

Pete Kaufman had his head buried in some court papers when Jodi looked into his office. "Got a minute, Pete?"

The sergeant looked up. "Oh, Jodi, come in. I was hoping you'd get back before I went home. Anything new?"

"Sorry, Pete, not a thing. Cornetti will be here in a little while and I hope he has something. I sent Connie out to the fire academy, but I'm grasping at straws. Nobody has seen anything."

His grandfather had told him, Jodi recalled, that nothing in nature goes unnoticed; there are always clues to the fact you've been there. The animals of the woods detect your presence by reading the signs you have left there, the scent on the ground; a scuff mark in the leaves, the snap of a breaking twig, the silence of the birds. The hunter can walk through the woods without making a sound, yet all the animals and birds know of him. But if you're there to observe, then the animals and birds won't mind and they'll come into view for you to see. They won't be afraid. So, if you are to see the animals you must think like the animal and not like the hunter.

If his grandfather was right, then there were clues to lead him to this killer of children. There were clues if only he knew where to look. Pete was right, the people in town were soon going to panic, and the death of Shirley Ng could well be the trigger.

"Your wife is on line one for you, Jodi." Miss Emma said, not getting up from her desk.

"Thanks." He said as he turned and walked quickly to his own desk in the rear of the office. "Send Cornetti back here when he arrives."

He dropped into his chair and picked up the receiver. "Hi, honey." He tried to sound cheerful.

"Jodi. Is it true? Did someone kill another child?" Eileen Eagle had just a touch of fear in her voice.

"Where did you hear that?"

"Lois Nelson called me. Is it true?"

"Yes, I'm afraid it's true. I don't want you to let this out, though. We're going to have enough trouble controlling the rumors as it is. Where did Lois hear about it?"

"I think Mary Lafferty called her at the beauty shop. You can't keep this quiet; people are going to find out, especially in a small town like this."

"I suppose so."

"Is it Shirley Ng?"

"Yes. Do you know the family?"

"Not well, but yes. We are both members of the garden club. Ruth is such a nice person. She is quiet, but she has a wonderful sense of humor. Her husband is nice too. You know all the flowers and shrubs where you come off the new freeway ramps onto North Bend Boulevard? They donated them all. And they planted them all. And they keep them weeded, and, well, they just spend

Chapter 3

a lot of time and energy making it look nice. Oh, Jodi. Why would someone do this to such nice people?" She was crying now.

"I don't know, honey. But I am sure going to try to find out. For now, just keep this to yourself. I'll be home as soon as I can. The Major Crimes team will be here in a few minutes to leave me a report. When I finish with them I'll be home. It might be a good idea to keep the kids close to home for a few days, just as a precaution." Jodi was instantly sorry he had said that

"I'm scared, Jodi. I don't know what I would do if something happened to one of our kids."

"It's not going to do any of us any good for you to lose control now. Just calm down and I will be home as soon as I can."

"I'm sorry. I'm just worried about the children, and I feel so badly for the Ng's. I'll be okay. You do what you have to do. I'll take something to the Ng's for dinner. I'd give Mary a break, but I don't want to leave our boys alone that long. I love you. And I'm sorry I'm such a big baby. I'll see you when you get home. Bye."

Jodi heard Cornetti in the outer office. "Come on in, Lew."

Lewis Cornetti came into the office holding a cup of coffee in one hand and his notes in the other. It was now after four in the afternoon, and neither Lew nor his team had stopped for lunch. The rain shower earlier in the day had given their tasks an unusual urgency.

He gave Jodi a wide grin. "It must be that Indian blood in your veins. You sure called it on the tire tracks and the prints on the guardrail."

Jodi was instantly excited. "You got a print from the guardrail?" he asked with some pleasure in his voice.

"Yup." Cornetti sipped his coffee, drawing out the drama of the moment. "As careful as this guy has been about leaving evidence, he sure screwed up this time. It looks like he was carrying the girl's body. When he stepped the rail he slipped on loose gravel. He must have fallen backward and grabbed the rail to catch his balance. We have a perfect hand print. Four fingers and half the palm on one side and the thumb on the other. We don't have a match yet, but we will get it into the computer as soon as we get back to town. I probably would have missed that print if you hadn't said something."

"Another thing." Lew put his coffee cup down on the desk so he could turn the page in his notebook. "We got enough of the shoe print to fix the size and the brand. It's a size 6 1/2 B, New Balance. This guy is little! If he is that small and could step over the guardrail while carrying the girl's body, he has to be pretty athletic."

"Damn, Lew. Maybe we finally got a break."

"That's not all. You know those tire tracks you put the cones around?"

Jodi nodded. "You're not going to tell me you got a tire print off them, are you?" He was sitting up straight now.

"Not quite. But we were able to get accurate measurements off the tracks. We have the wheel-base and width, as well as the tire size. We were able to cross-reference all this to our manufacturer's specifications book. We came up with the measurements that match a new, 1990, Toyota SE-5 standard cab. If it still has factory tires on it, it will be a sport model. When we finish our report I'll give you all the numbers."

"That checks out with the witness on the first body. Remember he saw a dark color Toyota pickup leaving the area. Good work Lew."

"It'll take a few days to get all the follow-up done and everything on paper. I'll see that you have a copy as soon as it's finished. In the meantime I'll get you a copy of my preliminary report and the Coroner's report, probably by late tomorrow. I would appreciate it if you would get me a copy of your report as soon as you can." Cornetti stood, picking up his papers and empty coffee cup.

"Let me walk out with you and I'll give you the film I took before you arrived this morning. You can take it to the lab with yours. I've marked all the canisters, and I'd like you to keep them separate from yours." He reached into a bottom desk drawer, withdrew a large manila envelope, and handed it to Lew.

Back inside again he asked Miss Emma, "Did Pete leave for the day?"

"Yes, he did. He has little league practice tonight. He'll be at the ball field with the kids until about eight o'clock. He has his radio if you need him."

"No. I'm going to leave here in a few minutes myself. Have you heard from Brice?"

"Yes. He called to say he'd have his report on your desk before noon tomorrow. He said something earlier about going into town for a ball game." She paused a moment to review the sticky-notes adhering to the railing around her desk. She selected one and handed it to Jodi. "That was a call from Earl Campbell. He said the chamber of commerce is worried about the recent vandalism of the grass by the freeway, and now, it seems, someone has done something on the Falls City road. I tried to have C-3 take the report, but Earl won't deal with anyone but you."

"Thanks Emma, I'll take care of it. I plan to stay until Connie gets back. Why don't you call it a day too. With all these reports coming in, you're going to have a lot of typing tomorrow."

"Mercy, just look at the time. I didn't realize it was so late. I'll make fresh coffee, then I'll be going." She began to close her file cabinets, clearing her desk for the day. "You should think about going home yourself. I think your family needs you at home tonight."

"I will, thank you Emma." The radio crackled; it was Connie reporting that she was out of her car at the station. "You go home, I'll see you tomorrow."

Jodi was pouring two cups of fresh coffee when Connie came into the office. He offered her a cup. "Learn anything?" Jodi asked.

"Thank, I can use it." she took a pensive sip, not wanting to burn her lips. "Yes, I think so. The academy is out of my usual patrol area, and I'd never been up there. It's really beautiful." She took another, longer sip. "There's a class of Coast Guardsmen up there. A group of them were out for their morning jog at 0430. They saw a gray Toyota pickup come through the gate. It turned around at the gate about fifty yards from the group. It was a sport model truck with white accents on the side. You know, the kind that is just white rectangles that become narrower and less distinct as they progress down the side of the truck. It also had a matching canopy. There was some disagreement about whether the canopy was metal or plastic. No one got a license number but several of them said it was a Washington plate. They couldn't see the driver because it was still pretty dark and the side windows of the truck seemed to be shaded. The driver just turned around and drove out the gate. There had been so much traffic through the gate today, that there weren't any tracks. The director of the academy gave me a printout of the roster and highlighted the names of the group I interviewed. That's about it." She took another long drink of her coffee, put her elbows on her knees, closed her eyes and gave out a long low sigh. "It's been a long day. I'm tired."

Jodi had been listening intently, "Good job. It fits with the information Cornetti gave me. Get out of here now and do the report in the morning. We have all had a long day … In fact, I have just one more call to make before I go home. See you in the morning."

CHAPTER 4

Jodi Eagle was nine years old when his mother died. It was a confusing and traumatic time for the young Dakota. His grandfather had tried to ease the boy's grief with love, but it was impossible. Though his grandfather had been the only real male guidance in his life, his mother had been his only true parent. The bond between mother and son was extremely strong. Jodi knew of the first of the sacred rites of the pipe, the keeping of the spirit, but did not understand it.

Before the white man came into this territory, there had been no true written Dakota language. Until the mid 1800s the legends of the Dakota were passed on by word of mouth; stories told from one generation to the next. One of the most important of the stories was the legend of the White Buffalo Woman. There were many variations of the story but Jodi could still hear the words as they were spoken by his grandfather that day, sitting atop the Devil's Heart.

Winter had been long and hard for the Dakota people. People in the village argued, children fought with their parents and parents lost patience with their children. The chief sent two good hunters, Blue Cloud and Black Knife to find the buffalo.

The two braves came upon tracks. Blue Cloud said, 'Someone may be lost. We must find them and offer them help.'

Black Knife said, 'I am too tired to chase after someone stupid enough to be lost.'

It was then that the two braves saw a beautiful woman in white buckskin and flowing black hair.

Black knife said, 'I want her and I am taking her back with me.'

To which Blue Cloud replied, 'She might not want to go with you. You should treat her with respect.'

Black Knife said angrily, 'She is only a woman. If she doesn't come, I will drag her.'

She came close. Blue Cloud said, 'Are you lost? Can we help you?'

The woman ignored him to look at Black Knife, 'You want to force me to come with you. I dare you to come and try.'

Black Knife lunged to touch her. A cloud descended. When it disappeared, only his bow and quiver lay on the ground.

She spoke to Blue Cloud, 'You are a good man. Go to your people and tell them what you have seen here. Tell them to make a great Tipi. They must work together and not argue or fight. When it is done I will come.'

Blue Cloud returned to his people and told the chief what he had seen. 'We must do this. Black Knife did not listen and he is gone.' He asked the tribal members, 'Will you listen now?'

One by one they agreed. They worked on the great Tipi without arguing. Even the children helped. When it was finished the chief sat in the doorway with the council behind him.

She walked into the village, singing, her hair floating around her. She carried a white deerskin bundle.

'I am White Buffalo Woman. I bring you a gift.' She placed the bundle on the ground in the center of the Tipi. She unwrapped it. Inside was a pipe. On one side a buffalo was carved. Attached to the stem were twelve feathers tied with sweet grass and four ribbons; black, white, red and yellow.

'You have shown yourselves worthy, therefore I bring you this pipe. The buffalo stands for the earth; the mother who gives us food. The eagle feathers stand for the sky and the twelve moons; the sky is our father and watches over us.

'The ribbons represent the four corners of the world. When you smoke the pipe, you must offer to each in respect of the earth.

'Black is the west, whose thunder sends the rain to make the seeds grow. white is the north that sends the cooling winds. Red is for the east, the home of the first light. It brings wisdom. The yellow is for the south which gives us summer sun to make the grass tall.

'You have shown yourselves worthy by working together in harmony. Use it with peace and you will prosper.'

She handed it to the chief and walked from the Tipi. As she walked away she was transformed into a magnificent white buffalo.

Just then a herd of buffalo were seen grazing on a hill near the village.

The people treasured the pipe, and whenever they were tempted to quarrel among themselves, they remembered that only through peace could they solve their problems and prosper.

Soon they offered the pipe to others and explained the meaning as White Buffalo Woman had told them; that it must be used with understanding of what nature gives and what the people must do in return. They hoped the message would travel to the ends of the earth, north, south, east and west.

There had been many other lessons to learn that day on the hill. He was to learn of the death of his mother. "She is with the Wakanjtanka now." His grandfather had said. "It is now time for the sacred rite of the pipe. There are seven sacred rites of the pipe, but this is the first, and perhaps, the most difficult for you to learn and to understand. It is 'the keeping of the spirit.'"

"In olden times when a family member died, the family would construct a mound on a hill with a good view. On the mound they would erect a platform. The body would be wrapped in the best blankets the family owned and placed on the platform. Each day the family would come to the place and speak with the dead. This would go on until spring if the person died in the fall, or until the fall if the person died in the spring or summer. The body would stay on the platform until only bones remained. The family would then take down the platform, remove the bones to be buried in the mound below the platform. More dirt and stone would be brought to the mound to cover the bones. This would keep the bones safe from animals."

"It is different today. Partly because of the influence of the missionaries, but mostly because there are more people in the countryside, the ceremony has changed. We now bury the dead soon. But, we will erect a tripod in the front of the house. From it we will hang a bag with personal things of the dead. For this one I have taken a lock of hair from your mother's head. We will treat this as though she were still alive and with us. We will discuss family matters, and tell her of the good things in our lives. We will ask her for advice in solving our difficult problems. Friends will come and leave gifts at the site. In the spring we will take down the tripod and we will bury the bag. We will have a powwow and we will give all the gifts that have been left here. You will see how good this will make you feel. After that, your mother will rest in the land of peace. You will see." There were tears in the old man's eyes.

It was during this time Jodi had decided he would not live on the reservation. He didn't know how he would leave, but he would find a way. Grief, Jodi was to learn, is not a condition but an emotion which must be endured, not dealt with. This he found true in every culture; grief was not the exclusive the property of the Dakota.

Chapter 4

During his senior year in high school, a Marine recruiter was to show him the way to leave the reservation.

From the time of his mother's death, his grandfather had raised Jodi. The old man had taught him to hunt and to fish. He had taken him to Freepeoples Lake and taught him to swim. He helped Jodi with his school studies as best he could. The old man taught him the Indian ways of honor and honesty. He also taught him respect and, unlike his father, Jodi learned a good work ethic. He spent a great deal of his time with other boys from the reservation, but never participated in the drinking parties or the pot smoking binges that many of his friends seemed to like so well. Many of those friends were now dead, victims of their own good times. Car crashes, shootings and suicide had claimed too many of his friends.

The Marine recruiter looked impressive in his sharply creased uniform. He assured Jodi he would have one just like it. He also told Jodi he could select a field before he enlisted. After much consideration, Jodi decided he would like to be a policeman. He qualified for military police school.

After basic training and M. P. school he was assigned to Camp Pendleton, near San Diego, California. The training had been physically demanding; a large percentage of the recruits didn't make it. Jodi loved it. He was used to climbing, running and general physical activity. He had played football in high school and now played on the camp team.

He was challenged by the study of regulations and law, but since he didn't drink, he spent most of his free time studying. He graduated third in his class. His grandfather was proud of his record and his promotion to corporal.

His first assignment was to gate duty at Camp Pendleton. It was only a short-term assignment. He was soon transferred to headquarters for investigations. He learned a great deal about police work in those early days. Then came the news that he was being transferred overseas. Embassy duty in Brazil. Jodi didn't care much for the assignment. It was hot and humid, and it was boring. He spent most of his off-duty time seeing the sights and in general, being a tourist.

While in Brazil he'd become acquainted with a U. S. Consul official. She was the one to get him interested in college after his enlistment. The country was grateful for the service her young men had given and would help provide for a college education to those qualified. As his term of enlistment came to an end, she had helped him apply for entry at the University of Washington. She was also a close friend of the King County sheriff. He agreed to interview Jodi for a part-time position with his department while he went to school. The Marine Corps provided him with enough money to pay his tuition and he had saved enough to live on for a while. The job with the sheriff's department would provide the rest.

Jodi liked football and tried out for the Washington Huskies. He made the team and played two years as a tight end, then moved to a running back position. It was here that he met Earl Campbell. He was an easy-going, energetic business major with a lively sense of humor and a ready-made answer for people who called him African-American Just call me the 'Black Guy.'" Neither Earl nor Jodi drank much, so when the team was on the road, they spent a lot of time together.

Jodi spent five years at the University of Washington. working for the King County Sheriff the entire time. After five hard years he graduated with a Master's degree in criminal justice. It was during his time at the university he met and fell in love with Eileen Littlewing. She was also Sioux, but from a band which had settled in western Minnesota. Upon graduation he took Eileen to Fort Totten to meet his grandfather.

"She is much like your mother," his grandfather had said. It was then that his grandfather invited Jodi to his first sweat lodge. "This is the second sacred rite," his grandfather explained. "It is appropriate that you come to this rite of purification before you are married."

Jodi enjoyed his return to the reservation, and especially his visits with his grandfather, who was very old now. He could no longer farm the land but maintained a few cows and some chickens to keep useful. Eileen's family had come from Minnesota for the wedding, which was held on his grandfather's ranch. It was a good time. Jodi visited with some of his old high school friends and decided he had made the right decision by leaving the reservation. This was not the life for him. Those days at home were happy ones. It would also be the last time he would see his grandfather alive.

Jodi and Eileen were living in North Bend, Washington when the news came about his grandfather. The tribal chairman called to give him the news. Jodi flew home for the funeral. His grandfather had given him, when he was twelve, a good hunting knife. He found the hunting knife and used it to cut a lock of hair from his grandfather's head. The funeral director was shocked at having someone disturb the body in the casket. He stepped forward to stop him but the look on Jodi's face made him reconsider.

Jodi erected a small tripod at the top of the Devil's Heart. There he hung a small deerskin pouch, and for more than a day he sat by the monument and spoke with his grandfather. He explained that times were changing and that the old ways were dying. But, he would do his best to observe the first of the sacred rites of the pipe. He could not stay a year or even six months, but he would make the mound and bury the lock. He would return as often as possible to visit him. He thanked the old man for making him a good hunter and a good Dakota. He thanked him for taking care of him after his mother had passed away. He asked to be forgiven for not returning home more often to visit. He said good-bye to the old man in the way of the Dakota.

Jodi gave the livestock to several of his grandfather's close friends. Clothing and household goods he distributed to the needy of the reservation. He left the sale of the house and property to the tribal chairman, who would treat him fairly.

In the house there was a pipe and a bow and arrows, all made by his grandfather. These Jodi took for himself, as a reminder of his proud Dakota heritage. He would never forget his grandfather or the love he had given him.

Jodi was alone in his little office when he heard the door open and someone enter the front office.

"Hello, anyone here?" It was his old friend, Earl Campbell.

"Back here, Earl. Get a cup of coffee and come on back."

The deputy heard footsteps approaching. Earl stopped by the office occasionally, but this didn't sound like a social call.

Earl stepped into the small cubicle. "How are things in the world of subdivisions and supermarkets?" Jodi inquired.

"We be sells-en-em fast as we can." He stated in his best Oakland Ebonics.

"When are you going to buy a bigger truck to haul your money to the bank?" Jodi asked jokingly.

"Got it ordered, my man, got it ordered." His smile faded and his manner became more serious. "Jodi, I know you can't say much but … " He looked down at the floor. "When I first called I was going to ask if you knew anything about the graffiti that has begun to show up around here. But I heard this afternoon there was another child killed. Is it true?"

"Yes, it's true. I can't give you any details, but the victim is a North Bend girl, Shirley Ng." The look on Earl's face was one of shock and sadness. "Earl, you know this is the third killing in a couple of months. When the press gets this story there's going to be a splash and I suspect they'll be calling them serial killings. We don't want a panic in town. Is there anything you and your chamber of commerce can do to defuse some of this?"

"You know we'll do whatever we can. What did you have in mind?"

"I really don't know. There must be something. The department is going to catch a lot of heat for not stopping the killer before he got this last victim. The parents are going to be afraid to let their children out of their sight. Our phone won't stop ringing."

"What have you got in mind?"

"I don't know, Earl. I just think that, in a small community like this, there's going to be a lot of emotion, and I'd like to figure out a way to make all that energy have a positive effect instead of negative. You know how small towns are, they tend to bind together in a crisis. There must be a way."

"Let me think about it a while. You're right, we need to find something to help folks focus on the good life we all have here. I'll call some of the Chamber members for breakfast in the morning and brainstorm it a little. We'll come up with something. Sorry I bothered you today, Jodi. You have enough on your mind without dealing with this other stuff right now." He stood to leave.

"Oh, Earl, it almost slipped my mind. What graffiti were you talking about?"

"Don't worry about that now. We'll talk about it later."

"No, come on Earl, I'll leave a note for one of the other deputies to look into it tomorrow. What about these graffiti?"

Earl was somewhat embarrassed. "You remember a couple of weeks ago when the new seeding job began to green up, and then in a few days there was a huge green message, "Jesus is Lord," printed in the grass. Whoever did that was a real artist. The thing looked like a professional job."

"I remember. We thought it was seeded to grow differently. Turned out, someone hit it with fertilizer. Made the grass grow twice as fast and twice as green. Pretty ingenious, really."

"Ingenious or not, it defaced the new seed job. And now it's happened again. Out on Falls City Road. There's a huge circle with a picture in it, we're not sure of what yet, it's just beginning to turn green. It's right beside the road in the hay field. You're right about one thing. Whoever is doing this is smart. By the time it turns green, any trace of them has long since been erased by the weather."

"Yes, I've seen them. I'm sorry, but my mind has been on other things and I never thought of it as important."

"I can understand that. But, take a look at them, Jodi. This one has the professional touch too. They must have a pump sprayer full of fertilizer and use it like a painter's brush. This one is a circle with the picture of a face in it. I think it's like the picture you see on a package of cigarette papers. We'll know in a couple of days."

"Okay Earl, I'm not sure what we can do, but I'll have someone take a look in the morning ... " He was writing notes to be given to another deputy in the morning. "And thanks for your help on the other thing." He stood and turned off his desk lamp.

"It's your turn to come to our place for dinner. What's a good day for you and your family?" Jodi asked as the two men walked to the front door. "Eileen has been badgering me to get you folks over."

"Let me check with Linda and see what Darren's little league schedule is. I'll call you. Thanks Jodi." He waved as he stepped into his car.

Jodi was about to climb into his own car when he heard the rumble of a pickup, with loud pipes, behind him. He turned to see a tall, four-wheel-drive Chevrolet, 1974 model. There were two identical trucks in town, owned by twin brothers, Einer and Aino Laxo. The trucks differed only that the paint scheme was reversed. Both boys were in the truck. Aino rolled down his window and shoved his smiling face through the open port. "Hi there, Jodi. What's up?"

"Not much. How about you boys? Staying out of trouble?"

"Dad works us so hard we don't have strength enough to get into trouble. He's heating the sauna tonight and thought you might want to come over for a while."

Jodi hung his head for a moment to mentally review his evening plans, then looked up at the boys. "Tell your dad I'll be over about eight."

The pickup sped off heading north, with an arm waving from the window of the passenger side.

CHAPTER 5

The last of the Park View Townhouses opened this month. The first had opened last fall. Brice Roman was one of the first to move into the complex. The townhouses were a new concept for North Bend, one which many investors shied away from, simply because they were not what North Bend residents were used to seeing. It was a well-thought-out complex, though, with each unit on the ground floor, and exits into a small green yard. A small stream ran through the property, which bordered scenic county property, adjacent to Si View King County Park. It had an indoor swimming pool. Green trees and pleasant surroundings made the venture an instant success.

If he skipped dinner, Brice calculated, he would just have time to make it to the King Dome before the game started at seven o'clock. He called in to tell Jodi he'd write his report in the morning. Jodi wouldn't like it. Tough.

Brice changed into civilian clothes, and was headed for his private car when a neighbor stopped him on the walk.

"Hi there, Brice." It was Tom Dillard, the maintenance man for the townhouse complex. Brice called him "the old man." Tom was fifty five years old and retired from the air force. "The word is that there was another kid killed last night. Is that true?"

"I'm afraid it is, Tom. How did you hear about it?"

"I just came from the hardware store. I heard two women talking about it. I'm glad I don't have any kids at home anymore. It would worry me sick knowing someone like that was out there. Do you have any idea who's doing it?"

"Not yet, Tom. But, we'll get him." Brice spoke over his shoulder as he parked himself in the driver's seat of the blue and white Buick Le Sabre. He managed a quick wave to Tom as he backed out of his reserved parking spot. It would take almost an hour and a half to get to the King Dome, find a parking spot and get to his seat.

About the time Connie Lupine was returning from her investigation at the fire academy, Brice was purchasing a hot dog and a Rainier beer from the concession stand at the exit above his seating section. The home team, The Seattle Mariners, was just taking the field as he took his seat. The noise in the Dome was almost unbearable. Johnson was pitching tonight. Ken Griffey Jr. was in right field and getting a lot of attention from the crowd. The Toronto Blue Jays had been hot this season, but Seattle was confident of a win on their home turf.

Jodi didn't expect his wife to be home when he came from work, but she was and had dinner waiting. The boys were fighting in the living room; a quick word from their father stopped it. He walked into the kitchen, dropped his duty belt, weapon and radio into a desk drawer and locked it. Eileen was just taking a casserole from the oven when Jodi came home. He sort of waltzed around the table, wrapped his arms around her and gave her a long kiss.

"I sure needed that," he said

"I love you, honey," she replied. "Are you ready to eat?"

"I haven't eaten all day. Been too busy. I'm starved."

"I'll set the table if you'll call the boys for dinner and make them wash up. They have been unbearable since I told them they couldn't play outside."

"We can't lock ourselves away just because some nut out there is hurting people. We still have to live our lives. I'll catch this guy, but I don't know how long it will take. Please, honey, try not to overreact on this thing. If the kids want to play outside, then let them. Keep an eye on them and make them stay together, but let them be kids and have fun."

"That's easy for you to say. You're not the one responsible for them all day. I couldn't live with myself if something happened to one of our boys." Panic was creeping into her voice.

"Come on, Eileen, settle down. You're not the bad guy here. Neither am I. It's some crazy out there. Until I can stop him we have to try to live a normal life. We can minimize our family's risk with a little caution. I just don't want you to lose your perspective. You know I love you and the boys and if I thought there was real danger for you I would get the three of you out of here for a while. I don't think we need to do that. I need you on my side." He hugged her and kissed her on the cheek. "I love you, honey."

He picked up his gear from the table. On the way to the bedroom to change clothes he found his two sons, Phillip, who was now twelve, and Kyle, a grown-up ten-year-old. They had quit fighting and were now watching cartoons on TV.

"Okay boys, get washed up for dinner."

Phillip was the one to respond. "We don't have to wash. Mom wouldn't let us go outside, so we didn't get dirty."

"I know. Wash anyway. I'm going to the Laxos for a sweat after dinner. When I finish I'll take all of you for ice cream. How does that sound?"

The sauna wasn't exactly like the sweat lodge. Torval, the owner, always wore bib overalls and the whitest T-shirts Jodi had ever seen. His family had come from Finland to settle in Michigan. When the mines began to close, his father came to the west coast to find work. After graduating from high school, Torval took a job driving truck. He had an opportunity to buy an old wrecker and in 1968 began towing trucks on Snoqualmie Pass.

When Jodi arrived he was on the front porch, smiling as usual. A cup of steaming coffee in his meaty hand. Beside him, on a small table was a bowl filled with sugar cubes. He would place a cube in his mouth and sip his coffee as his father before him had done. His father, however, had poured his coffee from his cup into his saucer, then sipped his coffee through the sugar cube from the saucer. Torval's wife had scolded him until he no longer poured his coffee into his saucer, but drank it from his cup.

"Good to see you, Jodi. I am glad you could make it."

"Thanks for inviting me, Torval. Sorry to be late."

"It's okay. I t'ink you got big trouble. You need a good sauna. My boys, they say, the people in town are getting nervous, eh?"

The two men walked to the rear of the house. The sauna was a small building. Inside, fresh towels were laid out on the benches. Jodi hung his clothing on a wooden peg on the wall. He wrapped himself in a fresh towel and joined Torval in the steam room. The older man was already relaxed as the steam enveloped his short, stocky body and his huge shoulders. Torval had a knack for keeping the steam at just the right consistency and the heat at a perfect degree. The two men were silent while in the sauna. The steam felt good. It cleansed the body inside and out and made tired muscles relax.

"I t'ink we are here long enough, eh? You can use the shower first, Jodi. You can use the sauna any time. If I'm not home you have the boys heat it for you."

"Where I come from the Sweat Lodge is used to purify your spirit so you can think more clearly; to see things as they really are. I hope this will work for me." Jodi looked at his watch. It was getting late and he had promised his kids some ice cream. The bone-weary feeling induced by the stress of today's activity was gone.

"Thanks, Torval. Gotta go."

The streets were virtually vacant. Only two cars were parked on the main thoroughfare. Jodi recognized both as belonging to people working tonight, one in the bakery and the other at the Mar T Cafe. The townspeople were nervous. Jodi knew that by morning, when everyone had had a chance to read the newspaper, it would be worse. Ice cream with Eileen and the kids seemed like a really good idea right now.

The Jays were down by six in the top of the eighth. Brice had a date waiting. Leaving the game a little early would get him out of the downtown area before the rest of the spectators got on the road. His date had an apartment on the south end of Seattle, near the Boeing plant. He couldn't stay long tonight because of the reports he must complete in the morning. Pete Kaufman was his supervisor, but Jodi was in charge of the case. Pete would be much more forgiving of a late report than Jodi.

Brice was about to walk down the concourse to the main exit when someone called his name. He turned to look and recognized Barry Mallette coming down the ramp behind him. Mallette was a lieutenant assigned to the downtown headquarters. His job was to coordinate all job assignments in the department. A good man to know if you were looking for a new job assignment or a promotion. At this point in his life Brice was looking for neither, but he liked to keep his options open.

"Hi, Barry. How did you like the game? I think the Mariners have a real chance at the pennant this season. With Griffey's hot bat and Johnson's pitching, we really stand a chance." He paused for a couple of steps. "How are things downtown?" He was just making conversation while they walked.

"It's much quieter downtown than it is in North Bend these days. I see you had another one today. I spoke with Cornetti this afternoon. He told me there was some fresh information on the killer. Any suspects?"

"None. I haven't seen Cornetti's report yet, but I was out there all day. We found some tire tracks and a shoe print. There's a handprint too, but that hasn't gone through the computer yet. Looks promising though."

"Well, good luck. I hope you get this guy pretty soon. By the way, Brice. Today I heard Pete was taking the lieutenant-captain exam. Are you going to take the sergeant exam? There could be an opening if Pete gets promoted."

"Not this time. I'm happy where I am and with what I'm doing. I just bought that townhouse and can't afford to move if I was transferred. If I was assured of staying in North Bend I might try for it."

"You let me know if you change your mind. Stop in and see me when you're downtown." The two men were now in the parking lot.

"I'll do that. Thanks." When he reached his Buick, Brice was still trying to figure out if Mallette was just passing the time of day or if he was serious.

It was 7 A.M. when Jodi parked in front of the office. He had stopped on the way to buy a *Seattle Post Intelligencer*, the morning newspaper. There it was, in bold headlines on the front page. "**Another Child Slain at North Bend**." Pete had been busy yesterday, too. The office door was open. Miss Emma was busy making fresh coffee. Her purse and jacket had been piled on her desk.

"Good morning, Jodi. Did you get rested last night?"

"Morning, Emma. Yes, I'm fine this morning. Looks like we're in the spotlight again today." He held the front page of the newspaper up for her to read. "Any new business this morning?"

"I just got here , so I really don't know. Gary hasn't come in yet. He must be taking one last look around town before he goes off duty."

Just then the door opened and Gary Durbin, the night shift supervisor, came into the office

"Good morning," he said cheerfully. "You two are in early this morning."

"The earlier you get behind, the more time you have to catch up," Jodi grinned.

"I saw the headlines this morning, so I know what you mean. We had a quiet night. The only call was an argument at the North Bend Tavern. Two guys with too much beer in them were about to get physical over the pool table. I had their friends drive them home. That was it for excitement last night." Durbin reported.

Miss Emma approached the two men with two cups of steaming coffee. "I checked with downtown and there's nothing urgent. The sheriff wants all the formal reports from yesterday. The television stations are hounding him for interviews. The P.I. has the story on the front page and the sheriff's not happy. He thinks they have more information than he does."

"Thanks, Emma. I don't suppose you've heard from Brice this morning."

"Not this morning. When I talked with him last evening, he said he would be in early to do his report. I haven't talked with him since. But don't you worry, he'll be here soon."

Gary went to his office and Jodi stepped into his. He dug out the Shirley Ng file and was reading Connie Lupine's report when Brice came in.

Brice was sipping a Coca Cola. "Morning. Anything new?"

Chapter 5

"The sheriff has been on the phone and wants your report right away. How long will it take you to get it written?"

"I have it all done in longhand. I just have to get it typed up. Shouldn't take more than a half hour."

"Get on it right away, will you, Brice? Pete will be in soon and he'll need to take the file to town for the sheriff. I wish you'd done it last night so I could have had more time to review it before we sent it on. None of us is going to like it if the sheriff asks questions that should have been answered in the reports."

"I know, Jodi. Don't worry, my reports are always complete. Lighten up."

Jodi was in no mood for Brice's flippant attitude. "If three murdered children aren't cause for serious thought, then I don't know what is. Come on, Brice, this is our job. We get paid to take care of the public, and these reports are part of that job. Just get it done and put it on my desk."

The front door opened and Connie Lupine said good morning to Miss Emma. The two men exchanged glares. Brice went to his desk. "I'll have this report in thirty minutes," he called over his shoulder.

Connie peeked around the corner into Jodi's office. "Things a little tense in here this morning?" she asked.

"Sorry, Connie, you weren't supposed to hear that. I read your report. Good job. I need that list of the people in class at the academy, though. Other than that it's great. You have no idea how much I appreciate your staying last night to finish that report, thanks again. As soon as Pete comes in and I have Brice's report, I'll go canvas the neighborhood between the Ng home and where her girlfriend lives. Maybe someone saw her or a stranger or something else that might help us. Would you like to come along?"

"Sure would." She liked being included. "I'll make a copy of that list for you." She disappeared around the corner. In less than a minute she reappeared in the doorway, the list in her hand. Pete was standing behind her.

"How's your morning?" Pete asked with more than a little sarcasm. "As good as mine, I hope."

"I'm going back to work. Call me when you're ready to leave," Connie said as she backed out of the small room.

"Have you seen the morning paper?" Pete asked.

"Oh Yes. I have. Emma told me you have to go into town this morning and explain to the sheriff. Good luck. I have the whole file here," Jodi explained, "except for Brice's report, which should be finished in about ten minutes. I suspect the whole town will be full of TV cameras and reporters by noon."

Pete's face was grim. "I don't know where the P.I. got the information, but it was pretty accurate. Not many particulars, but accurate. I'm worried about one thing in that article, though. Did you notice they referred to him as the "Mount Si Murderer"? That's going to sound really good on the six o'clock news," he said. "Like it or not, we're going to be the top story for every news program until we catch this guy. Reporters are going to be following us around like puppies. There's not much I can do about that. Just be careful about how much information you let them see. We still have legal obligations here."

"I got it , Pete. I'm taking Connie with me to check out the Ng girl's last walk before reporters start interviewing everyone about what we interviewed them about."

"Listen, Pete. If you want me to review the daily shift reports and make assignments for the day, you can take the file and head for Seattle. Brice should be about finished with his report by now."

"Good idea, Jodi. Have him bring me a copy when he's finished."

Ten minutes later Pete was out the front door on his way into downtown Seattle. He and the sheriff would be in conference most of the morning. Traffic from Issaquah across the floating bridge and into town would be fierce this time of the morning.

Jodi had accomplished all the daily morning chores in the office when Miss Emma told him Earl was on line one. He had forgotten Earl was going to call this morning.

"Morning, Earl. I still don't have anything on those vandalism cases."
"Mornin', Jodi. Hey, I know you're busy this morning, but I would like to have about five mutes of your time. I think you'll like what we came up with this morning … You know, the Chamber?"

"Oh, yeah. Sorry Earl, I've been so busy I forgot. Are you busy now?"

"As a matter of fact, now would be perfect. I have an appointment with a client in a half hour. I'll buy the coffee at the Mar T if you want to meet me."

"I'll be right there, Earl. If you don't mind, I'd like to bring Connie Lupine with me. We have to do some interviews this morning. We can meet with you on the way."

"That'll be fine. I'll walk to the cafe and order coffee. You want breakfast?"

"Thanks, but we won't have time. We'll be right there."

The KOMO-TV mobile television unit was coming up the street as the two deputies walked out of the office. The two hurried to the patrol car in hopes of avoiding the reporters. The truck stopped in the space vacated by the patrol car. Jodi was confident Miss Emma would keep them busy for a while. It was only three blocks to the Mar-T Cafe.

Earl had coffee and sweet rolls waiting. He motioned for the deputies when they came through the door. A stack of notes and what looked to be a schedule strewn on his side of the booth.

Chapter 5

"Connie, you know this bum, don't you?" Jodi asked, teasing Earl. "He and I played football together at U-Dub. He's been mooching meals off me ever since."

"Yes, good morning, Earl. Thanks for the coffee." She turned to Jodi, "Earl's wife is my aerobics instructor."

"Good morning, Connie. It must be tough working with this Indian. Is he still sending smoke signals or has he learned to use the police radio?"

"I don't mean to rush you, Earl, but the TV cameras are right behind us. If we don't get a move on we're going to have them with us during our interviews this morning." Jodi said seriously.

"Sorry. It must be the salesman in me." He paused to pick up and review the top sheet of paper from the mess in front of him. "Some of the Chamber people met with me this morning, and we came up with a plan. We have all the stuff for the Neighborhood Watch Program. We never used it because it never seemed necessary. We're going to start the Neighborhood Watch Program, beginning today. In addition we are starting neighborhood patrols. We will work in shifts, twenty four hours a day. There will be two pairs on foot patrol and one pair in a vehicle. That's six people per shift, twenty four hours a day, all chamber of commerce members. It's going to spread us pretty thin. We all have businesses to tend, but we agree on how important this is." Earl looked directly into Jodi Eagle's eyes. "It's also going to be important for you to catch this killer … soon. We would like your deputies to keep an eye out for our people. For their safety. We're contacting the school board and some of the teachers. We want to open the grade school and provide some supervised activities for the kids. We're still working on that one." He shuffled through his notes one more time. "Well, what d'ya think? Will it work?"

"Sounds great, my friend. I'll pass this along to Pete when he gets back from town. This program should do two things. It will make it more difficult for someone to abduct a child without being seen and it should help relieve some of the tensions the parents have about watching their kids. What do you think, Connie?"

"It sounds good to me." She had been taking some notes. "It might be a good idea to run this by the mayor. Just to save him some embarrassment when the reporters ask him about it."

Earl began to stuff the papers into his brief case. "Okay, you guys get back to work and I'll follow up on this." He stood, "By the way, Connie. My youngest son, Darren asked me to thank you for helping him with his swing and his grip. He hit two runs, a double and a single, in last night's game. I'll see you two later." He picked up the check and walked to the till where Ester greeted him with a smile. Earl was a good tipper.

CHAPTER 6

The morning haze had burned off. The sun shone and the air was warm and clean. It seldom became too hot in the valley, but today would be a scorcher. The Snoqualmie Valley, during the day, inhaled the warm air from the flatland below and in the evening it exhaled the cool mountain air down onto the flat farmland. This made North Bend a pleasant place in which to live.

Connie and Jodi had knocked on three doors each when the first of the reporters found them. When Jodi spotted the KING-TV truck at the end of the street, he motioned for Connie to come to this side and join him.

"I think we'd better stick together," he told her, as the first reporter advanced.

"Are you deputies Eagle and Lupine?" he asked while the cameraman hooked up his cables.

'Yes, I'm Eagle, this is Deputy Lupine."

Before Jodi could say anything else, the reporter stuffed a microphone in his face and asked, "Would you mind if I asked you a few questions about the child murders and the Mount Si Killer?"

"I know you folks have a great deal of interest in this story for your audience, but you will have to talk with our supervisor. We have a lot of work to do, and your presence is keeping us from it. Please, go back to the office and wait for the sergeant." Jodi was trying not to show his irritation.

"Deputy Eagle, can you tell us if this is the neighborhood from which the last victim was taken?" The male reporter in the brown sport coat asked, ignoring what Jodi had just said.

"I'm not authorized to answer your questions. How about turning that camera off for a minute so we can talk?" Jodi asked politely.

Chapter 6

"Sure." He motioned for the cameraman to turn off the camera. "I'm sorry. I guess I went about this the wrong way. Spontaneity is important on camera; it just looks better. I didn't intend to interfere with your work. I try to maintain a good working relationship with the local police departments. Is there anything you can give me? Is this the street the victim came from?" He sounded partly honest and partly sugar-coated.

"I would really like to help you but I can't." Jodi explained. "Sergeant Pete Kaufman will be back from Seattle right after lunch. He has all the information. He can give you a statement. We are out here trying to do our job. We can't do it with you folks tagging along. I promise I'll tell Pete you cooperated and that he should give you as much as he can."

"Okay, we'll back off a little. But, off the record can you give us anything?"

"Yes, maybe I can. If you check with Earl Campbell at his real estate office, I think he and the mayor may be able to give you some information on what the city is doing to protect its children from future harm." Jodi knew Earl would be a little miffed at him for this and hoped that he and the mayor had met to discuss their strategy.

The workload had not lessened because of the deaths of the children. Crimes, though most were minor, continued to take place. Brice was in his regular patrol area now with reports of two burglaries to investigate. Businesses were sparsely scattered in this area, making it a prime target for burglars. Either juveniles or people from out of town committed most these burglaries.

He had just completed his investigation of the first break-in when a white station wagon with a PRESS pass stuck to the window pulled in beside his patrol car. A twentyish, man wearing blue jeans and a striped T-shirt almost jumped from the car. He fairly ran around the nose of the vehicle as though he feared he might not catch the officer.

"Hi there. Are you Brice Roman?" He asked in a squeaky voice.

"Yes." Brice replied, looking up from the sheet of paper he had been writing on, "Who are you?"

He reached into his shirt pocket and produced a business card which he handed to the deputy. "I'm Jerry Lomax. I'm working for the *World Inquirer*."

Brice recognized the name of this supermarket tabloid with a poor reputation for the truth. He remembered a recent headline in the newspaper, which read, "GOD SEEN WRESTLING SATAN ON TELEVISION." Accompanied by a picture of a cloud shaped like two wrestlers, suspended over a wrestling ring in some unknown arena.

"I'm kinda busy right now. What can I do for you?"

"I understand you're one of the officers investigating the Mount Si Murders. My paper has authorized me to pay you for an exclusive interview. We will pay you extra if you can provide us with pictures of the victims and the crime scenes. We can be generous if you help us out. As you may know we are a national publication, well respected in the field of journalism."

"I don't think I can help you." Brice replied, concealing his amusement. "I have orders not to talk with reporters. In any event I don't want my name in your paper."

"That's not a problem, Deputy Roman. I can guarantee you complete anonymity. Nobody will ever know where I got this information. It would be like money from heaven for you; no risk, no loss. Come on. What do you say?" This was the standard sales pitch of the *World Inquirer*, worked every time.

Brice looked at the business card again, then stuffed it into his shirt pocket. "Jerry. Is it Jerry? I have certain legal responsibilities to look out for. I can't just grab a bunch of department photos. Maybe I can meet you later, but right now I have to finish with a burglary. I still have another one to investigate and then patrol my area. I'm busy."

"I can meet you this evening. What time would be good for you?" The young reporter asked, a little excited with his apparent success.

"Don't get your hopes up. We haven't made a deal yet."

"Okay, okay. I'll buy you a beer at North Bend Tavern at, say, seven o'clock?"

"I'll think about it." As Jerry turned to walk back to his car, Brice called him back. "How much are we talking about here?"

"We'll talk about that tonight." The reporter said with a cocky little bounce.

As Lomax drove away, Brice went back to his report. He was just finishing when Mary Alice Jade came out of the real estate office. She was blonde and beautiful, and dressed like a Nordstrom model. She was twenty eight years old and owned this office. Mary Alice was also single, which made her a target for almost every Romeo in town.

"How soon can I get back into my office, Brice? I have a tremendous amount of work waiting for me."

"Let me dust the window area for prints and I'll be finished. I would like you to write a statement for me on how you discovered the burglary this morning. Not too lengthy, just a short statement, and sign it on the bottom of the sheet." Brice gave her an official statement form.

He completed his work in less than a half hour. On the way out of the office he stopped to tease Mary Alice, he let her know she could call him any time.

It was just a mile to the next burglary scene. When he arrived he found an almost identical operation. The culprits had broken a rear window and entered. They took office equipment and computers. This was the local funeral home and it appeared

Chapter 6

the burglars took time to look for any drugs they might be able to use or sell. He dusted the rear entry area for fingerprints, interviewed the owner, Harry Makin. Makin told him that the front door was left open and if they had come to the front they could have entered without breaking the window. After taking pictures, an inventory of missing items was written. Brice wrapped up the investigation with a last walk-through. Outside a broken window, against the wall was a piece of paper. He retrieved it to learn it was a gasoline credit card receipt.

Back inside, he asked if the receipt belonged to any of the employees. It didn't. Slipping the paper into his notebook, he gave Harry a witness statement form and asked him for his statement. He could leave the completed form at the sheriff's office.

Brice was patrolling west, toward Falls City, when a highway patrolman flagged him down. Brice stopped behind the Highway Patrol vehicle. The two men met between the cars.

"How ya doin', Brice?"

"Pretty good, all things considered." Brice replied.

"Want to go for coffee?" Patrolman Cavanaugh asked.

"I can't, Gene. I still have some work to do on the death from yesterday and I have two burglaries to finish up today. The town is filled with reporters. They follow me around everywhere. It makes working a little tough. How are things on the freeway?"

"Oh, you know, a taillight here and a speeder there. I get bored sometimes."

"Be careful out there, Gene. Crime is moving out of the city. You just don't know when some coke freak or nut might pull a gun and shoot you for no reason at all. Look at us. We haven't had a major crime in years, except for a body now and then, dumped by some drug dealer from the city. All of a sudden we have three kids killed and left on the side of the road. We had two break-ins last night. We used to be a small town of farmers and loggers. Now, with all the new subdivisions, we're becoming the next Bellevue."

"Don't let them get you down, Brice. Hey, I almost forgot the reason I stopped you. We're planning a softball game and beer bust, the last weekend of July. How about getting a team of deputies together and joining in ... I already checked, the Mariners are out of town that weekend."

"Sounds great, I'll put up a notice in the office. We'll stomp your butts again this year." Both men laughed. "I have to get going, Gene. I still have a lot of area to patrol and reports to write. See you later." He pulled himself into his car, waving as he drove away.

When Jodi and Connie returned to the office, there were four TV trucks

43

and several carloads of reporters parked along the street. Sergeant Kaufman was doing his best to satisfy their questions. Jodi and his partner walked around the end of the building to a rear door where they entered unseen. Their first stop was the coffeepot; they had missed lunch.

Miss Emma had suffered a particularly busy and frustrating day. Reporters had been in the office and on the telephone all day long. She'd managed the problem pretty well by organizing a press conference on the front walk. No matter how confusing the day, Miss Emma always seemed able to cope.

"Anything new, Emma?" Jodi asked.

"Reporters, reporters and more reporters. Earl called, he wants to talk to you. The mayor called, he wants you to call him. Brice has a credit card number he wants checked. And your wife called, nothing serious, but call her as soon as you can. I guess you saw Pete out front with the news people. He has not had a good day since he came back from downtown." Emma ran her finger down the list again. "I think that's all for now. How about you two, did you learn anything new?"

"Not a thing." Connie answered. "It's like this thing never happened. Nobody saw anything."

"Give me that credit card number and I'll run it for Brice." Jodi said, "And would you get my wife on the line for me?"

The news hounds had tried to hurry the interview with Pete. It was getting late and their deadlines were creeping up on them. Pete didn't give them much outside of the prepared statement he and the sheriff had put together. When the last of them wouldn't go away, he just said, "Thank you ladies and gentlemen, that's all for today. If there are any further developments I will let you know." He turned away, walking into the office, leaving several reporters standing on the sidewalk.

The first person he spotted when he entered the office was Jodi. "Did you learn anything new?" He asked, crispness still in his voice.

"Nothing, Boss. We talked with every person on the route from the Ng house to the girlfriend's place. Nobody saw a thing. Connie and I talked about that, and we thought it may be because she was abducted close to her own home."

"Isn't it strange that all these kids were taken without any sign of a struggle? In all the interviews, the kid's parents say their children were instructed not to get into a vehicle with a stranger. If that's true, how is this guy getting the kids into his truck, assuming the Toyota is the suspect vehicle."

"Sorry Pete, at this point all I have is questions. I don't have any answers."

"I was just thinking," Connie interrupted. "Pete mentioned that each of

Chapter 6

the kids had been instructed not to get into a car with a stranger. That could mean that the kids don't see the guy as a threat. Maybe he's dressed like a priest or a cop or something like that. Or, it could mean that the killer is someone everyone in town knows and trusts."

"Keep on it," Pete instructed.

"Will do." Life suddenly became complicated around here, Jodi thought. But his grandfather had said a good brave can fight many bears if they attack one at a time.

"I'll go write up the report." Connie offered. "Anything else you want me to do right now?"

"Thanks, Connie. That should cover it. I'll talk with the Mayor and with Earl."

Emma was on the intercom. "Your wife on line two."

"Got it, thanks Emma." He picked up the receiver and punched the button for line two.

"Hi, honey. Is everything alright?"

"Everything's fine. I had a call from Earl. He's organizing some activities at the school for the local children, and has asked me to help supervise the kids. I just wanted to know if you had any objection to my doing that." The tension was gone from her voice.

"I think it would be good for both the kids and for you. When will he be able to open the school?"

"He said he'd get back with me on that." The thought of taking positive action had almost entirely relieved her of earlier frustrations. "It might mean you have to fix your own lunches."

"The way things are going around here, I won't have time for lunch anyway." He gave a small chuckle. "I am supposed to call Earl as soon as I hang up here. This is a really good idea, honey. Let me finish up here and I'll try to get home on time tonight."

He called Miss Emma. "Emma, if you have that credit card number I'll do that now."

While he waited for Emma to bring the memo with the number, he dialed his friend Earl. He knew the telephone number by heart. "Earl, Jodi Eagle."

"Jodi, thanks a lot buddy. I've been up to my hip pockets in reporters all day. When I finally thought to ask why they were chasing me, they said you put them onto me. I owe you one, pard."

"I would never give you a problem you couldn't handle," Jodi said, laughing into the receiver. "Eileen tells me you've worked out a deal to open the school. She wants to come and help. How soon will you be in operation over there?"

"I met with the mayor this morning. He met with the school board today. He called me just a few minutes ago to tell me we had a green light for Monday. The school board also authorized pay for five teachers to organize the activities. I want Eileen to help register kids in and out of the building. You know, check to be sure the right parents are picking up their kids. We hope this will ease some of the fears the parents have about the safety of their kids. People are really worried about this killer, Jodi. Two of my salespeople asked for time off to be with their families. We have to put an end to this and soon, man."

"I know how high tensions are, I have kids too. We're working on this as hard as we can. If we had any real suspects we would have them in here now. The whole department is working on it. I want this guy, but we can't just go out and arrest someone without evidence. We have to be sure. I feel responsible for not finding the guy. But he hasn't left us much to go on."

"I'm not blaming you or anyone, pal. I'm sorry, I didn't mean to sound like I was blaming you personally. I guess I'm getting wound as tight as everyone else in town. Tell you what. Tonight, you get Eileen and the kids, I'll pick up my bride, and we'll go to Bellevue for Pizza. I'll buy."

"Sounds good to me. I should be out of here by five. I'll pick you up in the station wagon. See you later. By the way; Linda said you had been to the doctor for a check-up. Is everything okay?"

"Nothing serious, Jodi. Just a little high blood pressure. He gave me some pills; I'm fine."

With no computer link in the office, all data checks had to go through the main office, downtown. It was usually done on the radio, but things like credit card numbers were phoned in so that people with scanners didn't have access to the numbers. A printout would be sent to the office by fax. It would probably be here by the time Brice came in off the road.

Next on his list of things to do was a call to the mayor. Tom Altman had been mayor for fifteen years. A city term limit bill, passed last year, would make this his last term. City hall was in the same building as the police station, but the mayor, being a part time city employee, had a business of his own to run. When Jodi called, the mayor answered the phone.

"Mountain View Golf Course, Director Altman speaking, how may I help you?"

"Mr. Mayor, Jodi Eagle. I had a message to call you."

"Jodi, I was about to call you again. Have you talked with Earl?"

"Yes sir, I have. He filled me in on the school thing."

"You two fellas have come up with a pretty good idea. I know you've been working hard on this case. I don't envy your job. We'll do anything within our power to keep citizens calm. By the way, I had a lot of reporters here today. I want to thank you for giving Earl and me some time to get prepared. Now, is there anything the city can do to help out?"

"I can't think of anything right now, Mr. Mayor. If I do I'll be sure to call you. Thanks again for your help."

At the end of each day, Jodi had a habit of reviewing his activity for the day. He checked his notes and reviewed his reports to be sure he had completed everything. He was about finished with his last report when Connie came into the office. She had compiled more paperwork for the Ng file. He looked up when she came in.

"If you want to look these over, I'll file them. I think everything else is done for today," she said.

"You've done a great job with this, Connie. Earl, his wife, my family, and I are going to Bellevue for pizza after work. How about joining us? It's nothing special, just a family thing. We'd sure like to have you come along."

"Thanks, Jodi. I'll take a rain check, if you don't mind. You have worked me to a frazzle. I'm going home, getting into a hot bath and relax. I'm beat."

"I understand. Maybe another time. See you Monday."

Together, Pete and Jodi left the office. It had been a long and not too rewarding day. Driving past the Mar-T Cafe, Jodi saw two press cars parked at the curb. He wished this publicity would just go away. The Laxo twins were cruising through town, each in his own pickup. Both waved as they passed the King County Police car.

At home, Jodi discussed the day's events with his wife. He teased the boys and told them they were going out for pizza. The whole family seemed relaxed tonight.

CHAPTER 7

Brice came to the office less than ten minutes after Jodi and Pete had gone. Emma was just leaving when he walked in. She gave him the printout from the credit card, said good night and went home for the day.

Scanning the information he decided there was nothing in it that couldn't wait until morning for action. He put the burglary reports in manila folders and dropped them into the sergeant's IN basket. The deputy looked through his notebook to see if he had forgotten anything. Tossing his empty Coke can into the recycle bin, he left the office.

He drove home, and backed his patrol car into the reserved parking space. There was an hour before he was to meet Lomax. Inside his townhouse, he turned on the stereo. This was not going to be an easy decision. The probability of losing his job was pretty high. Brice opened a Heineken and sat on the couch. What to do? That stupid bitch in town wanted more money for supposed medical expenses. The payments on the townhouse were eating more of his monthly check than he had anticipated. The payments on the Buick seemed to come around more frequently than once a month. Would it be worth the risk to deal with Lomax?

Forty minutes later he had showered, changed clothes, finished his beer and was on his way to the tavern. He hadn't yet made a decision, which led him to wonder what kind of money the reporter was offering. The streets were nearly deserted. It was strange; no people walking, no kids running down the sidewalk, no one on the benches in the park even though it was such a warm evening.

The white PRESS car was parked on the side of the brick building. Inside, Brice found Lomax seated at a table in the back of the room, behind the pool tables. He had a small notebook on the table next to a draft beer. He looked up as Brice approached the table.

The cocktail waitress had followed Brice to the table. "What can I get you?" she asked.

"Heineken," he answered.

Lomax waited for the girl in the tight white blouse and short black miniskirt to go back to the bar. "Mr. Roman, do you mind if I call you Brice? How was your day?"

"About like all the others," Brice replied. The girl was returning with his beer.

When she walked away again Lomax continued. "I understand you're having some tight financial times, Brice."

"How the hell did you find that out?"

"My paper has been in this business a long time. We have many sources. Don't get me wrong, this isn't a shakedown. I only mention this so we can start a meaningful negotiation here."

"You listen to me, Jerry. It's true, if I didn't need money I wouldn't be here talking with a sleazebag like you. I'm telling you up front, if my name appears in any of your newspapers, I'll be knocking on your door. You got that?" There was no anger in his voice, just cold determination.

"Don't get your tail in a twist, Brice. We're after the same things here. A mutual interest, you might say. Your personal life isn't germane to this story. All I want is the photos and the files. And, I'm willing to pay good money for them. Are we on the same page now?"

"That's more like it, let's get down to business." Jerry Lomax knew he had the deputy by the short hairs. "I'm willing to pay you a grand for the files on the three killings. I'll give you another grand if we get photos of all three crime scenes and the bodies. The price is not negotiable and I would advise you not to try to come back later and try to shake us down. We're a big company and we don't like to lose. We can have some good times if we keep it friendly. What do you say?"

"I don't like you, Jerry. I'll meet you on the south side of the Edgewick Road overpass in an hour. I want the money in cash, no checks. Don't get the idea this is going to be a long and lasting relationship, because it isn't." Brice stood. "Thanks for the beer." Sarcasm dripped from his icy voice.

Brice walked out the front door of the tavern, looking neither right nor left. He was going to do it, he didn't have to like it, but he was going to do it.

He drove directly to the office, knowing he would be alone there. He had a key to the file cabinet which held all the files from this and the other two deaths. It was easy enough to make copies of each of the files. Some of the photos had as many as three copies. He sorted out several pictures from each of the cases, dropping them into their respective files. By hand, he wrote names on three file folders, placing stacks of papers and pictures in each. He returned the originals to the secure cabinet, locking it again.

He had finished his business and walked out the front door just as Larry Piedmont, assigned to business district patrol, pulled to a stop in front of the office.

"Working late, Brice?" he asked.

"No, just stopped to pick up some stuff from my desk," he lied. "It's really quiet in town tonight. Looks more like a Monday evening than a Friday."

"You've got that right. See ya later." He walked into the office.

Brice cruised slowly east on old U.S. Highway 10. Even at this pace he would be twenty minutes early at the rendezvous. Maybe Jerry would also be early. It might be better if he didn't have too much time to think about what he was doing. At Edgewick Road, he turned right and crossed the overpass. On the south side of the freeway he stopped, parking so he could see traffic coming from three directions. He turned off his engine and began to think of the possible ramifications of his deal with the reporter. Just as he was having serious second thoughts the white station wagon came up the off-ramp, interrupting his guilt.

Jerry made a U-turn, stopping his car alongside the blue Buick. "Did you get it?" He asked through the open window.

"Did you bring the cash?"

"I have it. Where are the files?" Lomax was anxious to view his success.

Brice handed the three folders through the window to an expectant hand. Jerry quickly dropped them on the seat next to him and thumbed through the contents of the files. This was even better than he expected.

He turned back to the window, handing a thick, white, business-size envelope to his new colleague. "There's more cash where that came from. If you get anything more on the killings I'll pay you for it. Don't worry, Brice, nobody will ever know, you have my word."

Somehow, Brice found no comfort in that. "You just stay away from me. I'll call you if I get anything else. Until then, you don't know me. You got that?"

"Whatever. See you around." He was grinning like a Cheshire cat as he drove off. Brice found no reason to smile. He looked into the envelope, tossed it on the seat and drove back to town.

He had planned to go home, then decided instead he needed company and conversation to stop him from thinking about what he had just done. He drove west on the Falls City road to the real estate office of Mary Alice Jade. The lights were still on. He walked up the path to the office and opened the door. The receptionist had gone for the day.

Chapter 7

"Is anyone here?" he called.

"Be right with you." Came a voice from an office. A moment later the pretty blonde realtor stepped out of her office.

"Hi, Mary Alice. I know it's late, but I saw your office lights were on. I just thought that, with the day you've had, you might like to have dinner." He used his smoothest style.

"That was thoughtful of you, Brice." She looked at her watch. "I think I will. Give me a minute to lock up. Where would you like to go?"

"If you want to ride with me, we can go out to the Falls. I'll bring you back later to pick up your car. Can I help you lock up?"

"No thanks, I'm all finished." She picked up her purse, turned off the lights and locked the front door. Outside, the evening breeze was cool and the air fresh.

Dinner was relaxed. The food in the old power company hotel was excellent and the view of the falls spectacular. The small talk over dinner was exactly what Brice needed. They spoke of the new subdivision being planned, south of I-90, at the end of North Bend Avenue. They talked about how the character of the town was changing.

After dinner and a drink, Brice drove his date back to her office, stopping next to her car.

"Thank you for dinner, Brice. It was nice."

"I should thank you. Tonight is the first nice thing I've experienced all week. By the way, I may have a lead on the burglars. Don't hold your breath until you get your stuff back, though."

"Just put them away. I had to buy another computer today. I can't afford to do that too many times. Thanks again for dinner, Brice. Good night."

Brice was much less tense on his drive home. In town he passed Jodi's station wagon. That looked like Earl Campbell in the front seat with him. He must have taken the family out to dinner. At home, Brice turned the cable television to the Vanguard station, opened another Heineken and stretched out on the couch. He'd done it; now he'd have to live with it.

Monday morning was bright, no morning haze. Today would be a scorcher. Eileen was to meet Earl this morning at the school. The neighborhood watch was working. The patrols had been on the streets all weekend. Anxiety among the citizens had diminished some; people were taking action, fighting back, and they felt good about it. Earl was a great organizer; his plan was beginning to have a positive effect on the small community.

Pete and Jodi were both in the office early. Connie and Miss Emma came shortly after. Brice called in to say he was going directly to his patrol area. The rest of the shift prepared for a normal day. Jodi had just finished reading the coroner's report when Pete poked his head around the corner.

"I just had a call from the funeral home. The funeral for the Ng girl is today at one o'clock. I'm going to ask you to escort the funeral motorcade. You know the Ng family. Just try to keep the reporters away from them. If you have an opportunity to speak with them, please, give them our sympathy."

"Thanks Pete, I will. This has to be the last one of these. I can't think of anything worse than losing a child."

"You have the duty then, one o'clock." He stopped at the coffeepot on the way back to his own office.

A short while later, Jodi had cleaned off his desk. He stepped into the outer office to speak with Emma Garson, who had already written a large stack of phone messages this morning. Most were from reporters wanting to know if there was further information to be had about the Mount Si Killings.

"I'm going out on patrol. I should be back around ten. Unless it's a real emergency, I won't be available this afternoon. Pete gave me the escort duty for the funeral."

Connie Lupine overheard him and called out before rounding the corner to the front office. "Jodi, hold up just a minute. I need to see you before you leave."

She came striding toward him. "If you don't have anything holding you here, why don't you ride with me this morning. We can cruise your area while we're out there. We can discuss all this in the car."

Jodi turned to look into the sergeant's office. "That okay with you, Pete?"

"Yeah, go ahead. Just be sure everything is covered."

Five minutes later the two were moving east on old Highway 10. The Laxo boys were just going out to the yard to begin work for the day. They flashed their big toothy grins and waved to the two deputies cruising slowly by.

"Let's drive up to mile 38, just for the heck of it. I know the area has been looked over by M.C.U., but let's look anyway."

"You read the coroner's report this morning. Was there anything in there that might help us, anything we didn't know?"

"Not a thing." Jodi said. "Death was caused by a choke hold, just like the other two. He did it right, too. He cut off the blood to the brain while allowing the person to breathe. That way the victim doesn't struggle as hard, fighting for breath. The victims are all small. It looks like he lays them face down, keeps his weight on them, puts an arm around their throat and pulls back. All the victims were done the same way. That piece of information isn't for the press."

Chapter 7

The two officers drove silently until they were off the highway at Exit 38, which led to the small concrete bridge. Jodi parked across the road on a stretch of abandoned paving. Lenny or his crew had replaced the guardrail. The memory of the dead child lying face down on the rocks above was still strong.

Jodi pointed to the spot. "That's where she was found. He stepped over the railing here." Faint chalk marks were visible here and there.

"Lots of people have been here since that day. I'm going to walk down the road a couple of hundred yards and back, just in case we missed something. Why don't you do the same in that direction? I'll meet you back at the car in a few minutes."

It was a fruitless exercise. Traffic and weather had obliterated even the tire tracks and shoe prints. Jodi was leaning on the fender of the patrol car when Connie returned.

"Find anything?"

He shook his head.

"Me neither."

Back in the car, they continued to patrol. "I wish the FBI would get on the ball with the evidence we sent to them. Maybe there was a hair, a fiber, a blood spot, or something to give us a lead. Nobody can commit a crime without leaving something of himself at the scene. It can't be done. I get really mad at myself for not being able to see it. I don't think my grandfather is proud of me as a hunter right now."

"I think you're just being impatient. You have found evidence. You have to wait for all of it to be processed. Be patient." They were back in town now. "Before we go out to my area, let's call and see if they got a match on that hand print."

"Good idea." Jodi agreed, turning right toward the station.

Connie sat across the desk from her partner while he dialed Lewis Cornetti of the Major Crimes Unit. Miss Emma brought two cups of hot, fresh coffee.

"Lew, Jodi Eagle. I was calling to see if you had anything new for me."

"Sorry, Jodi, nothing new. You got the Coroner's report, didn't you?"

"Yes, I did. There's not much doubt it's the same guy. But we need physical evidence. Did you run those palm and finger prints you took from the guardrail?"

"Yup, and you won't believe it. This guy doesn't exist. We ran him in State, NCIC, FBI and XYZ. My guys have to draw the print into the computer by hand. Once he's in there, we'll have him forever. If he ever turns up, anywhere, we'll get him."

"You're telling me this guy isn't in the fingerprint files anywhere?" Jodi asked again.

"That's right. We're checking Interpol to see if he might be a foreign national. It will be a couple of days before we have an answer from them."

"Well, thanks anyway, Lew. Let me know if anything turns up."

Jodi hung up the phone. "Nothing," he said. "We might as well finish that patrol in your area."

It was just after noon when Jodi and Connie returned to the office. Miss Emma was eating a sack lunch at her desk when they arrived. There were no new messages for him, so Jodi went to the locker room to put on a fresh, sharply creased uniform. He donned his Smoky the Bear hat and slipped a black armband over his left sleeve. They'd stopped at the car wash before returning to the office. He gave himself an inspection in front of the full-length mirror, looked at the clock above the door. It was time to go.

The Ng family was Catholic, not Buddhist as both their families had been in the old country. The priest condemned the killer and praised the family. The bulk of the ceremony was traditional with added testimonials from several of the town's notables including the Mayor and Earl Campbell. The crowd was one of the largest seen at a funeral in the history of this small town.

Jodi stood at attention during the entire lugubrious affair. He had no chance to speak with Earl. The Ng's were so consumed with grief during the funeral rite that he thought it best not to approach them.

It had been a long slow drive to the gravesite. The graveside passages were read, prayers offered and condolences passed. Jodi stopped to give his sympathy to the family. Both mother and father stood and hugged him tightly, thanking him for his efforts. Jodi felt his stomach knot and his eyes become hot.

"We will have some food at our home after. Won't you please come, be with us for a while?" Mrs. Ng asked.

He escorted the limousine to the family home. Television cameras were set up on the street. Jodi parked his official car and walked down the street to where the media folks were gathered.

"Please, give them some peace today," he asked, then turned and walked back to the place that had once been home to the murdered girl.

CHAPTER 8

"David Bennett, come to the Maintenance Supervisor's office. David Bennett, to the Supervisor's office, please."

David was mopping in the upper stands, section G, at the King Dome. The young man had worked in the sports arena as a sweeper for more than two years. Usually, this was only an entry position, but David liked the work and the freedom from supervision it gave him.

His boom box was positioned on the railing above the last row of seats in section G. He had finished sweeping this section and was beginning the chore of mopping the aisles and between the rows of seats. David was a show all by himself. While the stereo belted out rock music, the muscular young man practiced his dance moves, using his mop as a partner.

When the announcement came, he picked up a towel that had been draped over the pipe rail, wiped his face and walked to the office where the maintenance foreman waited. The sweaty young man thought he could use a break.

The King Dome was a gigantic building located on Fourth Avenue, not far from the waterfront and just across the street from Pioneer Square, a restored section of old Seattle. A nostalgic section of town, with its narrow brick streets and antique streetlights, and was a favorite with tourists, this section of Seattle became a terrible traffic bottleneck during special events like Mariner baseball, Seahawk football or Supersonic basketball.

The King Dome itself, was a monster of a place to keep in good repair, with its thousands of leaking faucets, burned-out light bulbs, clogged drains, and, and, and, the list never ended. The Dome had its own power generating-plant as well as its own heat and air conditioning units. George Towles managed a crew of about ninety maintenance workers with varying skills, including about thirty sweepers and moppers. These were usually part-time employees and as a rule didn't remain long on the job. David had been on the crew longer than anyone, and George delegated supervision of this motley bunch to him.

George looked up when David knocked "Have a seat, David. I'll be right with you." He continued to write. When he finished he called the secretary.

"Sorry, David. Work orders for some contractors. The renovation on the freight dock starts today and it makes a lot of added paperwork."

"No problem, George."

"I called you down here because one of my regular electrician helpers is quitting. The city offered him a job with Parks and Rec. I would sure like you to take that opening. It would give you a chance to learn a good trade and the pay is almost double what you make now. I need someone I can depend on and you've proven yourself. You have a good work record. What do you say, do you want to give it a try?"

"Geez, George, that's really nice of you. How much time do I have to think about it?"

"You'd begin two weeks from today. I need an answer by the middle of this week. I really hope you take this offer. I like you, and I know your work is good. You think about it and get back to me."

"I'll let you know by Wednesday. Thank you for thinking of me for the job." David walked from the office he heard George calling for Miss Randolph, the secretary.

The two met in the hallway, halfway to the exit. Jolene Randolph was slightly pudgy but attractive. She wore a black leather mini-skirt, high-heeled shoes and a bright red silk blouse, which she filled quite adequately.

"Call me sometime when you're going dancing" she said, as they passed in the hall.

David took the stairs two at a time to the top of the bleachers. He had a lot to think about. At the top of Section G he turned up the stereo and picked up his mop. The physically demanding work kept him in shape for dancing, his first passion. Almost any night of the week he could be found in one of the hard-rock dance clubs practicing his art. Partners were never a problem. Young women were constantly calling him, leaving notes on his car or dropping by the King Dome to talk with him.

After graduating from Tacoma High School David had taken a job as a roadie for a rock and roll group called the Zippers, taking care of the instruments and setting up the sound equipment and lights for each of the group's road appearances. The work was hard but he loved it. Everywhere they went groupies threw themselves at the band. It was while working for the Zippers that he became interested in this kind of dancing. His small stature, five feet six inches, and muscular frame made it easy to accomplish fancy dance moves more easily than someone with a higher center of gravity and longer limbs. Mostly, he just loved to dance.

The Zippers were hot for about three years; then they couldn't get a booking. Like most rock and roll bands they had a bright flash and burned out quickly. The public wanted a new sound. The band broke up with the members scattering to the winds. The roadies were all out of work. David came back to the Northwest to take a sweeper job at the King Dome.

There was a lot of work to do, which made the afternoon pass quickly. His long blonde hair became tangled and stringy from sweat as he danced with his mop. At the end of his day, David carried his stereo to his locker, showered and walked out of the arena. His pickup was parked in the employee area of the main parking lot. The first of the Mariners baseball team were arriving when he drove out the main gate.

At home in south Seattle, he had much to think about. The job offer was fabulous. But, what about his future plans? His current love affair was falling apart. The more he thought about that, the angrier he became. He took a diet Coke from the refrigerator. It would be unfair to take this job and then leave in a few months. George deserved better than that. After all, he'd always treated me fairly. Not like that bitch who was trying to dump him without any kind of compensation for all he'd done to keep this relationship going.

The deep anger was welling up inside him again. The sound of the phone saved him. Sometimes the anger became overwhelming and uncontrollable.

It was the third ring. He had taken several deep breaths to calm himself. "Hello," he said, calmly.

The soft female voice on the other end was that of Jolene. "Hi, David, it's Jolene."

"Oh, hi there, Jolene. What can I do for you?"

"I just heard that a new group is auditioning tonight at the SST CLUB … you know, down in Federal Way? I thought if you didn't have any other plans for tonight that you might want to go see them and dance for a while."

He looked at the clock on the end table at his side. "I'd love to. Have you had dinner?"

"No," she replied. "Would you let me buy you dinner on the way. Maybe we can go to Bob's in Renton."

"Want me to pick you up at your place?"

He wouldn't have to sit at home and think about new jobs and old loves tonight. He dressed in his black silk shirt, black slacks and black patent leather shoes, adding a silver belt, and three long silver chains around his neck. He picked two large silver rings from his jewelry collection, then inspected himself in front of the mirrored closet door. He was going dancing.

At about the same time, Earl Campbell and his family arrived at the Eagle residence. They would have been here much earlier, but young Darren had a little league game. Connie's coaching was paying off for the young outfielder. He had hit two singles and a home run tonight.

Jodi was broiling hamburgers in the back yard. Earl pulled a beer from the refrigerator and stepped out onto the back porch. Phillip and Kyle were off on a run when they saw Earl, knowing his two sons were somewhere around.

"Who are you burning at the stake there, Savage?"

"We leave cooking and eating people to your tribe, Lion Hunter," Jodi returned.

Earl walked to where Jodi was cooking and parked his large frame in a lawn chair. "Things seem to be returning to normal, downtown," he reported. "There were a few folks on the sidewalks when I drove through. God, I wish we could get a break and end this tension."

"Me too, buddy, me too." It had been a particularly slow day for Jodi. He had managed to review the case files on the killings. Nothing new. The Ng girl was abducted and killed one week ago today.

"Tomorrow I think I'm going to go to the parents of the first two kids, and interview them again. There must be something we missed." Jodi turned the burgers. "I'm happy with what you have done with the patrols and the Neighborhood Watch Program. At least we haven't had another missing kid in the last week." He sipped his lemonade.

"I don't know how long we can continue the twenty-four hour patrols. Our members are spread pretty thin. Nobody is complaining yet, but they all have businesses to run. I know it's hard on them."

"They have done an outstanding job of easing the fears of most of the town's parents." Jodi said sincerely, "I want to thank you for all your help. In a small town like this, emotions get real high real fast. You and your group have put some of those emotions to positive use. It could have been really ugly. Thanks, Earl." He began scooping burger patties from the grill. "Every law enforcement officer in the Northwest is working on this thing. But, like I told you before, we don't have much to go on. You remember the Green River killings. It took years to get that one. Bring my glass for me, would you, Earl? These burgers are done."

From inside came a cacophony of voices, kids screaming in play and women visiting. Connie Lupine sat in the kitchen with Eileen and Linda. Matthew, the youngest of the Campbell crew ran into the kitchen to tattle on his older brother; Darren wouldn't let him play the Nintendo.

"Come and make your hamburgers, kids." Jodi called. "Hi Connie, glad you could make it."

It was nice to have a normal, if not quiet, evening with family and friends.

Nothing new came from the repeat interviews done later that week. The parents of the victims were extremely upset at the lack of progress in the case; they wanted revenge over justice, and they wanted it now.

Jodi had discussed it with his wife. He would go to the top of Mount Si to pray to Wakantonkah: the Great Spirit God of the Mdewakantonwans; the Spirit People of the Lake.

In ancient times, before the Spaniards introduced horses to the Indians, the Dakota had been nomadic people, following the buffalo, the deer and the fish, and going to secret places to dig camas root and wild onion, traveling many miles as they did so. Everything they owned was packed up and carried on their backs or on the backs of dogs. It was, therefore, important to be frugal in the volume of goods one family owned. In the mountains, goods were rolled in hides from the Tipi. On the plains, lodge poles from the Tipi were used to make a travois for transporting goods. On these trips, sacred objects such as the pipe were handled with great care.

Early Saturday morning Jodi drove to the trailhead at the foot of Mount Si. The State of Washington Division of Parks had provided a nice hiking trail, which led to the summit of the beautiful mountain. Jodi carried only a small daypack on his back. In it were a flask of water and a roll containing his sacred pipe. It was a long and enjoyable climb to the summit of the 4000-foot viewpoint. At the summit he took a long and well-deserved drink from his water canister. He rested only briefly before beginning the task for which he had made the climb.

From the roll he took the pipe and a small deerskin pouch filled with Indian tobacco. He filled the pipe and puffed gently as he lit up the sacred icon then offered the pipe to each of the four directions as the ceremony demanded, and asked his grandfather to come and speak with him, to give him advice. He gave thanks to the Great Wakan and asked his grandfather to intercede for him with the Spirits. The powers of all the spirits would be needed to help him in the hunt for this killer of young children. As he sat on the top of this hill in the mountainous west, he hoped his voice would carry to the top of the Devil's Heart, from there he knew the spirits could hear him.

Jodi hadn't kept track of time. He was sitting cross-legged, among the pines and fir trees. He heard footsteps behind him and turned to see one of the Laxo boys topping the rise. He raised his hand in recognition.

"Hi, Jodi. It's Einer." The boy knew few people could tell which brother they were dealing with. "Sergeant Kaufman sent me up to get you. He said to tell you there was another one."

Jodi hung his head and muttered to the Spirits as he rolled his pipe and stuffed it back into his daypack. He took another long drink from his water bottle. "Come on," he said, finally. "Let's head down."

CHAPTER 9

Einer could give no details of the latest abduction. All he knew was that the sergeant had contacted him to ask if he would go to the top of Mount Si and get Jodi to come to the office. Sergeant Kaufman was not one to request an officer to come in on overtime unless it was absolutely necessary. His budget was stretched to the limit as it was, with the current investigation requiring so much manpower.

Jodi drove directly home where he switched to his patrol car. He didn't go into the house, but thanked Einer for his help and drove to the office. Pete was waiting for him. The look on his face was grim.

"Come into my office and have a seat, Jodi." His voice had a nervous tone. "I think we'd better talk before you go out to the scene."

"What's up, Pete?"

"Have a seat, Jodi." Jodi sat. "Patrol found another body this morning … no, let's back up. We had another missing child reported last night. I had patrols looking all night. They found the body this morning at Railroad Park. Just off the Falls City road."

"Why didn't you call me last night, Pete? I should have been out there looking, too. This is my case. I should have been the first one called."

"I know, Jodi." Pete seemed to be deliberately stalling. "I gave my word not to call you."

"Why, Pete, why would you do that?"

"Jodi, I … " Pete looked down at his desk, his eyes sad. "Hell, Jodi. There just isn't any easy way to tell you this. The missing kid is Earl Campbell's boy, Darren. They … " His voice was weak.

Jodi broke in. "That can't be. They were at my house for dinner last night. Earl took the family home about nine thirty. It can't be." Stress raised his voice about a full octave.

"It's true, Jodi. That's why I asked for you to come into the office. I want to be sure you can handle this." The sergeant looked into his officer's eyes. "I know how close you are with Earl and his family. I need to know, are you going to be able to handle this?"

"Can you give me a minute to think, Pete?"

"Sure, take your time." Pete stood, stepped around the desk, giving Jodi a consoling pat on the shoulder as he passed. He walked to the coffeepot where he poured two cups of steaming brew. He loitered a moment before returning to the office where he handed one of the cups to the deputy.

"Thanks," He had a far-away, pained look in his eyes. He was silent for several minutes, thinking, crying, screaming, hating-all within his own thoughts. He wiped his eyes with the heel of his hand, sipped his cup of coffee and took a deep breath. "Sorry, Pete. I shouldn't let it get to me like that, but I've known Darren from the day he was born. I was best man at Earl and Linda's wedding. He's my best friend. I'll be okay, I just need some time to accept it."

Kaufman sipped his own coffee, evaluating his number one investigator and good friend. "Okay, if you want to stay on the case, I'll leave you on it. I am going to caution you though. If it gets too personal I'll pull you off and turn it over to someone else. Understood?"

"Yeah, Pete, I understand, thanks."

"Cornetti is out at the scene now. The coroner just left. Connie is with the family now. They want to see you as soon as possible. I told them you would be there after you went to the scene. They're feeling really guilty, Jodi. They're blaming themselves for not watching the boy closer. He climbed out his bedroom window and sneaked out. His brother said he was headed for your place. Move slowly on this one, Jodi. You're too close and you could make mistakes."

"I'll be careful, Pete." Jodi said as he left his supervisor's office. He walked to his locker, where he kept a black windbreaker with "SHERIFF" in white lettering on the back. He slipped the jacket on as he walked from the office to his car.

Railroad Park was a collection of old steam engine era cars and engines with nostalgic value to citizens of the Northwest. A chain link fence surrounded the display. The entrance to the park was a locked vehicle gate about two miles from the police station. The deputy drove slowly to the scene in an effort to give him time to compose his stressed emotions. As he approached

Chapter 9

he saw the Major Crimes Unit truck. Several King County Police cars, with lights flashing, were parked on either side of the spot. Officers directed traffic and kept the spectators moving. The sun was hot now. He parked his car in the grassy ditch off the roadway, he spotted Cornetti and made his way past the yellow marker tapes to where the gawky deputy stood.

"How are you doin', Lewis?"

"We're almost finished here, Jodi. Same as before, just a disposal site. We found him face down like the others. Left hand under his face and his clothing piled neatly by his left elbow. Coroner says the cause of death looks the same, too. No evidence, nothing this time. Not even a footprint."

"We have to catch this guy, Lew. I know this family. They were at my place for dinner last night. I'm going there now. Let me know if you get anything, anything at all."

"I got a fax from Interpol this morning. You know, on that guardrail print. Nothing. I guess we have to assume he's an American, he's never been in the military and he's never been arrested," Cornetti reported.

"Don't you ever have any good news?" Jodi asked, as he walked away. He reviewed the scene and walked around the area, hoping to see something the others had overlooked, but he didn't. He did spot Brice's Buick parked on the other end of the line of cars. He also noticed a Channel 4 Television van approaching.

"What would Brice be doing out here on Saturday morning?" Jodi asked himself. "It's not like him to come out on his own time." Jodi didn't notice Lomax parked several cars behind the Buick Le Sabre.

Deputy Eagle had spent about a half-hour at the scene. The body had been removed before he arrived. That was good, since he wasn't sure he could deal with the sight of his friend's dead child. He did his best to keep emotion from his thoughts, but hate for this killer was creeping into his consciousness. This latest death added even more urgency to the need to catch the person responsible for these crimes. His personal involvement was making it difficult to concentrate on proper investigative techniques. He was beginning to realize how difficult it was going to be to remain detached and objective.

Back in town, only six blocks from his own residence, he pulled his patrol car to a stop in front of the large, well-kept home of Earl Campbell. Connie Lupine's patrol car was parked at the curb. Jodi found his station wagon in the driveway. Eileen was there. He knocked gently on the door.

Connie opened the front door. "Hi, Jodi. Your wife is in the kitchen with the children. Earl and Linda are in the den. Earl's holding up pretty well, but Linda is coming apart. We may have to call her doctor and get her a sedative," she reported. "Have you been to the scene?"

"Just came from there. Nothing new. Cornetti is handling the scene. Too many people out there," Jodi responded. "Have you interviewed Earl and Linda?"

"I got names and birth dates, all the statistical stuff for the forms. They don't know anything. His brother, Matt, said he climbed out the window last night, around ten fifteen. He was going to your place to stay with Phillip. The boys were going to play Nintendo. You know, Jodi, just kid stuff. He never got to your place, obviously. Phillip said he didn't call because he thought Darren had been caught and wasn't coming." She hung her head; there was a deep sadness in her voice. "I'm having trouble staying on track here. My mind keeps vacillating from official to personal. I really loved that little kid, Jodi." A tear formed in her eye.

"I'm having the same trouble. I find I'm getting mad at the killer, then crying for the Campbells, then mad again, because my own kid is partly responsible for his being out. But we have to quit thinking about ourselves and get on with the investigation. It'll be tough, but we have to do it. I'm going to talk to Earl and Linda now. Would you tell Eileen I'm here, and that I'll be in to see her in a few minutes?"

"Sure. I'll be in the kitchen with her."

Jodi walked to the door of the den. He reached for the door knob, then paused. He took a deep breath, attempted to compose himself, then entered. Earl was on the couch with his arm around Linda. She was sobbing uncontrollably, her eyes swollen and red. Earl, normally an emotional and outgoing man, was reserved, and a pillar of strength for his wife. Jodi thought it strange for Earl to show this much composure under the present circumstances. He stepped into the den and closed the door.

"I don't know what to say, Earl. I know there isn't anything I can say that will take away the hurt, but I want you to know that if there's anything I can do, as a friend or as an official in the investigation, just ask."

"I know that, Jodi, and I thank you for being there." Linda was still sobbing. "We're going to have to lean on you and Eileen for help in the coming days; with the funeral and all. I'm going to need your help. Right now I just have to take care of Linda and Matthew."

"I'll be there for you, buddy, whatever you need."

Jodi turned his attention to the distraught woman next to Earl. "Linda, I know you're suffering all sorts of feelings right now. In fact, I'm having trouble with that myself. But don't blame yourself. You did everything you could to protect your kids. Sometimes things get out of our control and bad things happen. That doesn't mean you're a bad parent. If you have any feelings of guilt, forget them. You are not the bad guy here. Darren did what every kid does at some time in his life. The guilty party in this is the nut who seized that opportunity to do harm to a child, your child. I suppose there's no greater pain in a person's life than that of losing a child, but you have another son who needs a mother. He has suffered a loss too. Please, Linda, we have been close friends for a long time. Let us help, let us stay close."

Linda looked up at Jodi through red, puffy eyes. "Thank you, Jodi. You and Eileen have been our best friends for all these years. But, you can't stop the grief I feel. I know it will ease, in time. And, I know I'll have to live with it. It's just so hard. I keep thinking there was something I could have done to prevent this." She was blurting words between sobs. "I should have watched Darren closer." She was crying harder now.

Earl spoke. "She is going to have to cry it out. Thanks, Jodi, for everything. I know you want to help, but like she said, we'll have to deal with our grief as best we can." He pulled his wife closer. "I would appreciate it if you could keep the reporters off the front porch. They are going to want to sensationalize all this, and I don't think we can deal with them right now."

"I'll do what I can. Can I get you some coffee or something?"

"No, thanks."

At the door, Jodi turned to look again at the grieving parents. Linda would be all right in time. Earl, on the other hand, was another thing. Something was wrong. He was too composed, too cool. He had lost his outgoing nature. He was trying to be strong for Linda, but something was wrong, something Jodi couldn't put his finger on. He opened the door and walked to the kitchen.

Kyle was first to spot his father. "Hi, dad."

"Hello, son." He turned to his wife. "How is everyone in here?"

Eileen had been busy at the stove. "Oh, Jodi, I'm glad you're here." Relief sounded in her voice. She walked across the kitchen, put her arms around her husband and held him tight.

Jodi caught Connie's eye and, with a nod of his head, indicated he wanted her to take the children to the backyard. While Connie and her little parade marched outside, Jodi held his wife. When they were alone, he kissed her.

Eileen looked over her husband's shoulder to be sure they were alone. "This is so awful, Jodi. I don't know what to do."

"I know, honey." Jodi was still holding his wife. "There isn't much you can do. Just be here for them, so they're not alone." He loosened his grip on her. "Connie and I will have to go back to the office soon. The kids need you, and we can't leave the family alone right now. As soon as I finish at the office, I'll come back here. The news cameras are going to be here soon. There's no way to stop them. Don't let them in, and don't let them interview Earl or Linda."

Jodi said good-bye, called Connie and drove back to the office where Pete waited. Reporters were gathering on the sidewalk. Pete had set up a press conference, which was due to start in ten minutes. Emma was in the office when the two deputies entered. It was happening again for the fourth time in just two months.

Lomax had heard the news on his police scanner. He called Brice early in the morning to tell him of the latest killing. He seemed excited; after all it was his story. Brice had dressed and driven to the scene. His official status as one of the investigators on the case gave him access to the area behind the yellow tapes. He arrived just minutes after Cornetti and his crew of skilled technicians. With his camera in hand he walked around the area, taking pictures of everything from the gates of Railroad Park to the ten-year-old black child lying lifeless in the grass next to the gates. He talked with Cornetti a moment, then left him alone to do his work. Cornetti had confirmed there were no clues at the scene. He also confirmed what everyone already suspected, it appeared to be the same killer. He walked back to his car, put the two rolls of newly shot film in a manila envelope and walked back along the line of parked cars. Several cars back in the line, his new associate waited. As Brice walked by the car, he dropped the film through the open window and paused only long enough for a short statement to the young driver.

"A grand, tonight, same place. I'll have the paperwork with me. Seven o'clock." He walked back, past two more cars, crossed the road and returned to his own car.

Before Brice could get back to his car, Lomax was addressing the manila envelope. He would personally deliver it to the office. His work ten days earlier had won him praise from the chief editor and a phone call of congratulations from the publisher himself. This week's issue would have his by-line, with his pictures and text on the front page. Here he was, twenty-three years old and already a force on the paper. Some reporters struggled all through their careers and never achieved what he had done in such a short time. Hard work, he thought to himself, pays off. He put the old white station wagon in gear and sped off toward Seattle. He would scoop all the competition.

Jolene gave the young maintenance worker a broad smile when he entered the office. "Good morning, David," she said in her sultriest voice.

"Hi, Jolene. You look really great today. Sorry I haven't called to tell you how much fun I had the other night. You're a great dancer. We should do that again soon, if you would like, that is."

"I had a great time too." she said, her eyes half closed, attempting a sexy look. "Call me sometime when you feel like dancing. I loved it."

Chapter 9

"I will. Is the boss in?"

"Yes, I'll tell him you're here."

Before Jolene could tell him to go back to the office, George Towles was in the hall. "Come on back, David."

He took a seat behind his old, scarred, chipped and generally well-used desk. "I was hoping to hear from you today. Have you made a decision on the offer I made?"

David looked down at the floor for a moment, then back to George. "Yes, I have," he said, "and I hope you don't take this the wrong way, but I can't take the job. It wouldn't be fair to you. You have been really good to me here, but my life is getting complicated right now and I'll probably be moving on soon."

"Listen, David, I know you don't make much money as a sweeper. That's why I offered you the job as an electrical apprentice. You have a good work record and the crews like you. This wasn't charity, you earned it."

"I thank you for that, George. But that isn't it at all. My whole life is a wreck right now. I'm having personal problems that I'm not sure I can work out. The person I'm in love with is trying to leave me. I'm trying to save money for some surgery I need, and quite frankly I don't think I can deal with the accumulated stress. Taking this job would be wonderful if I was going to stay here, but with my personal problems, I don't think I'll be able to stay. I want you to know I enjoy working for you, George. This has nothing to do with the job. You have always been more than fair with me. In return I have to be fair with you. I really have no choice but to pass on your offer. I'm sorry, George."

"Well, I can't say I'm not disappointed, but you have to do what's right for you. I hope you change your mind about leaving. If you stay, I will try to find you a better-paying position. As for your surgery, I didn't know you had a health problem. If you were to take another position here, a permanent position, you would be eligible for better health insurance that may pay for your surgery. I can't help you with your personal problems, but I am sorry they are interfering with your work. You can stay on the job as long as you like, and if you leave I will be sorry to see you go. Good luck, David."

"Thanks, George. I'd better get back to work before I get fired," he said, trying to be cheerful.

He went back upstairs to his work area, turned up the boom box and began to dance the afternoon away. There was a double-header today.

It was just after six in the evening when Brice stopped at the office. He knew Saturday afternoon was not a busy time for administrative types. The morning would have been chaos, but now there was only the regular duty shift, and most of them would be out on the road.

He walked into the office with little thought of being caught at what he was doing. After all, he was involved in the investigation and had a right to the information. He unlocked the file cabinet and found the manila folder containing the information he needed today. It took longer to warm the copy machine than to make copies of the necessary forms, and was in the office for a total of less than five minutes. He replaced the folder in the file and re-locked it. He stepped out into the fresh evening air, took a deep breath and walked to his Buick. The radio came on when he turned the key.

As he drove away from the office he heard the announcer say, " … going into the top of the seventh, the score: Yankees, eight, Mariners, five. We'll be right back after this." The action cut away to the main studio and recorded commercials.

Brice drove slowly to the Edgewick Road exit. Again parking his blue car at the end of the freeway exit where he could view all the roads leading to his parking spot. The radio was tuned to the baseball game. He wished he were there instead of here waiting for Jerry Lomax. The large brown envelope lay on the seat next to him. Why had he gotten himself into this? It was stupid. Any time an officer let his personal life get mixed with his duty, he was making a mistake, a lesson he'd forgotten. The reminder was painful. Before remorse overtook him, the white car appeared at the foot of the exit ramp.

Lomax made a sweeping U-turn, parking with his driver's side window next to that of the deputy. He was grinning his Cheshire cat grin. He turned off the engine in the old white station wagon: oil fumes and a loud exhaust made it almost impossible to talk otherwise.

"I have something for you, Brice." He said, handing a newspaper through the open window. "This week's edition of the *World Inquirer*. We're famous. Front page. They promised me front page next week with the stuff on this new murder. If it's as good as before, I'll get you a bonus. This is our big break, old buddy."

Brice took the paper. "I'm not your buddy. I'm not your friend. I hate your guts, Lomax. I'll take your money, but that's where this relationship ends." He opened the newspaper to be struck with color photographs he had taken from the Shirley Ng file, and bold headlines which read **MOUNT SI KILLER STRIKES AGAIN,** with the subtitle **POLICE HAVE NO LEADS IN KILLINGS**. He could only stare at the photo of the nude body of the frail little girl. He felt sick.

"I have the reports from today's scene. Give me my money and get out of my face," Brice said angrily.

Lomax knew he had the upper hand now. "I have a thousand for you now. This edition hits the newsstands on Monday. If you are able to keep the information coming, and I can stay on the front page for a couple more weeks, I'll be able to get you a large bonus. You need the money or you wouldn't be here." The power was intoxicating.

Brice couldn't resist the bait, "How much of a bonus are you talking about? Because this may just be the last envelope you get from me." He knew he was in too deep to quit now, but the threat might humble the reporter a little.

"This is not the time to get righteous on me, Brice." Lomax sneered. "I'll be out of your life soon enough. In the meantime we have an agreement, and I expect you to live up to it. I have enough on you to get you not just fired, but prosecuted. So don't get cute with me." He started his car. "I'll be talking with you."

The envelopes containing the new information and the new payment were exchanged. Lomax drove away. Brice sat a few minutes before reaching for the newspaper on the passenger seat. He read the story. This was one of the few times in his life that he felt shame.

In the ninth inning Ken Griffey Jr. hit the wall, injuring his right wrist. Seattle lost the game eight to six.

CHAPTER 10

Saturday had been a horrid day. After the interview with Earl and Linda, Connie and Jodi went back to the office. The reports had to be done and reporters were waiting for their chance to interview the investigators. Pete had scheduled a press conference which, as it turned out, was a carbon copy of the one the week before. Jodi waited on the street, behind Pete, for the public information session to end. While waiting, he spotted the brown sport coat among the reporters in the street.

The formal press conference had ended and the television folks were reeling up their cables. Most of the trucks had departed when the reporter in the brown tweed sport coat approached Jodi inside the office.

Miss Emma notified Jodi there was someone in the outer office to see him. Stepping out of his little cubicle, he recognized the reporter.

"Hello there again. What can I do for you?" Jodi asked in a friendly voice, though he wasn't in the mood for questions.

"Could I get you to step outside for a minute?" The brown coat asked. "I would like to speak with you privately."

"Sure. I'm pretty busy today, but I can give you a minute. What's on your mind?"

Tom Logan had a reputation as a good reporter. Known as a tough newsman, he had been fair and respectful of law enforcement agencies in his reporting. He was not afraid to take on a bad cop or an agency with a poor reputation, most law enforcement people liked him. He spoke with a soft, deep voice that put people at ease and gave him an air of authority.

"I'm not one to betray my own profession," he began, "But the rumor around the press table is that there's a leak in your department. Bad leak. I

Chapter 10

haven't seen the copy yet, myself, but I understand there's going to be an issue on the street Monday that is going to make your department look pretty bad. Like I said, I haven't seen the copy yet, but there is supposed to be some pretty graphic pictures and copies of reports that could only have come from your files. How they got the information, I don't know. But, Deputy Eagle, if any of the rumor is true, you guys are going to take some heat next week."

Jodi was shocked. "Where did you get this information?"

"Sorry, I can't tell you that. You were honest with me last week and I figured I owed you. But I can't betray my profession." Jodi was sure Tom Logan knew no more than he had already told. "My professional guess is that, since the publication is coming out Monday, this is a weekly. The type of story would lead me to believe it is one of those supermarket rags, but all that is pure speculation on my part."

"Thanks Tom. I'll repay you for this somehow." The two men turned and began the walk toward the office entry. "The victim this morning was a good friend of mine. I played football in college with the child's father. We're close. I don't want anything to upset the family. They're pretty fragile right now. I would appreciate it if you would let me know if you learn anything else, but I would be really grateful for any help you can give me in holding off the interviews with the family. They don't know anything anyway."

"I'll do what I can. It must be tough investigating the death of a friend's child. I couldn't do your job."

Back inside the office, Jodi reported, at once, to Sergeant Kaufman. Pete was not given to emotional outbursts, so when Jodi gave him the news, he merely leaned back in his chair, rubbed his eyes with his thumb and forefinger, then pinched the bridge of his nose. He gave a long sigh as his face flushed.

"Thanks, Jodi. That's just what I needed to make this a perfect day. Were you able to get any specifics?"

"My source didn't have any. I believe him though. I don't know what we can do about it except be prepared for Monday. Did you have any idea this was happening?"

"Not a clue," Kaufman said. He thought a moment. "Why don't you and Connie finish your reports and get out of here. There will be enough to do next week. Cornetti won't have his reports for a couple of days."

"Thanks, Pete."

It was almost four hours before the final touches were put on the reports. Connie Lupine had done most of the work. She was proving to be a real asset in this investigation.... efficient and hard working and doing an excellent job of staying on track when Jodi was, at times, distracted.

The two deputies were finalizing their reports when Emma Garson came in to say she was leaving for the day. She asked if there was anything she could do for the Campbell family, there wasn't.

Connie and Jodi were about to leave the office when Jodi remembered, "Hey, Connie. I wonder why Brice isn't here. I saw him out at the scene this morning. He's been acting so strangely, I hardly recognize him. There was a double-header at the King Dome today, and he didn't go. It's not like him to be out on a scene on his own time. Especially on a Saturday with the Mariners playing at home. The whole world must be going crazy."

"I know. He's supposed to be working on this case with us, but I've hardly seen him. I didn't want to say anything, but he hasn't contributed much." She tried to change the subject. "I'll be home all weekend if you need anything. I'll be glad to help at the Campbells if there is anything I can do ... you know, watch the kids or cook or anything."

"Thanks, I may just call you."

It was late afternoon when Jodi arrived back at the home of his friends. Eileen was in the kitchen when he arrived. Linda and her husband were still in the den. The boys were in the back yard. Something on the stove smelled delicious; Jodi hadn't eaten all day.

"How's everyone doing?" he asked.

"The boys are okay. Linda came out of the den to go wash up and put on some makeup. Earl hasn't been out of the den. I'm worried about him. He doesn't say anything, he won't eat, and this thing plays havoc with his blood pressure. It's been out of whack for a long time, anyway. He just holds Linda and stares into space. How did things go at the office?"

"We did the reports and held a press conference. Pete stayed all day. Emma came in, handled the phones, and kept everyone off our backs so we could work. She's a real sweetheart."

"I was about to call the boys to eat; would you like something?"

"I sure would. I forgot to eat today. Have you asked Earl and Linda if they want to eat?"

"Linda said she would have something later. Earl refused to eat. Maybe you should talk to him."

Eileen began to set the table. Jodi walked to the den to speak with the grieving parents, and found the scene almost identical to the one he had left earlier in the day. The two parents sat on the couch; Earl had his arms around his wife.

Linda spoke, "Come in, Jodi. Did you find out anything new today? About ... you know, about Darren's death?"

"I wish I could say yes, but I can't. I want you to know I will get this guy. If I never do anything else in my career, I'll get this guy."

"I know, Jodi. Please, I don't want revenge. I just want to know my son didn't suffer. And, I don't want any other parents to lose a son. I want to know why anyone would do such a thing to a wonderful little boy like our Darren." Tears were coming from her eyes, making little wet rivers appear on her cheeks. Even in her grief she had maintained her poise. Linda was not only beautiful, she was a real lady. She didn't deserve this tragedy in her life. But then who did.

"Can I bring you something to eat, or better yet, would you come out to the kitchen and have something with the boys?" Jodi wanted them to begin accepting a normal life again.

Earl had not spoken, in fact, not acknowledged Jodi's presence. He just stared, withdrawn in his own thoughts. They didn't want anything but to be left to themselves for the time being.

It was after eleven when the couple came from the den. They went upstairs to their room, not saying good night to the other son, who was asleep in his own room. Earl walked like a zombie. "His spirit has followed the spirit of his departed son. The Great Wakan will have to help it find its way back to the place where it belongs," Jodi thought. "A man cannot live long without his spirit, for though he walks he is already dead."

Eileen stayed the night with the Campbell family. She busied herself cleaning the kitchen, washing dishes and puttering. She stayed busy to keep from thinking about the events of the day, a day that seemed so terribly long. Eileen and the children were Lutherans, as were so many families from the upper Midwest. She was strong in her faith and prayed for the family and their lost son. Jodi had maintained his Indian beliefs. His faith was as strong and, in some ways, more logical than the Christian faiths. Jodi knew why things happened. Nothing was given based solely on faith. Times might change and the reasons for people acting as they do may change, but the Great Wakan made things happen for a reason; so it would rain in spring, so it can snow in winter and so the flowers will bloom in summer. There was a time to be a child and a time to be a warrior. There was a time to learn and a time to be wise. The White Buffalo Woman would provide for them if they worked in harmony and peace. Life was simple for those who believed in the way of the Dakota. Earl would have to deal with his grief in the manner of his own faith. No matter what your belief, losing a child was one of life's greatest tragedies.

Sunday went by pretty much the same as the previous afternoon. Earl showed little improvement; as Linda gained strength it seemed Earl became more depressed He sat in the den without speaking. Linda began to move around the house and to take interest in her life again. The healing process would take a long time. Eileen made arrangements for someone to take her responsibilities with the children at the school. Monday would be a traumatic day for the entire community.

Jodi was in the office early Monday morning. He had done the regular weekly and daily chores required of his position. Emma Garson also came to work at an early hour. She made coffee and checked the messages on her recorder as well as the written notes left her by the off-going weekend shifts. There was always a lot of administrative duty on Monday morning. The King County Police Department covered a large area in which the usual amount of crime was a daily occurrence. Things like the recent killings took priority and added to the workload of the entire department. The North Bend detachment was suffering the brunt of the added duties. They also suffered the greatest frustration for allowing the crimes to continue.

Jodi had completed a stack of weekly and daily reports to be forwarded to the downtown office. He handed them to Miss Emma and returned to his office. He suddenly had a second thought.

"Emma, you read those supermarket tabloids, don't you?"

"I like the Star. Some of those papers are nothing but fiction and sensationalism. I'm not a fanatic like Lois, the woman who accepts the donations at the Salvation Army store. She never misses an issue of any of those papers."

"Would you know what time those papers hit the newsstands on Monday?" he asked.

"I buy mine at the grocery store. They usually get there around noon, perhaps a little earlier." Her curiosity was aroused now. "Is there something in there about us this week?'

"I'm afraid so. I had a tip we were on the front page of one of them. The word I got was that we didn't come off too well." He stopped talking for a moment, thinking. "When you go to the post office to mail the weeklies, would you stop by the grocery store and look over the tabloids? If you see any with a story about our case, pick up some copies for the office and I'll reimburse you."

Jodi was standing at Emma's desk when Pete signed in for the day. "Come into my office, Jodi."

Jodi stopped at the coffeepot to pour two fresh cups, then proceeded to the sergeant's office.

It was Emma's habit to prioritize the morning mail for the boss. He thumbed through the stack and pushed it aside. "I just came from a meeting with the mayor," he said. "He wants to call a town meeting to discuss the case and inform the citizens of our progress. The town is in a virtual panic. Earl is a prominent citizen and the death of his son has folks worried. I want you to handle this. People have confidence in you and since you and Earl are so close, they'll listen to what you have to say."

"Come on, Sarge. I have a lot of work to do. Can't you assign this to someone else?"

"I could, but I won't. The Mayor asked for you, and I think you're the best I have for this job. People here trust you, Jodi. This isn't a pacification detail, the people really do need to be informed. I just think you're the best man for the task." Pete paused a few seconds, soliciting any response, there was none. "Today at the elementary school gym, Five o'clock."

"Anything in particular you want me to say?"

"No. Use your own judgement. Tell them as much as you can without jeopardizing our case. Most important is to answer questions. The Mayor is right, since you and Earl are so close, people are going to look to you for answers. Give them what you can."

"That tabloid story is supposed to hit the newsstands today. I have Emma looking for a paper. If that story is as graphic as I was told, the town mood is going to get worse," Jodi noted.

Brice was in the squad room at his desk by the time Jodi left the sergeant's office. He had avoided contact in the front office this morning.

Connie Lupine reported in a half hour later. The added duties of the case did not exempt her from her regular patrols, so Jodi had told her to use her driving time to think about the killings and the case. So far she hadn't come up with any new thoughts or ideas.

Before noon each deputy had finished with office work and returned to the road. Jodi was patrolling east on the old highway, past Torval Laxo's business when he noticed the older Finn sipping coffee on the front porch of his home. Jodi turned into the drive, parked and stepped up onto the porch.

"Do you think Marge could spare another cup of that coffee?"

"Youbetcha, Jodi. Ma, bring a cup of coffee for Jodi." He called. "I t'ink you got big troubles in town, eh?"

"Bigger than you know, Torval. I wanted to thank you for sending Einer up the mountain to get me on Saturday."

"I hear on the radio, that the Mayor is having a town meeting. They say you will be there. That is a good t'ing. People like you, Jodi. And they trust you. I know you and Earl Campbell are good friends. But, you must set that aside for now. You must do your job as if you didn't know any of the people. It is hard, I know. My boys, they say you take this hard. We give you any help

75

we can. Maybe you need a sweat tonight. You t'ink so? I have the boys heat the sauna."

"Thanks, not tonight. Too busy." He set his cup down and stood. "Thanks for the coffee. I have to get back on the job."

"Before you go, my boys have to say something." Again he turned to call into the house. "Ma, send the boys out here."

The two boys had a guilty look about them. Einer gestured for Aino to do the talking. "Well, … I guess, … well, we have done something we need to tell you." Both boys were nervous. Aino looked at Einer who motioned for him to continue. "We, Einer and me … we're the ones that have been making the signs in the grass around town. We didn't mean to harm anyone, we were just having some fun making people wonder who did it."

It was the first chuckle Jodi had had in several days, but he didn't dare let it out. "You mean you two are responsible for the artwork in the grass?"

"Yes." Jodi could see how painful it was for Aino to make this confession. "We didn't put anything that looked bad. The first one, "Jesus is Lord," we used a fertilizer sprayer and wrote it on the new grass by the highway. Then we got the idea of doing some pictures. I guess we have done about six or seven. We did our best to draw good ones … no dirty pictures." Jodi looked serious.

"This is a serious situation. What do you think I should do with you two, arrest you?"

"Pa said we should leave that up to you. He said you were fair and that, whatever you did, we deserved," Einer pleaded.

"All right, boys. I'm not going to arrest you right now. But, don't leave town without telling me first. I'll talk to the sergeant and determine what should be done with you. Now, get back to work." It was all Jodi could do to keep from laughing out loud.

Torval laughed. "You have the boys worried. I t'ink it is a good t'ing to make them stew a while." He laughed again.

"This should be a good lesson for them. I think I'll have them work with the kids at the school. I would like for them to apologize to the Ng's for messing up their display. Maybe they should help them weed and water for the rest of the summer." Jodi was laughing. "I can deal with kids' pranks. Your boys are good kids. In fact the pictures showed a great deal of talent. We'll make their lives miserable for a while, then let them off the hook." Jodi stepped off the porch. "Thanks for the coffee. You're a good friend, Torval."

Jodi chuckled several times that morning, thinking about the Laxo twins. He continued his patrol, finishing just before noon. He called Connie on the radio and asked that she meet with him at he Mar-T Cafe. If Emma had a paper for him, she was to bring it with her. After lunch he would see the Campbells.

When Connie came into the Mar-T Cafe, Ester Parks was busy telling all about the report in the *World Inquirer.* She had given Jodi a Readers Digest version of the story and was now asking a million questions, the same questions the rest of the community would be asking before the day was through. "How did that paper get those pictures?" Ester was asking as Deputy Lupine dropped into the booth.

"I don't know, Ester. That is one of the things we will have to find out." He nodded to Connie. "Give us two specials and two coffees, would you please, Ester?"

"How did you know?" Connie asked in a quiet voice, while watching the waitress walk to the coffeepot. "Have you seen this?" She presented him with the folded copy of the supermarket newspaper.

"No, I haven't seen it. Is it as bad as I think?"

"Worse. How did you know?"

"Old Indian trick." He said, laughing for the second time today. "Did you read the story?" He held the paper open to see the photos on the front page. They were shocking photographs from the files of the murder cases. The top half of the front page was filled with a color picture of the nude body of Shirley Ng, where it had been placed on the large stone only a few miles from where they now sat.

Connie watched him thumb through the pages. "No, I haven't read it thoroughly. I read the headlines and scanned a few photographs. Jodi, I think someone in the department furnished those pictures and the details about the investigation. There are things in there that could have come only from our files."

Ester was approaching the booth with their lunch order. "I am making fresh coffee for you. I'll be right back with it." She stopped to point at the tabloid in Jodi's hands. "What will the families of those kids think when they see that?"

"There are going to be a lot of questions like that one asked today. Most of which I can't answer." Jodi folded the paper and picked up his fork. Hot roast beef sandwich, today's special. Ester returned with the coffee.

"You realize you and I are going to be the number one suspects for this." Connie made it more a statement than a question. She poked her fork into the mashed potatoes. "I'm scared about this, Jodi. In this business you have to be able to trust the people you work with. This violates every trust we ever had. Worse, we don't know who did it."

"If I know Pete, he is already hot on the trail of whoever gave out this information. When he finds out who it was, he'll fire him on the spot. The Sarge won't have anyone around he can't trust," he said between bites.

"What's the plan, then?"

"First of all, I have to go to the Campbell's. Emma is going to have her hands full with telephone calls this afternoon. The phone is going to be ringing off the hook. Everyone from the Mayor to the dogcatcher is going to want to know what happened and what we're doing about it. I think you should go back to the office and help Emma. Try to sort out the calls and answer them as best you can. Make a call-back list for Pete and one for me." He flipped the paper open to the front page. "The byline is someone named Jerry Lomax. See if you can contact him and his paper and get any information. Downtown isn't going to be happy with this story. If you get anything, give it to Pete so he can pass it on to the sheriff." He finished his meal, wiped his mouth with the napkin and took a long drink of the last of his coffee. "This is one of those times I think I should have listened to my grandfather and become a farmer."

On the way to their patrol cars he said, "Call me at the Campbell's if you need me. I'll be back in the office in about an hour."

CHAPTER 11

Eileen Eagle opened the door when Jodi arrived at the Campbell home. She was beautiful. Jodi couldn't remember the last time they'd been alone together … it seemed as though it had been forever. The two of them needed some time together. Eileen had worked hard at the school, keeping track of the comings and goings of the children. It was important to her. The lines on her face told Jodi that it was time for her to get away from it for a while; it was wearing her down.

"Hi, honey," she said, kissing him on the cheek.

"Hi. How's everyone here?" He gave her a hug and kissed her.

"Linda is doing fine, but Earl isn't doing well at all. I'm worried about him, Jodi." The two of them stepped into the house. "Do you want some coffee or juice or anything?"

"No, thanks, honey. I just had lunch at the Mar-T." He handed her the folded newspaper in his left hand. "This just came out this morning. I think there's going to be hell to pay in town, soon. I'll have to get back to the office as soon as I can. I know things have been difficult for you the last few weeks, I promise I'll make this up to you as soon as it's over." He held her gently, looking into her eyes. "I love you."

"I love you too." She kissed him again. "Earl and Linda are in the kitchen." She stepped back from him, opening the tabloid to see the front page. A look of shock came over her face when she viewed the horribly explicit photos.

"I know, honey. Don't let them see this. It's hard enough on them already."

Jodi walked to the back of the house where the kitchen was located. He tried to be cheerful. "Hi, folks. How are you doing this morning?" Linda looked fresh and, though sad, he could see she was coping pretty well. Earl hadn't shaved, and he still had that vacant look in his eyes. He didn't look up, just stared at the breakfast in front of him. Jodi wondered just how much more of this Earl could take.

Linda looked first at Earl then at Jodi. "Okay, I guess. Earl is having a difficult time." There was a small tear in her eye. "The office is closed today, but I think I'm going to go down and try to talk with the staff. There will be mail to answer and a million things we can't let get out of hand. Eileen said she would stay here with Earl while Matthew and I are at the office." She paused, then asked. "Have you found out anything yet?"

"Sorry, Linda, we haven't. We're waiting for some information from the Major Crimes Unit. They have sent some evidence off to the FBI, and we have some fingerprints we're working on." He'd better prepare her for the article in the *World Inquirer*.

"Linda." She could tell he was uncomfortable with what he was about to say. "One of the tabloids has some pictures and information on the crimes. We don't know how they got it, but it's pretty bad. I just want you to be prepared if people ask you about it."

"How bad is it? Is it about Darren?" There was that look of horror again.

There was no way to soften what he was about to say. "No, nothing about your son, but the pictures and story are pretty graphic. I think you should be prepared to see some of the same kind of story, next week, about your boy. If they have the pictures and information, there isn't any way we can legally stop it."

"How can they do that? Are they monsters? Don't they have any feelings?" She paused to get a handle on her outrage; trying to control her emotions. "Thank you, Jodi," she continued. "You and Eileen have been just wonderful through all this. We'll never be able to thank you enough. I know you're doing the best you can."

"Thank you for that." He patted her on the shoulder. "I have to get back to the office now. There's a lot to be done."

"Will we see you later?"

"Yes, after work." He looked at Earl, who was still staring at his plate. "Don't you think we should have a doctor look at Earl?"

"I'm taking him to see Doctor Dennison in the morning."

The news on the radio was filled with stories of the Gulf War and of Saddam Hussein, the Iraqi dictator. It was tragic news. "Two of the local youth sent to the Persian Gulf, one a helicopter pilot and the other a National

Guard Infantryman, were killed yesterday in separate battles on the Iraqi border. Helicopter pilot George Simons was killed when his craft was knocked down by missile fire while attempting to rescue a tank crew close to enemy lines deep in the Iraqi desert. Loren Boswell was killed when his unit came upon an Iraqi tank unit north of Kuwait City. The tanks fired on the infantry unit killing Boswell and two other members of his squad. Three others were wounded in the battle."

Jodi turned off the radio. He had heard all the bad news he could handle for one day. There was no clue as to who was responsible for the deaths of the local children. He had serious misgivings about the health of his friend, and was about to be asked a lot of questions about the article in the *World Inquirer* for which he had no answers. A line from Rudyard Kipling kept going through his mind, *If you can keep your head while those around you are losing theirs and blaming it on you ...*

He took a detour of several blocks, driving through the neighborhoods, delaying his return to the office. He noticed that lawns were manicured more neatly this year. Flowerbeds were better tended and more of them were visible. Homeowners with children were staying home more this summer, keeping the children busy with yard work and home repairs. Some residents had used their fears to produce a positive result. Earl had tried to do that, too, but he and his family were victimized anyway.

North Bend was a microcosm of America. Its population was diverse. The area was a melting pot of all nationalities and religions. Though people differ in background and culture, they were united to form a close community, a community now in crisis with the population banding together for strength. Standing in a united front against an unknown but common enemy. In this case the enemy was anonymous but his work was well known. Tonight there would be tears for each of the dead youngsters. The community would remember and mourn the deaths of its two offspring killed in a far-away war.

Jodi parked his patrol car at the curb near the front door of the office. Miss Emma was talking with Brice, something about the burglaries last week. Connie was at her desk, head down, working on a report of some kind. Pete was on the telephone; Jodi couldn't hear what was being said. He waited for Emma to finish with Brice before walking through.

"I have several messages for you, Jodi." Emma said.

"Put them on my desk, will you? I want to talk to Pete first." He stepped to the doorway of the sergeant's office.

Pete motioned for Jodi to come in and have a seat. He covered the mouthpiece on the phone and said softly, "I'm about done here." Then returned to his conversation. It was the sheriff, downtown. "Okay, will do." He said and hung up the receiver.

"Well, Boss, do you want the good news or the bad news first?"

"Better give me the good news. I don't think I want any more bad news."

"The good news is that I solved the great pictures-in-the-grass mystery. It's a kids' prank. I would like it if you would let me handle it and not make me arrest the kids."

Pete grinned. "The Laxo boys, eh?"

"I was hoping that wouldn't get out. But, yes, it was the twins. How did you find out?"

Pete was still grinning. "Last week when they stopped out front to talk to you I saw a couple of backpack weed sprayers in the back of the truck. I thought at the time they might have used them for fertilizer. It's the kind of thing active high school kids do for a prank. How do you intend to handle it?"

"I talked with Torval this morning. I'll have the boys help the Ng's with their gardening for the rest of the summer. Make them do some community service things. They're good boys. I don't think they need criminal charges on their records. Their dad and I have already given them a scare. I think I could give them some personal probation, you know, just keep their attention for a while."

"Okay." Pete chuckled aloud. "Don't let them off too easily. You're right, they are good boys."

"Thanks, Pete." His mood darkened. "Have you heard the news about the two local boys killed in the Gulf?"

"The sheriff just told me. How much more is this town supposed to take?" He shook his head and sighed.

"Have you learned anything about who passed information to that newspaper?"

"Not yet." He dialed the intercom, and asked Connie to come to his office.

She came to the office with a jumble of notes clutched in her left hand, a ball-point pen in her right.

"Did you call that news office in Seattle?"

"Yes, I did. Boy are they some nice people." She looked through her notes. "I talked with a secretary there. I have her name here somewhere." She shrugged and restacked the pile of notes; it wasn't important right now.

"They refused to give me anything. She said if it wasn't in the latest issue of the *World Inquirer*, she wouldn't help me. I asked her for the number where I could reach this Jerry Lomax. She basically told me to go to hell."

"I might have a source to find Lomax." Jodi volunteered. "I'll see what I can

Chapter 11

do. I don't look for it to be productive though. I think he'll tell us the same thing as the secretary."

"Yeah, you're probably right, Jodi. But check it out anyway." He looked at his watch. "I have a meeting with the Mayor in ten minutes. I wish I had more to tell him."

Jodi found Cornetti's name on one of the messages Emma had placed on his desk. He picked up the phone and dialed the Major Crimes Unit.

"Got anything for me?"

"That's what I was calling about. I got the preliminary report from the FBI this morning. I have sent a copy to you by mail."

"Great. Is there anything in there we don't know?"

"As a matter of fact there is. Now, this report only covers the first three victims. But we have some carpet fibers. They are like indoor/outdoor carpet, black. We're speculating that the fibers came from the back of the truck. We think he has carpet on the bed of his pickup."

"I guess that will help us identify the truck if we find it. It doesn't do us much good until then, except to tell us what we already suspected; he's assaulting his victims in the truck."

"We have something else, Jodi." Cornetti continued, "There was a lipstick smudge behind the left shoulder of the second victim, the Wilson boy. It looks like the killer tried to wipe it clean, but there was enough residue to get a sample. The shade is Pink Pearl, the manufacturer is Revlon. Standard department store brand and shade. You might check with the mother and see if she wears that brand."

"It might tell us something else too, Lew. It may be the reason none of the kids was afraid of him. He could be dressed as a woman."

"That's what we thought. A couple of other things. Two of the victims had some blonde hair strands mixed in the clothing. None of the victims was blonde. And, something we didn't find … there's no evidence he used a condom during the assaults, but there was no semen present in any of the victims. We don't have a full profile on this guy yet, but we think the assaults maybe ritualistic rather than sexual. We're hoping there will be a psych profile in the final report from the feds."

"Great job, Lew." Jodi was trying to put all this new information into perspective. "Let me know when the rest comes in."

Lew couldn't resist. "Shall I send all this directly to the *World Inquirer* or can you handle that from your office?"

"Not funny, Lew," Jodi said, more embarrassed than insulted. "Talk with you later."

After hanging up, he called Connie on the intercom. She met him in his office where he shared the latest information from the MCU. He also cautioned her about sharing this information with anyone outside the investigation. He didn't want this showing up in next week's edition of that rumor-rag.

While Jodi was on the telephone with Cornetti, Brice was loading his car with goods returned from several burglaries. He welcomed the chance to leave the office and be on the road. He also welcomed the opportunity to see Mary Alice Jade once again. Her office would be his first stop.

The sky was overcast, but Brice paid little attention to such things. The air was thick with humidity and low clouds obscured the top of Mount Si.

The deputy stopped his car at the rear of the real estate office on the Falls City road and walked with long strides, his head bobbing to and fro in a weird pecking motion. He tapped gently on the back door. The door now had new locking hardware, which allowed for exit but was locked to outsiders. The secretary opened the door. She smiled when she recognized Brice, who looked handsome with his neatly trimmed blonde hair contrasting starkly with his dark, neatly creased uniform.

"Is Mary Alice in?" he inquired. "I'm returning some goods from her burglary."

"Oh, good. Bring them in, I'll hold the door for you." The secretary said. "She has a client with her now, but she should be finished in a couple of minutes."

He carried the merchandise into the office, piling it along one wall, out of the way. When he finished he took a seat in the outer office and waited. He had just picked up a magazine when the door to the boss's office opened.

" ... That seems fair. We should have an answer on the offer by Wednesday." There were handshakes and acknowledgements as the couple and their briefcases departed through the glass doors.

"Hello, Brice. What can I do for you today?" She was smiling. "Are you ready to trade your townhouse for a nice single family dwelling? I have some nice ones."

"Nope. I can't afford to move. This is an official visit." He smiled back. "I brought some of your office equipment back. If you would check the serial numbers for me to verify they are the right ones, you can have them back." He checked his notebook. "A Compaq computer with monitor and printer. Three calculators, two electric typewriters, IBM, and three office telephones. That's all I have."

"I think that's everything they took, except for one computer and printer. I'm really happy to see them again. Did you get the burglars?"

"Yes, some road deputies caught them over the weekend. Dopers looking for cash. I found a credit card receipt out back of the mortuary. It turns out one of them threw it away while they were breaking in the back door. We had a license number and one of the road deputies found them down by Renton. They still had most of the stuff in the car."

"They aren't smart, are they?" She laughed, then turned to the secretary. "Gina, would you check the serial numbers on this equipment for Brice?"

"I'll need your signature as soon as we check the numbers. How would you like to have a drink this evening? To celebrate the return of your office equipment."

"I'd love it, but it will have to be after seven. And as a reward I'm buying. You earned this one."

"I'll pick you up at seven."

Gina confirmed the numbers on the office equipment. Mary Alice Jade signed the receipt for the returned goods. The deputy exited the same door through which he had arrived. As he drove away he felt good for the first time in many days.

His next stop was the mortuary. A black Cadillac hearse was backed up to the service entrance. Harry Makin and two of his young assistants were moving a black body bag from the car to a gurney. When their task was completed, the two young assistants rolled it into the mortuary. Harry walked to Brice's car.

"Hello, Brice." He pointed back over his shoulder with his thumb. "The coroner just released the body of the Campbell boy. We're going to prepare it now. The funeral will probably be Wednesday or Thursday, whichever is best for the family."

"I won't hold you up too long, Harry. I have some of your stolen equipment here. If you will check the numbers for me, I'll have you sign for the stuff and get out of your hair."

The afternoon shift was taking to the road when Pete came back to the office. His meeting with the Mayor had taken longer than he had anticipated. Inside the office, Connie and Jodi continued to work on the reports and the new information given by Cornetti. Miss Emma was locking her files and preparing to go home for the day. She would make fresh coffee before leaving.

Pete called his two investigators into his office for a short conference. He thanked Jodi for cleaning up the vandalism case; the Mayor was grateful. He reported that the neighborhood patrols were going to continue for now. The energy levels were wearing thin, but with the death of Darren Campbell there was renewed interest. Everyone liked Earl and his family.

Jodi reported what he had learned from Cornetti. He was hopeful this new information would bring some results. The psychological profile should be here, in the mail, tomorrow morning.

The two deputies were leaving the office when their sergeant called Jodi back. They both said good night to Connie before returning to Pete's office.

"I got a call from the sheriff today," Pete began. "It seems I've been promoted to lieutenant."

"That's great, Pete. Congratulations. You deserve it. How soon will you be making the move?"

"The bars go on tomorrow. I've been a lieutenant for a whole day now," he said, somewhat embarrassed by the conversation. "I move downtown the first of the month. I'm the new head of MCU. Cornetti and his boys will be part of my responsibility." He looked down at his desk. When he looked up again, he had deep creases across his brow and sadness in his eyes.

"You and I have been doing this together for a long time, Jodi," he began. "I want to get this Mount Si Killer before I move to town. But whether we catch him or not, I want you to be the new supervisor here, be my replacement. The men respect you. The business people in town like you. You have a deep interest in the community. You have the education and the skill to run this place. I think you'd be better at it than I am. I talked with the sheriff about you. He agrees. What do you say, Jodi? Will you consider it?"

"I'm proud that you asked me, Pete. A couple of months ago I would have jumped at the chance, but right now, I don't know. May I sleep on it tonight?"

"Sure, Jodi. But please, give it a serious consideration."

He and Eileen would talk about it tonight. He would also ask the Great Wakan for assistance in making his decision.

"I'll let you know in the morning. I hate to see you move downtown, Pete, but you deserve this promotion. Congratulations again."

Connie had gone from the office for the day. Jodi closed his files. His mind raced through frayed and unrelated thoughts as he walked to his car. He took a deep breath and looked up at the clouded sky. He would stop and see Earl on the way home.

CHAPTER 12

Eustice Clayton Belmonte had moved to North Bend after his retirement from the Boeing Fire Department. He had joined that department right out of high school and continued to work there for forty two years. Everyone at Boeing knew him as Monte.

Monte was a volunteer on the North Bend Fire Department. Today, however, he was a member of the Neighborhood Watch patrol. He liked everyone and everyone liked him.

The King County Police patrol car was making a last tour of the neighborhoods before going off duty. It was only a five-minute task, which Jodi had made a daily habit. One block from the school he saw the foot patrol. Monte recognized the deputy and flagged him down.

"Hi, Jodi. Looks like we might get wet tonight."

"Sure does. Is everything okay?"

"Yes, boring at times. That's why I stopped you. I had forgotten until this morning. You know that Toyota you asked us to look out for? I think I saw it Friday night."

"Where?"

"We were right here as a matter of fact. The Nielson boy was out running around. We stopped him and asked him why he was out. While we were talking to him I saw a dark color Toyota Pickup driving slowly toward us. He turned to his right a block up, going toward town. It had a fiberglass canopy painted to match the truck. It was really clean and shiny. We escorted the kid home and in the process I forgot about the truck."

"Thanks, Monte." Jodi thought a moment. "Your patrol probably saved the Nielson boy's life. What time did you see the truck?"

"It was just after nine. It was getting dark and I couldn't see the driver."

"My guess is that he was stalking the Nielson boy when you stopped him. He cruised around until he saw Darren Campbell and picked him up instead."

"How is Earl, anyway? You know, Earl started these patrols. I truly regret we weren't able to save his son. Any child would have been a bad thing, but Earl's boy ... My God, what a tragedy."

"Yes, I know. I'm afraid Earl isn't taking it well."

"I saw Linda at the office when we walked by there. I wish there was something we could do."

"I know the family appreciates that, Monte. But you're doing a lot by being a part of these patrols. I know Earl would thank you, and will thank you when he gets better. See you later."

Monte waved as the patrol car pulled away from the curb.

Jodi waved back in his rear-view mirror as he pulled away. He needed to stop at Torval Laxo's place to ask if he could use the sauna. Monte was right, Linda was in the office. He could see her at the desk as he turned the corner by the office. There was a deep sadness in his heart. He stopped the car and walked back to the office.

Linda looked up as Jodi opened the office door.

"Hello. I just stopped to see if you were all right."

"Yes, I'm fine. It's been a trying day. The mortuary called and I made arrangements for the funeral on Thursday. I wanted to get it out of the way as soon as possible. I don't know how long Earl can go on without some kind of finalization to this. I don't mean to sound callous, but we have to get on with our lives. I am Darren's mother, I hurt too; I just want it to all go away." There were tears in her eyes.

Jodi put his arms around her shoulders to comfort her.

"I know, Linda."

She sat up straight. "They asked me for a list of pallbearers. I asked them to call you. Do you mind?"

"It would be my honor."

"One other thing, Jodi. Would you ask Eileen if she and the boys would sit with us during the funeral? Earl isn't himself and I don't want to be alone."

"Of course she will, Linda. Anything at all we can do." Jodi looked down at her sagging shoulders. "I think you should call it a day. Would you like me to drive you home?"

"No, thanks. I am going to quit for tonight, though. There just isn't any way we can thank you and Eileen enough for being there for us. We love you both."

"No thanks needed. That's what friends are for." He turned to leave. "I'll stop later, at the house."

Chapter 12

He drove east, toward the Snoqualmie Towing yard. The sky was threatening rain and daylight was now fading. His lights were on as he pulled up to the front of the big old house.

Torval came out the front door, fastening the strap on the left side of his bibb overalls. He grinned when he saw it was Jodi.

"You come to put my boys in jail?"

"Not this time, Torval." Jodi chuckled too. "I came to ask a favor. Can I use the sauna this evening?"

"Youbetcha, I have the boys heat it up for you. You want company?"

"Thanks, I have some thinking to do. The sweat is the best place for me to do that."

"You got big troubles?" Torval asked, a deep crevasse appearing between his bushy eyebrows.

The two men sat on the front steps.

"I've been offered a promotion. I have until morning to decide if I will take it."

"That is good. You will make a good boss."

"Thanks, Torval. It would affect my job and my family in a lot of ways. I need to think about it."

"Okay, you come have a sauna. I have the boys start it up."

Linda was home with Earl and Matthew when Jodi arrived. His own children were in the back yard playing. He said hello to Earl, then asked Linda if she could manage for a while without Eileen. He wanted to take her home for a family meeting.

At home he told the family of the offer for a promotion. The boys were all in favor of their father being promoted to sergeant. Eileen thought for a while, then told Jodi it was his decision to make. He must feel comfortable in his job; he must do what he thought was right. Jodi would need to think about that and determine what she really meant. All policemen's wives suffered fears for their husbands. Would this increase or alleviate some of her fears? He didn't know and she wasn't saying.

It was nearly nine o'clock when he stopped his station wagon in front of the sauna. Inside, Torval had laid out towels and fresh water. Jodi stripped down, walked into the steam and leaned back on the bench, trying to sort out all the details and make a decision.

It wasn't just the family issues he must address. There was the problem of dealing with all the varied personalities of the department. He didn't know if he had the expertise to handle the personnel problems. Then there was the political side, dealing with the downtown office. He thought he could be effective in that area, since he had known the sheriff for so many years.

The Dakota call the sweat lodge *Intipi*. It was usually made of willow or birch boughs covered with hides or blankets. It was just large enough to sit in, naked, and sing. Jodi didn't feel much like singing. The Great Wakan would find him here and help him with his decision.

The voice of his grandfather came to him as he basked in the heat of the sweat lodge. Jodi sipped cool water and remembered the lesson his grandfather had given. In the Dakota tradition, all male descendants of the father are referred to as sons. Because they are a male dominant society, and females did not aspire to leadership, male descendants of the mother are uncles or cousins.

"Life is made of choices, my son, not responsibilities," his grandfather said. "If you lead, it is because you choose to lead, not because others ask you to lead. If you lead with a true heart and for the good of your people, you will be a good leader. If you lead only because you are asked to lead, you will fail your people. It is for them you lead, not for yourself. If you do this you will be a great E-ton-chon."

Jodi thanked his grandfather for the advice. He also asked his grandfather to speak directly to the Wakantonka on behalf of his friend Earl; he was afraid Earl's spirit was leaving his body and mind behind.

There was a knock on the door, jolting him back to present-day realities. It was Torval.

"I just came to check on you, Jodi. Are you all right?"

"Yes, thank you, Torval. I was about to come out."

After a cool shower, Jodi dressed and walked to the house. Torval was on the porch with a pot of fresh coffee and two cups. No conversation passed between them while the two men drank coffee and enjoyed the evening. The coffee tasted good. Jodi was relaxed.

Jodi stood, put the cup on the small table, then stepped off the porch. He turned around to face his friend. "Thanks, Torval, for everything." Torval gave a wave of his hand. "I thought you should know. I've decided to take the new position."

"Good."

It was after ten when Jodi returned home. The boys were in bed. Eileen was watching television. She looked up and smiled as he came through the door.

"Have you made up your mind?" she asked.

He looked at her for a moment. She was so beautiful. The light from the single table lamp accented her black eyes, dark skin and raven black hair. She understood him nearly as well as his grandfather had. She had helped him meld his traditional culture with the culture of modern America.

"Yes, I have. I've decided to take the promotion," he announced. "My education and experience qualify me. Pete and the sheriff think I have the intelligence. It'll be a challenge, but I think I can do the job. We have to catch this guy we have out there, and I hope to have that done before I take charge of the detachment. It should be better hours for us as a family, too."

"I have never objected to your hours, Jodi, but it would be nice to have you home more. You know I'll support your decision, whatever it is. I love you."

Pete was in the office, wearing shiny new silver bars on his collar, when Jodi made his appearance on Tuesday morning. Emma was busy at her desk, arranging her day.

"Got time for me, Pete?"

"Sure, come on in, Jodi. I was hoping you would get in early. Have you made your decision?"

"I gave it a lot of thought. I had some doubts … about myself. But, if you still think I can do the job, I'll give it my best."

"Congratulations, Jodi … er, uh." He reached into his desk drawer to retrieve a small plastic box. He tossed it to Jodi. "Congratulations, Sergeant Eagle. I've talked with the sheriff. He thinks you're the right man for the job. You can put those stripes on your collar now. It'll be official as soon as I can call the office downtown. You can't have the office until the first of the month, though." He laughed, then reached out to shake the hand of Sergeant Jodi Eagle, Supervising Deputy for the North Bend Detachment.

CHAPTER 13

David had awakened in an ugly mood. His lover had promised to visit last night, but failed to make an appearance. It was getting to be a habit within this relationship, promise to come, then not be there. Promise to bring money, then wait several days before bringing it. Promise to go out to dinner, then cancel at the last minute.

His mother had known all along men couldn't be trusted. After all, his father had left them when she became pregnant with David, and he'd grown up in a home with an absent father. His mother was a domineering, foul-tempered woman who hated anything masculine. She had even dressed David as a little girl until he reached school age. She had insisted on a neat and orderly life for the two of them. She would scold him terribly when he failed to put some item back in its proper place after he used it. His clothing must be folded properly and placed in the proper place, neat and orderly, neat and orderly.

David had few male role models in his life. At the age of five he occasionally had a babysitter, a teen age boy who lived across the street. The boy had abused David, a fact his mother didn't learn until David was eight. it gave her even more reason to hate men. It also further confused David.

Early in his life David's mother had enrolled him in dance class, hoping he would someday be a great ballet star. Once he was old enough to make up his own mind he changed from ballet to modern dance, which he loved immensely, never missing an opportunity to practice his new art. He danced with many young girls, but found himself fantasizing that he was the girl in the dance pair. He kept this secret to himself and welcomed any invitation to go dancing.

Chapter 13

Upon completion of high school, David left home. He never returned and seldom corresponded with his mother. She was now a sickly, bitter woman with few friends. David called her each year on her birthday and, once a year wrote her a nice letter, which he included in her Christmas card. Once David began to mature, they were never close. Except for the mandatory Christmas and birthday occasions, he never contacted his mother. She, on the other hand, never contacted David for any reason, and in fact, was not friendly to her son during his annual telephone call.

David spent the morning cleaning his apartment, waiting for the telephone to ring. It didn't. His mood was even angrier when he sorted through some cassette tapes to take with him to work. Just a few more paychecks, he thought, and I'll be able to quit this job and leave this heartless town. He stood beside his pickup, studying the hazy morning before driving to the King Dome. He had come back to Seattle because it was a mecca for people, who like him, resided in one of life's great gray areas. He took several deep breaths, closed his eyes and tried to calm himself before getting into the truck.

"Those stripes look good on you." Connie commented when she met him in his office. "I didn't know a promotion was in the works. Congratulations."

"I didn't know it myself until yesterday, thanks."

Jodi called Channel 5 which put him through to the reporter in the brown tweed sport coat. He asked the reporter if he knew how to contact this Jerry Lomax.

"Sorry, Deputy. I don't have any idea. Have you tried the local office for his paper?"

"Yes, and they were a little less than helpful."

"This story is his. At least as far as his paper is concerned. You might keep an eye out there in town. He won't be far away. He drives an old white station wagon. I don't know what make but it's easy to spot because it belches blue smoke when the engine is running."

"Thanks, Tom."

"Before you hang up, is there anything new on the case this morning?"

"Nothing, but if anything comes up I'll let you know first."

As he hung up the telephone, Jodi heard the commotion of rattling toolboxes and strange voices in the front office, at Miss Emma's desk.

"Telephone company, I have a work order to modify your phones." He said.

Pete Kaufman was the next voice Jodi heard.

"It's okay, Emma. I ordered it. You fellas go ahead and do what you came for."

Jodi returned his attention to Connie. "My source said Lomax drives an old white station wagon. He doesn't know the make but says it smokes pretty badly. He thinks Lomax is in town somewhere, keeping an eye on his story. Watch for that car and try to talk to him if you see him."

"I'll do that. I'm going out on the road now. Anything you want me to do for you this morning?"

"No, just be visible. Townspeople need to know we are out there."

"See you later then."

It was just after eleven o'clock when Emma Garson dropped the large stack of mail on Jodi's desk. As was her custom, she had prioritized the stack from most important on the top to less important on the bottom; the packet from Cornetti was on the top of the stack.

Jodi eagerly opened the thick manila envelope. Inside was the FBI report. With its scientific information neatly formatted, and a file number issued by the Federal Bureau of Investigation on the top line. On the next line, under *Name,* was the notation *Unknown.* Jodi read through the report to find only what Cornetti had previously given him. The file was broken down into sections. First the identification section. Copies of fingerprints, also filed as unknown, and other standard identification items, each with the word "unknown" typed on the line.

The next section was for evidence and the scientific analysis of that evidence. Jodi again found Cornetti had covered all the important points-the tire tracks, the shoe prints, the fibers found in the clothing, the blonde hairs which yielded a result of blood type O Negative and the lipstick smudges. It took quite a long time to thumb through the thick report.

Finally, in the last section of the FBI report, the psychological profile. This section, too, was several pages long. Jodi had read psychobabble in other cases and would read this entire report another time. In the meantime he turned to the last page of the report to find the paragraph titled *Summary* and began to read about the person he was attempting to apprehend.

Psychological Profile, Identity unknown. SUMMARY: This individual is likely 25 to 32 years of age. In many ways, this male is likely to live a normal life, hold a job, take care of normal adult responsibilities, and have few, if any, other legal violations. This individual has some type of sexual or personality disorder. He knows the difference between right and wrong, but is likely to have disturbed sexual issues. He is likely to value privacy, and have order in his life. This individual is likely to come from a single-parent home with an absent father. Look for an individual for whom sex and power are related. Anger is likely an element to this individual's psychology, most likely directed at one of his parents. These are willful crimes with a ritualistic element given the pattern of clothing and the manner the body is found. Review of the evidence also suggests a feminine element to the crimes. It is clear that these crimes have been perpetrated by a male assailant but there is a feminine element in the care of the bodies and the placement of the clothing. There is likely an obsessional aspect to the offender. It is probable that he is living within five miles of the victims. He has a strong sexual preoccupation with children, both in fantasy and in the amount of time spent around them. He probably has a prior sexual offense. However, if it was as a juvenile, the files would be sealed and not available for review by adult criminal justice elements. END SUMMARY.

Jodi rubbed his eyes and leaned back in his chair. He tried to envision what all this information meant in terms of a real person. He stood and walked to the coffeepot. As he stepped into the hall he saw the telephone repairman in the blue coveralls leaving the office. It was getting difficult to concentrate so he decided to clear his desk and go out on the road for a while.

David Bennett was full of conflict and confusion as he drove to work that morning. The big day was here, and he was terrified. He'd met his goal and had already made up his mind to go ahead with it. Financially he was ready, mentally he was ready and emotionally he was ready. His dream was so close he could touch it. Could it be true? What if he went ahead and it didn't work out? Once he started he couldn't turn back.

He parked his truck in the employee parking area and stepped out into the morning air. There was an onshore breeze, which presented his senses with a strong smell of salt water. He closed his eyes, tilted his head back and took a couple of deep breaths.

"Today is the day," he thought. "I'm going to do it."

He walked to the administrative offices with purpose in his stride. The decision was made and he was going to put it into motion. Jolene looked up and smiled as he entered.

"Does George have a minute to see me, Jolene?"

"I think so. Let me check." She dialed the extension. "David Bennett would like to have a minute of your time, Mr. Towles. Can you see him now?"

She hung up the telephone and gave David another big smile. "Go on back, David. He'll see you now."

He said thanks and walked down the hall to his supervisor's office. This would not be easy; George had been good to him the past two years. He stepped into the office where George was again busy signing work orders.

"Good morning George."

"Mornin', David. What's up?"

"Do you remember the talk we had the other day?"

George nodded.

"Well, things have come together for me and I am going to go ahead with my plans. I'm giving you my two weeks' notice. I want to thank you for everything you have done for me, George. I don't want to seem ungrateful by leaving. I will be happy to train someone to take over my position. It's just that it's time for me to go on with my life and in order to do that I have to leave the Seattle area."

"You told me you might be moving on. I'll miss you. You will always have a job with me when you want one. Good luck, wherever you go. What day do you want to terminate?"

"The end of the month would be best for everyone, I assume. That's a week from next Saturday. I'll make that my last shift."

CHAPTER 14

It seemed inconceivable to Jodi that no one had seen the gray Toyota pickup. The description of the vehicle was detailed with everything except the license number. Every law enforcement officer in the state was on the lookout for the truck. The Washington State Highway Patrol was making a concerted effort to locate it, but so far it had not been spotted on the state's highways. Where could it be?

Jodi had maps of the area scattered across his desktop and on the floor surrounding his desk. He had marked the locations where each of the children had been found. There was no pattern to the sites. Each was close to town except for the first and it was not that far away. Each was on a well-traveled roadway, which meant that each body was discovered almost immediately. Each of the children was abducted from a main street in town. It appeared that in each case the child willingly got into the vehicle with the killer. Every indication was that this killer wanted to be caught and yet he was careful not to be spotted. There were so many inconsistencies and contradictions in the case it made his head hurt.

And what about the psychological profile? Jodi had studied it for hours. Every town had weirdo's and North Bend was no exception to that rule, but he could think of nobody who, even vaguely, fit the description given in the FBI report.

There was a reason the killer had picked North Bend for his rampage. What that reason was eluded him. Sometimes the rabid fox became bold and attacked chickens in the middle of the barnyard in broad daylight. Being rabid didn't make him any easier to catch. He was, after all, still a fox; still cunning and still quick.

Jodi wondered if that was the case here. Were they trying to credit a rational thought process to an irrational mind? Was this killer cunning in the commission of his crime and yet committing them for some crazed reason? It didn't seem reasonable that these were crimes of passion; they were certainly sex crimes but without viciousness. The crimes didn't show anger toward the victims. The crimes didn't seem to be motivated by revenge, as neither the children nor their families seemed to be connected in any way. Crime for profit didn't work either. Jodi could discern no rational reason for these killings.

Emma Garson had gone home for the day. Pete was somewhere in the office as Jodi began to pick up the files, papers and maps that had littered his office all afternoon. He hadn't realized how late it had become. He'd promised to stop and visit with Earl and Linda on his way home. Earl seemed to become more fragile each day.

There was a stack of file folders on his desk, which had to be put away before he could leave the office, and he wanted to make one last inspection of his patrol area before he went home. Pete poked his head into the little office as Jodi finished stuffing maps into his desk drawer.

"Are you about to wrap it up for the day?" Pete asked in a tired voice.

"Yes." Jodi replied. "I want to make a lap around town before I quit for the day. I have to stop and see Earl too. Is it me or are the days becoming longer?"

"Don't let it get you down. Sooner or later we'll get this guy and you'll be able to get back to normal. Speaking of that, give some thought to delegating some of the investigation work. You're not going to have time for it. What with the responsibilities of the office and personnel you will have to find someone else to fill your shoes. Have you thought about who you will get to be your investigator?"

"Connie Lupine would be my first choice. A couple of other deputies could handle the job. Brice would have been my choice until this case came along, but he has sure dropped the ball on this one, and I don't know why. I suspect he is going to be one of my first personnel headaches."

"Connie will be a good choice. She works hard and has a good head on her shoulders. As for Brice, there are some things you need to know. We'll have to go over personnel file tomorrow okay?"

"That will work out just fine." Jodi picked up the stack of files from his desk to take them to the file cabinet. "Did you see my leave request for Thursday? That's the day of the funeral for Darren. I need the whole day, not just for Linda and Earl but for my own family. We were all close and my boys will need me there. I'll sure be glad when all this is over."

"I guess Emma didn't give it to you. I signed your request. In fact I'm glad

Chapter 14

you're taking the day off. You're getting wrapped a little tight. You're too close to the investigation. It's time to pass it on to Connie."

"I know you're right, Pete, but it's difficult to let go." With the files in their proper drawers, Jodi began to lock the cabinets.

"Go home, I'll see you tomorrow."

The town was quiet as Jodi made his last patrol around town and through the residential neighborhoods. The Neighborhood Watch Patrols were out and waved to Jodi as he passed. The lights were on in the school and several cars were parked in the faculty parking lot.

Jodi made a tour past the wrecking yard on the east end of town. Both the boys' trucks were parked in the yard. Torval was keeping them close to home. He chuckled, thinking about the twins, as he drove east toward Edgewick road where he turned around and made his way back to downtown North Bend. There were few cars out on the streets. The Mar-T cafe was almost deserted. Across the street, the lights were out in Earl's real estate office. The town was quiet.

Jodi parked his patrol car in front of Earl Campbell's home, walked to the door and was met by Linda before he could knock. Matthew was at her side. She gave Jodi a weak smile.

"Please, come in. I was hoping you'd come this evening."

He kissed her on the cheek. "How is Earl?" he asked as he rubbed Matthew's head.

"To tell the truth, I just don't know. I don't like the way he's acting. He just isn't his old self. I don't expect him to be joyous and playful, but he is so melancholy. I'm really worried about him. I took him to Doctor Dennison today. He said that physically, nothing much has changed. His blood pressure's no good but it's been that way. It's the depression that has me worried."

"Anything I can do?"

"The two of you have been close. Would you talk to him, maybe try to make him understand what he is doing to himself? I have some business things he should take care of, but he won't even look at them. I'll do the best I can, but I don't have his experience."

"I'll talk to him." He turned to the boy by her side. "How would you like to come and spend the night with Philip and Kyle?"

He looked up at his mother. "Can I mom? Please?"

Linda smiled at her son. "Yes, you can go. Go get some pajamas and your toothbrush. I'll put a change of clothes in your backpack." The boy turned to run up the stairs. "You have to promise to be good," she called after him.

"I will, mom." He said, taking the stairs two at a time and not looking back.

She turned back to Jodi with tears streaming down her cheeks. "I miss Darren so much," she sobbed.

Jodi put his arm around her shoulders. "I know, Linda. I know." He walked her into the living room where she sat, wiping her eyes with a Kleenex.

Jodi walked into the den where Earl, seated on the couch, stared into space. It seemed he hadn't moved since he had last seen the grieving father.

"How are you doing, Earl?"

Earl looked up, shrugged his shoulders then returned to staring into space.

"Linda and I are worried about you, Earl. Don't you think it's about time to come out and join the world?" Earl only stared as before. "Come on, Earl. Say something. How long are you going to sit here like this? You have a life that needs tending. You have always been a fighter, fight now. You can't just sit here for the rest of your life."

Earl looked blankly at Jodi, then said softly, "It's my life. I'll waste it any way I want." Then his gaze returned to that faraway place.

Jodi returned to the living room just as Matthew and his mother returned. She was giving him instructions; be good, brush your teeth, mind Mrs. Eagle. She kissed the boy, then swatted his rump as he walked toward the door.

"Mo-om" he said.

"Yes, I know, you're too old for all this attention."

"Wait for me in the patrol car, will you Matthew?"

The boy left the front door open as he ran to the police car. All kids liked to ride in the patrol car and Matthew was no exception.

"I have taken Thursday off. If there's anything you need done, please, don't hesitate to ask. Eileen and I will be with you all day. Some of the neighbors are planning to have food here for you and anyone who wants to come to pay their respects. I think you should be prepared for the news media to be there. I'll try to keep them away, but there are bound to be those that won't show any mercy."

"Thank you, Jodi. I don't know what I would do without you and Eileen. There isn't any way I can thank you enough."

"No thanks necessary. We are glad to be able to help." He looked into her sad eyes. "I had better get going. Matthew will be playing with the radio and the siren if I don't get a move on. See you tomorrow."

She waved good-bye to her son from the front porch, then went back inside.

Matthew jumped from the car the instant it stopped in the drive next to his friend's house. He snatched the little backpack from the front seat and raced to the door. Philip was waiting. Matthew dropped his pack on the front porch and ran with Philip to the back yard where Kyle was waiting. Jodi picked up the pack and opened the front door.

Chapter 14

"Does anybody care that I'm home?" He shouted as he removed his duty belt.

Eileen stepped into the living room, smiled at her husband and put her arms around his neck. "I care," she said.

Later in the evening, Kyle and Matthew were upstairs in the boys' room when Philip came out to the back porch and sat beside his father. "Can I ask you a question, dad?"

"Sure, Philip, what do you want to know?"

"Well, I go to church with mom, and I understand about where people go when they die. If I die, and I believe in Christ, and have lived a good life without hurting people, then I will go to heaven. That's where Darren is going now, because he believed in Christ and he never hurt anybody. But, what I want to know is what is going to happen to Darren's dad? He's not the same as he used to be. I know he's sad because of what happened to Darren, but what will happen to him now?"

"That's a pretty grown-up question. I don't know if anyone can answer what will specifically happen with Darren's father, but I can tell you about what has happened to him according to the Dakota ways. Is that what you want to know?"

"Yeah, that's what I want to know. If I am Dakota, then I should know about Dakota ways, right?"

"Yes, that's right. You are old enough now to understand some of the Dakota ways. You will have to make up your own mind as to which ways you will want to follow. Your mother and I can only tell you about the Dakota way and the Christian way. It is up to you to make up your own mind." Jodi was proud that his son was interested enough to ask.

"To understand what I am about to tell you, you must think differently than your Christian beliefs have taught you. In the Dakota belief, life is like the light or the sunlight. Death is like a shadow. Each is a part of the same and it takes light to make a shadow. The Dakota word for this shadow is *nagi*. When the Indian spirit passes into the shadow world it is called *wanagiyata iyaya*. This means *gone to the spirit land.*"

"Earl has looked down the path to the spirit world. He looked to see if he could find Darren. There is a great deal of sadness in Earl. We can only hope that he will realize that he cannot go with Darren. He has to decide if he will come back to us here in the light or if he will follow Darren down the spirit path, which is called *wanagi tacanku*. One thing is for certain. A man cannot live for long without his spirit." Jodi looked into the eyes of his eldest son. "Do you understand any of what I have told you?"

"I think so. It's kind of mystical, but I think I understand. You have told me enough about the Dakota Way of doing things that I feel like I should know more. I believe in the things I learn in church, but I want to be able to understand your beliefs too."

"You have asked some pretty deep questions, so I think you are ready to learn. I will be happy and proud to teach you because it is the way I believe and I would be proud to have you follow the ways of your Native American heritage."

Philip stood to return to the house. "Thanks, Dad."

Jodi watched his boy open the screen door and walk inside. His family was growing up. He, like Philip, wished he could reach down the spirit path and pull his friend back into the light, but he knew that if Earl was to return he would have to find the way by himself. It was Jodi's duty to be there, in the light, when he returned to welcome him back and tell the others of his return. He, like his son, hoped Earl would find his way back, soon.

CHAPTER 15

Pete and Jodi had spent Wednesday in the office with their heads together pouring over personnel files, duty assignments, goals and objectives and a myriad of other important things that would affect the future of the North Bend Detachment. In a few days Pete would be moving on to his new assignment and he needed to bring Jodi up to speed on what went on behind the everyday menu of events seen by the public and, for the most part, by the officers of the detachment. By mid-afternoon Jodi had acquired a king-sized headache.

Late in the day he started his patrol car for the first time that day. Two hours later he had made a cursory inspection of his area. He was driving west on the old highway when he spotted Einer working on his pickup in his father's yard. He nosed his car up close behind the Laxo boy's truck, poked his head out of the side window and called to Einer.

"Hey you, garden painter."

"Hello, Jodi. I heard a car but didn't pay attention to who it was. How are you?"

"I'm doing just fine. Is your dad here?"

"No. He went into Seattle to pay some taxes and renew his towing license. Anything I can do for you?"

"I thought if you weren't using the sauna tonight I might take a sweat. My oldest boy is growing up and I might bring him too, if he is interested."

"Dad told us to heat it up any time you asked, so it will be ready. What time will you be here?"

"About eight, I think. I have some work in the office to finish. By the time I go home and eat dinner, yeah, about eight o'clock. That okay with you?"

"I'll have it ready. I'll set it up for two."

"Thanks, Einer. Say hello to your folks for me." He put the car in gear and started to back out of the yard. "See you tonight."

That evening at home, he asked his wife about taking Philip to the sweat with him. What he thought would be a simple yes or no became a fifteen-minute discussion. In the end she agreed that the boy was old enough to make up his own mind about his future and his beliefs. Jodi agreed he should not force manhood on his son, but shouldn't a parent be proud when their son, at last, left childhood behind and became a brave, a man in the tribe?

The matter was moot if the boy decided not to participate. But the lad was excited when asked if he wanted to go. It was a sign he was growing into a man. Jodi gave him the history and objective of the sweat lodge. It was not a playhouse and should be taken seriously. If Philip was to become a man, it was time for him to purify his body and to cleanse his mind. Jodi was proud to take his son with him; tonight his son would earn his first feather.

Eileen Eagle met her son and husband at the door when they returned. "How was the sweat?" she asked the boy as he stepped past her at the doorway.

"It was good," he said in a quiet voice. He was tired from the sweat and went directly to his room and to bed.

She looked at Jodi with sad eyes. She no longer had a boy. She was now the mother of a Dakota brave. In the two hours since she had last seen her son, he had changed from boy to man. Jodi said nothing. He kissed his wife, then went upstairs to bed.

It was 6 a.m. when Jodi came down the stairs to make coffee. While it perked, he stepped onto the back porch to enjoy the morning. The sun shone brightly. There were some wispy, high clouds above the mountains. Wind, up high, foretelling the storm that would arrive tonight just after dark. Back inside he poured two cups of coffee. He was about to take one to his wife, upstairs in bed, when she came into the kitchen.

"Good morning, honey. What time did you come to bed? I was so tired I didn't hear you."

"Morning, sweetheart," she replied. "I came up about a half hour after you. I started to feel sorry for myself last night. I just want to say you were right. The boys have to grow up some time. I guess they will do that whether I'm ready or not."

"His voice will change soon. How are you going to take it when he starts thinking about girls?" he teased.

She set her cup on the kitchen table, put her arms around Jodi's neck and held him tightly. "I love you," she said.

Chapter 15

They sat at the table for a long time, Jodi holding her hand as they sipped coffee.

It was Jodi who broke the silence. "We should be at the Campbells' by ten. The limousine will be there to pick up the family at ten minutes of eleven."

Jodi showered and put on his seldom worn suit while Eileen awakened the boys and fixed their breakfast. By ten o'clock the group was loaded into the family car, driving in the bright morning sun to the Campbell home just a few blocks away. As they turned the corner several vehicles met them.

Jodi parked in front of the Campbell house. "Go inside." He instructed.

Connie Lupine was doing her best to keep the television and newspaper reporters away from the house. She asked them to stay a block away from the dead boy's home. Jodi walked down the street to where she was talking with some of the reporters. A reporter in a brown tweed sport coat stepped from the Channel 5 News truck. He waved to Jodi who turned to meet him.

"How are you this morning, Deputy?"

"I don't think this will be one of my better days."

The reporter spoke quietly as the two men approached each other. "Your friend from the *World Inquirer* is in town. He'll probably be here in the next few minutes."

"Thanks." Jodi replied, also quietly.

Connie saw him coming and walked down the street to meet him.

"Morning, Jodi. They seem to be cooperating. I asked them to stay a block from the house and they agreed to do that. I talked with some of them who told me they were just after some pictures of the family leaving for the funeral. They aren't planning to do any interviews."

"Lomax is in town. He is supposed to be here in the next few minutes. If you see him, lean on him a little. I don't think he will give up his source, but you might make him nervous. See what you can do. I'm going inside now

"I have the escort duty today, but I'll try to have a talk with Mr. Lomax. I'll see you tomorrow. I hope you don't even think about the office today."

Linda opened the door. "Good morning, Jodi," she bravely held back her tears.

"Good morning, Linda. How is Earl this morning?"

"The same," she said, shaking her head. "I have asked Eileen and the boys to sit with us during the service. I think it will be best for Matthew if the other children are with him. I will be with Earl. And, of course, you will be seated with the pallbearers."

Everyone waited in the living room. Linda sobbed occasionally, but there was no conversation. Even the boys were quiet, not knowing how to act or what to say; they had never been to a funeral before. Just before ten the limousine arrived. Harry Makin gave a rundown on how the event was to be run and where he expected everyone to be. He checked the time, then escorted the family to the waiting car.

Jodi followed the black limousine in the family station wagon. At the funeral home a parking spot was reserved for him. A large crowd of mourners stood outside the funeral home waiting for the family to take their place. Jodi helped Linda get Earl to his seat, then took his place with the pallbearers, just across the aisle.

After the service a long procession of cars, with lights on, followed the hearse down the Falls City road. Jodi choked a little as the procession passed the Railroad Park where the boy's body had been found. Painful memories of the last few days brought tears to the eyes of this man who rarely showed emotion.

The family held up well during all the service and the rites given at the graveside. Earl stared into space and seemed to be unaware of the ritual taking place around him. An announcement was made that the family was having some food and beverages served at their home for anyone interested in paying respects to the family.

The pallbearers stood in a line until the end of the ceremony ... the Mayor, two school board members, Jodi, and two businessmen, members of the chamber of commerce. As the somber group began to depart the cemetery, several of them came to Jodi to ask what was being done to catch the person responsible for this heinous crime. It seemed to Jodi that the group was more interested in vengeance than in justice. He recognized that emotions were running high and decided it was not a good time to discuss the case.

Back in the Campbell home, Jodi sat on the back porch out of the sun. He spoke only to those who ventured out into the backyard. This was going to be a long day.

CHAPTER 16

Linda Campbell was up early Friday morning. She had tried, but couldn't sleep. Earl had come to bed late and slept fitfully; he was sleeping soundly now. It was just before six in the morning when she stepped onto the back porch with a cup of freshly made coffee in her hand. She needed to make some kind of decision as to what direction their lives should take from this point. Matthew was their primary concern now. Earl would need time to recover from his depression. The business needed tending. Linda had held her real estate broker's license for several years. If the business was to continue, it was up to her to oversee things at the office.

She finished her coffee, ate some whole wheat toast, showered, and picked a dark green business suit from her closet. As she dressed she thought it was good for her to get back into things. It had been a long time since she'd had to go to the office every day. Perhaps this was good therapy. Earl and Matthew were still sleeping. She left a note on the kitchen table for them, letting them know where she was going to be.

Every office has someone who knows where everything is located and organizes the office activities. For Earl's realty office it was a 32-year-old whirlwind named Loretta Moser. She had been married a couple of times but was single at the moment. Her official title was secretary, but she functioned as a combination receptionist, secretary, and executive assistant. She kept the books, filed all the contracts at the courthouse, did title research and a hundred other things that made her an invaluable part of the company.

Loretta was in the office when Linda arrived. "Good morning, Mrs. Campbell. I didn't expect anyone in today. How is Earl? Is he going to be okay?" she asked.

"Good morning, Loretta." She looked at the stack of mail on Loretta's desk and wondered if she had bitten off more than she could chew. "Earl is the same. He is going to need time to get back to his old self. Thank you for the beautiful flowers and card. Everyone has been so nice, but that was thoughtful of you."

"I've worked here for a long time and I feel like a part of the family. I hope there is some way we can keep the company running. You know I'll help all I can."

"Thank you. I am going to need all the help I can get if I am going to run this business. Keep an eye on me and let me know if I am getting out of line somewhere."

"You'll do just fine, Mrs. Campbell. Which reminds me, you had a call this morning from some banker in Bellevue. He said it was important and wants to meet with you." She handed Linda a piece of yellow paper. "This is his number."

"If we are going to work together, I wish you'd call me Linda. I think we have known each other long enough for that."

"I didn't know if I should call you by your first name here in the office."

"This is a small town. Everyone is known by his or her first name. Let's not change that tradition." She looked at the telephone message. "Do you know anything about this fellow, what's his name? Aderle, John Aderle."

"He said he was with People's Bank. I haven't checked it out yet. He didn't tell me what he wanted."

"Thanks, Loretta. I'll call him."

Linda walked into what was now her office. A stack of mail, mostly sympathy cards, lay on her desk. She took a moment to sort the personal mail from the business mail, setting the personal letters on the credenza behind her desk. The remaining stack was left on her desk to be opened after she made this phone call.

She dialed the Bellevue number. A female voice answered, "Peoples Bank and Trust Company. How can I direct your call?"

"This is Linda Campbell of North Bend Realty returning a call to Mr. Aderle."

"Please hold and I will forward your call."

There was a short pause, some Muzak and another female voice. "Mr. Aderle's office. How can I help you?"

"Good morning, Mrs. Campbell. John Aderle here." Aderle's voice was a soft baritone. "I know this a difficult time for you. Please accept my deepest sympathy. I wouldn't have troubled you so soon if it weren't important."

"Thank you Mr. Aderle."

"Please, call me John."

"John, thank you. We are just attempting to get on with our lives. What is it I can do for you?"

"I represent some investors who are interested in one of your properties. I would like to meet with you and discuss this. I could come to your office if that would be convenient."

"When did you want to meet?"

"I can be in your office by eleven. We could discuss our business and then have lunch. Would that fit your schedule?"

"Yes, I hadn't scheduled anything for today. Can you tell me which property you are interested in?"

"I would rather not say anything until I meet with you. I assure you this is not just a fishing expedition. My investors have researched this quite thoroughly and are willing to make this a profitable venture for you."

"All right Mr. Aderle. Eleven o'clock."

Linda called Loretta into the office and motioned for her to sit.

"John Aderle wants to meet with me here at eleven. Is there any way you can check him out for me, discreetly? I don't know anything about him and he wants to discuss some business deal. I would hate to get swindled on my first day in the office."

"I'll see what I can do."

Ten minutes later she returned to the boss's office. She had written notes on her steno pad.

"Are you ready for this? John Aderle is vice president of the Bellevue branch of Peoples. He has been with them for more than twenty years. He travels in high dollar circles. He's known for being honest but tough. The person I talked to said he was really a nice person. His exact words were, 'If John Aderle said it, it's true.'"

"Sounds like a testimonial. Do you trust your source?"

"Implicitly."

"Thank you Loretta. I have some mail to take care of this morning. Would you see to it that there is fresh coffee and maybe some apple juice when he arrives?"

It was precisely eleven o'clock when her intercom rang to announce the arrival of John Aderle. Loretta showed him into the office and asked if he would like coffee or juice.

The banker was a tall well-built man of, she guessed, about sixty. He was attired in a blue suit, sparkling white shirt and a conservative maroon tie. His hair was dark with specks of gray showing here and there. A proper introduction was made and he took a seat in front of her desk just as Loretta returned with the coffee. She placed the tray on the credenza, served each a cup of steaming coffee, and then closed the door as she exited.

"I would like to say again, Mrs. Campbell. I am anxious to discuss this business with you, but if you would rather wait, I will understand. I can sympathize with you. I lost a son a few years ago in a boating accident. So, I have some idea of how you feel."

"Thank you. I came back to work to have something to think about besides our son. Only time is going to ease the pain. What can I do for you?"

"You and your husband own eighty acres on the other side of Interstate 90. I have three investors who would like very much to develop that eighty acres for a subdivision. One of the principals is a general contractor. He proposes to build the homes. I have two businessmen with a large amount of free cash who want to finance the whole thing. There is enough timber on the property to pay for development of the roads and utilities. The plan is to build homes of not less than 2,500 square feet. The contours of the property allow for a magnificent, unobstructed view for each of the proposed lots. We have worked out a general idea of the cost and have an outline of percentages for members of the corporation. I would like to leave a copy of the proposal for you to review. If you like it, and we hope you will, we will have the attorneys draw up a formal corporate agreement."

She rocked back in her leather desk chair, closed her eyes and thought a moment. "Do you have any idea how much this will cost?"

"Yes, we do. Believe me, Mrs. Campbell, the money is not the problem. I am only the facilitator. I will be involved in the corporation but only for a small percentage for putting the thing together. Will you think about our offer?"

"Of course I will." She made a note to call her lawyer after lunch.

When she came back from lunch Loretta followed her into her office.

"Well … ? Can you tell me about it?"

"I will, but let me talk with Lloyd first. Would you get him on the phone for me?"

Lloyd Bemis was an institution in western Washington business law. He had handled some of the biggest and highest-profile cases on the West Coast, and had been Earl's lawyer since he started the realty business. He was never too busy to talk to the Campbells.

The lawyer was a crusty little man in his early seventies. He dressed like Ben Matlock. His wrinkled suit and bow tie gave him the country hick look he wanted to present. "Throws them city fellers off guard," he would say.

The two spent more than an hour going through the papers Aderle had left on her desk. Bemis had a yellow legal pad on his lap and took notes as he

Chapter 16

read through the papers. There were contracts, plates, legal descriptions, maps and proposed subdivision covenants. A thick packet contained the rules for the new corporation, Emerald Empire Investments, which Lloyd said, would take him some time to review.

"I don't see anything here, so far, that would scare me," he said. "You would all make more money if there was more land there to subdivide. You're going to do all right as it is, but there's going to be a lot of outlay before you see a return."

"Are you saying that the cost per lot would be less if we had more lots?"

"That's exactly what I am saying. Let me take this to my office and spend some time with it. I'll get back to you about it on Monday."

"Thank you, Lloyd."

She sat in her office trying to read the cards and notes she had received. It was upsetting her. She couldn't get her mind off what Bemis had said. If there were more land, the costs would be lower.

She picked up her purse. "I have something to do, Loretta. I'll be out of the office the rest of the day. Lock up for me, will you?"

Linda rolled down her car window, put on her sunglasses, checked the traffic and pulled onto the street. She drove to Mary Alice Jade's office, hoping to catch her in. The receptionist showed her into the office where Mary Alice was busy at her desk.

When the door opened she looked up and smiled. "It's good to see you working, Linda.".

"Thank you." Linda hoped there wouldn't be any conversation about the family loss. "Can I have a few minutes of your time?"

"Sure, what can I do for you?"

"Do you still have the option on the two forty-acre parcels across the interstate?" she asked. "The ones on either end of the eighty acres we own?"

"Yes, I do. As a matter of fact, I just renewed those options. Are you interested in them?"

"Possibly," she began. "We have worked well together in the past. I wondered if you would be interested in a new venture?"

"If it takes money, I am afraid I can't. I'm extended about as far as I can afford to be right now."

"What I am about to tell you is in strict confidence. If I didn't know you as well as I do, I wouldn't be here," she said slowly, carefully considering her words "I had an offer today. An offer that, if everything is as they say, will make a lot of money and be a real asset to the community. I think there is room for you in this offer. It would entail no cash investment other than what you have in the options on those parcels on the other side of Interstate 90. Are you interested?"

"Does someone want to develop that area?"

"I can't give you any more information unless you think you want to become involved."

"You have certainly piqued my curiosity." Mary Alice was interested.

"Will you meet with me and Lloyd Bemis in my office on Monday morning?" Linda asked. "Lloyd is going over the proposal this weekend and will have something for me on Monday. If you are interested at that point, then we will present a counter offer and see if they accept. I'm sorry I can't give you specifics, but this is still on the table and I really haven't confirmed that the offer is legitimate, but Lloyd seems to think it is." She watched for Mary Alice's reaction. "Can I call you Monday morning with a time?"

"I'll be looking forward to your call. Thank you for thinking of me. See you Monday."

Linda drove slowly back toward town. Near the farm equipment dealership she saw a King County Police car parked in a turnout. Brice Roman was talking to some young man in an old white station wagon. It was getting late. She should get home and fix dinner for Earl and Matthew.

CHAPTER 17

Saturday was a beautiful, warm summer day. The annual baseball rivalry between the Highway Patrol and the King County Police Department would once again be played out. Brice Roman would pitch and Gary Durbin would catch. In recent years, Jodi had played first base and had been the number one hitter for the team. The families usually began to congregate at the picnic grounds around noon or shortly before. Kids would play a game of baseball, wieners would be roasted and burgers grilled. Officers off duty for the weekend would consume a large quantity of beer while those with duty assignments would skip the alcohol. The annual picnic was a happy occasion for the officers and their families.

Jodi Eagle had not planned to participate in this year's event but his family had insisted upon going. The boys looked forward to seeing their friends and to playing ball; games and picnics had almost ceased to exist this summer. Eileen was also anxious to see some of the wives she wouldn't see again until next year's get-together.

Jodi called Linda to invite her to come along, but she wanted to spend the day with Earl. Would they mind taking Matthew with them? Linda thought the kids would have fun playing together.

By the time the car was packed with picnic supplies and baseball gear and the family loaded into the beige station wagon, the mood was light. They made a stop at the Campbell house to pick up Matthew, who was waiting on the front porch. Linda gave him his instructions and waved at them as they drove away.

It was early evening when they loaded into the car for the return trip. Eileen asked why it was that police officers never took a day off even at the picnic the only thing they talked about was their work.

"Cops are cops." Jodi said. "Policemen spend so much of their lives on the job, and become so emotionally attached to their work, they seldom have time to develop other interests. Cops usually associate only with other cops. Most decent people don't understand their sense of humor. They talk about things they aren't allowed to share with anyone outside the fraternity. It may seem they don't leave the job at work, but this picnic is one of the few activities that make them feel like real people."

Eileen smiled. "I've been married to a policeman for a long time. I guess I shouldn't have had to ask that question." She chuckled quietly. "I had a good day. I sure do love you, Jodi Eagle."

He looked into her eyes and smiled. "I love you too, Mrs. Eagle."

From the back seat came the unified voices of a group of conspirators. "We want some ice cream."

They were still licking ice cream off their fingers when they dropped Matthew off at his home. It had been a good day. Jodi's muscles ached from playing baseball but he felt good. His mind had been cleared of the thoughts that had filled his every moment for the past two months, and he was glad the family had persuaded him to go.

Together they unloaded the car and put the equipment away. The dishes were done. The boys had shed their clothes and taken their baths. They were so tired they gave no argument when their mother suggested they go up to bed.

Jodi finished his coffee, then followed his boys' example. He showered and climbed into bed, exhausted from the day's activity.

Eileen put a load of clothes in the washer and, she too, indulged in a hot bath before falling into bed. She read for an hour before turning out the light, listening to the quiet, rhythmic breathing of the man lying beside her. There weren't enough of these family days. She put her arm over her husband, pressed her body against him and was asleep almost immediately.

The irritating sound interrupting his sleep was the telephone. It took several rings before he was conscious enough to realize what it was. He looked at the clock as he reached for the ringing phone. It was almost five a.m.

"Hello," he said groggily.

"Hello. This is King County Police Dispatch. Is this Sergeant Eagle?"

"Yes, it is. What can I do for you?"

"I have some bad news, sir," the dispatcher said.

Jodi sat upright on the edge of the bed. "What is it?"

"First of all, sir, one of your patrolmen has been involved in an accident. There are fatalities."

Chapter 17

"Where?"

"The Fall City road. Almost to Redmond. He was in pursuit of a suspect in the child murders when a vehicle pulled out in front of him. The officer is on his way to the hospital, he's critical. The two people in the other vehicle are dead at the scene."

"Which officer?"

"Gary Durbin, Sir."

"Okay. I'll be in the office in ten minutes." He started to hang up, then spoke again into the mouthpiece. "Dispatch. Has the State Patrol been notified to investigate this accident? We can't investigate one of our own."

"Gene Cavanaugh is the State Patrolman on the scene. Larry Piedmont, from your office, is there too," the dispatcher reported. "I called Lieutenant Kaufman before calling you."

"Thanks. I'm going to the scene before I go to the office. I'll be on the radio."

He found a clean uniform in the closet, and was snapping on his duty belt when his wife asked in a sleepy voice. "What's going on, Jodi?"

"There's been an accident, honey. Go back to sleep."

It was just becoming daylight when Jodi drove quickly from the neighborhood. He didn't turn on the red lights until he had turned onto the Falls City road. Traffic was light and he made good time to the scene. It was at the driveway to the Bjustrom Tree Farm. As he approached the scene he could see the Chevrolet patrol car on its side in the left ditch, the front end smashed. On its top in the highway was an older Ford sedan. Jodi recognized it as belonging to Nels and Hilma Bjustrom. He parked on the side of the paved roadway, but left his red lights flashing.

Piedmont was flagging traffic on this side of the accident. The officers had managed to get one lane open to allow traffic flow. He could see another sheriff's deputy on the other side of the accident scene directing traffic, but because of the lights he couldn't tell who it was.

"What's the story, Larry?"

"It's really bad, Jodi." Piedmont began. "The guy killed another kid tonight. Gary saw him putting the body on the sidewalk at the office. He jumped into his truck and drove off toward Redmond. Gary chased him after he made sure the victim wasn't alive." He stopped talking while he flagged another car through. "Anyway, he chased him down the Falls City road and up to here. Mr. and Mrs. Bjustrom were pulling out of their drive when Gary hit them. They pulled right out in front of him. He couldn't stop. All that blackberry brush must have obstructed the view and they didn't see Gary coming."

Nels Bjustrom had owned a dairy close to North Bend for many years. He had sold it five or six years ago and bought this tree farm for retirement. Their grandson had just graduated from Lutheran seminary and was giving his first sermon to his new parish this morning in Tacoma. The Bjustroms were leaving early to have breakfast in Renton before going on to Tacoma for church. They had been killed instantly when they pulled out in front of the speeding patrol car.

"How is Gary? Is he going to make it?" Jodi asked with concern.

"I don't know. He was pretty bad."

"Thanks, Larry. I'm going to talk with the Highway Patrol."

Gene Cavanaugh had just finished taking measurements of the skid pattern and was making notes in his book. Nels and Hilma were still in the car and would not be removed until the captain arrived and released them. By 6:30 this morning there would be only an oil spot and some tire tracks to mark the location where two nice people ended their lives in a tragic accident.

"Hello, Gene. How does it look?"

"Looks like pure accident, Jodi." He was still writing. "It looks like they came out of the driveway without seeing Gary coming. You can see there's a slight right turn. And with the brush growing up over that fence that way, they probably never saw the car coming, even with his reds on. Gary was doing about seventy, I would estimate. Hit the Ford in the left door post. There's only 22 feet of skid marks, so Gary didn't see them in time either."

"Will you get me copies of the pictures and reports as soon as possible, Gene?"

"Sure thing, Jodi." He hadn't stopped writing.

Jodi looked into the broken patrol car, climbed back onto the paved roadway and looked again at the crumpled bodies of the elderly couple. He walked back to his own car, turned off the red emergency lights and drove to the office.

When he arrived he could see a small crowd in front of the King County Police offices. A blanket covered the body he knew was on the concrete walk in front of the office. Connie Lupine was standing there, notebook out, scribbling information on the pad. Brice's patrol car was parked across the street.

"Everything under control?" he asked Connie. "How soon before Cornetti and the coroner get here?"

"The coroner should be here any minute. Cornetti," she looked at her wristwatch, "should have been here by now." She turned as a set of lights rounded the corner and headed in their direction. "This looks like him now."

"I'm going inside to see Pete. Have Lewis come see me as soon as he gets finished. Do you need any help out here?"

"Not now. Cornetti and his boys will take it from here. I can keep the crowd away for now."

Chapter 17

Jodi walked into the office where he was surprised to see Miss Emma Garson busy at her desk. It always amazed Jodi how she always knew when she was needed. She lived alone and, day or night would be in the office when a crisis arose. The rail around her desk was covered with yellow Post-It notes.

"Good morning, Jodi," she said.

"Good morning, Emma. How long have you been here?"

"Not long. I thought you would need a hand with the phones and the paperwork so I came in for a while. I will have to go at ten o'clock, for church, but I'll come back afterward."

He poured a cup of coffee, then stepped into Pete's office. "Morning, Pete." He sipped his coffee. "I just came from the accident scene. It's a mess. Gene said they would have it cleaned up in about an hour. Have you heard how Gary is doing?"

"I just got off the phone to the hospital. They aren't saying anything yet." He wiped his face with an open hand, then let out a long sigh. "Do you want me to go to his house and notify his wife?"

"I guess I had better do that." Jodi said. "I wonder if Larry Piedmont's wife would stay with her today. She is going to want to go to the hospital. She has that little baby to care for; maybe Nancy Piedmont would sit with her."

"You go on to the Durbins. I'll call Nancy and ask her if she will go there. Larry should be back in from the accident in a little while. I'll have him drive Lois down to the hospital."

"Okay, I'll be back as soon as I can."

As he walked from Pete's office he met Connie Lupine in the front office. "How is it going out there?"

"Cornetti has it under control. I have to get to the Texaco and notify the boy's mother. She is the night cashier there. I need to do that right now before someone else goes in and tells her."

"You know the boy then. Who is he?"

"Bobby Carstairs," he told him. "I've busted him a couple of times for juvenile stuff. His mother works nights and when he gets bored he gets into trouble."

"Well, go and see the mother. I'll have Pete call Barney Peters to go and relieve her at the station. Is there a relative or friend who can stay with the mother?"

"I don't know. She was having troubles of her own. She was kicking the drug habit and trying to support that boy of hers. I don't know who her friends are. I'll try to find out from her and have one of them come to sit with her." She turned to leave the office with Jodi right behind her. As they stepped out of the office they could see Cornetti's men had strung yellow barrier tapes around the street. The five men were all busy collecting evidence.

At the corner, Connie turned right while Jodi turned left. It was only a half mile to where Gary Durbin lived in a rented house with his wife Lois and their four-month-old baby girl. Nancy Piedmont's was just arriving when Jodi stopped in front of the house. She lived only a few doors down in another rented house, almost identical to the one he must now visit.

"Hi, Nancy. Thanks for coming." He could see she had been crying. "Are you going to be all right?"

"Yes, I'll be just fine. It was such a shock to get a call from Pete. At first I thought it might be Larry. I feel so guilty for feeling relieved that it was Gary."

"Let's get it over with. We'll have to wake her up." He looked at her again. "Are you sure you're okay?"

"Yes."

"Larry will be here in a little while to take her, and you, to the hospital. I don't know how Gary is doing. The hospital wouldn't release any information on the telephone. If you need any help, call Eileen. I haven't told her anything yet, but I'll call her as soon as I get back to the office. She will be ready to give you a hand if you need it. Just be there for Lois, right now. I appreciate the help, thanks"

The two walked to the front porch where Jodi knocked on the door. A sleepy young woman answered the door. Almost immediately she gained a look of shock as tears came to her eyes.

"No, no! Has something happened to Gary? Please, Jodi, not Gary," she almost screamed at them, backing into the living room. "Where's Gary?"

Nancy rushed to her support. "Take it easy Lois."

"Lois," Jodi began, He hated doing this.

CHAPTER 18

Connie pulled into the Texaco station. She could see Mona Carstairs seated inside the little locked office which held the cashier's booth for the self-service station. Mona was a local girl with a bad track record with her men. She'd been married twice and had the one son by her first husband. She divorced him when he was sent to prison for dealing drugs. She'd been using drugs in those days, mostly cocaine, but she had been off drugs for almost three years now, and lived alone with Bobby. She was thin, frail and had a nervous twitch in the left side of her face. She'd been a pretty girl once, but that was now gone. Broken and bitter, she faced a doubtful future.

Connie stepped to the window and, through the money slot, asked to be let inside. She walked to the end of the little building where the entry door was opened from the inside by Mona Carstairs. With the door open only a crack, Mona peered out to see if anyone was with the deputy.

"Hello, Deputy Lupine. Bobby isn't in trouble again, is he?"

"May I come inside, Mona? I need to talk to you for a minute."

"I'm not supposed to let anyone in here, but I guess it'll be okay for you to come in."

"I called your boss and he will be here in a few minutes to take over." Connie knew she had to deliver the news of her son's death but was unable to just come out and say it. "Mona, I have some bad news."

"I knew it. Bobby is in trouble again, isn't he? I told him not to leave the house after I left. Why doesn't that boy ever listen to me?" Her voice became shrill.

Connie took the woman by the shoulders and sat her on the stool in front of the cash register. "Calm down," she said, "calm down, Mona."

Headlights stopped in front of the little office. It was Barney Peters. He had a set of keys of his own and opened the office door from the outside. There was little room for the three of them in the tiny office.

"Do you want me to wait outside, Connie?" he asked.

"No, I think I'll take Mona with me now. Thanks for coming down with such short notice."

He looked at the confused employee. "You go with Deputy Lupine now, Mona. I'll take over here. Leave me your keys. I'll handle it until you can come back."

"What's … what's happening, what's going on?" she asked as she dropped her key ring on the desk.

"Come with me Mona, I'll explain on the way to the office," the deputy said as she escorted her to the patrol car.

In the car, Connie broke the news as gently as she knew how. Mona first stared at her in disbelief, and then she screamed so loud that she could be heard inside the cashier's office. Barney looked out to see the woman, with her face buried in her hands, crying uncontrollably. He watched from the window as the patrol car pulled away from the gasoline station in the direction of the King County Police station.

When they arrived, the Coroner had just finished loading the boy's body into his county car. The mother was asked to make an official identification. As the black body bag was unzipped and the face of her son appeared, she again began to wail and scream. It was all Connie could do to hold the woman, and keep the young mother from climbing into the Coroner's car with her dead son. Finally, with the help of Cornetti, she was able to escort the Mona into police headquarters. She sat sobbing in Jodi's office, and refused Connie's offer of coffee or a drink of water, but the distressed woman refused anything. She busied herself retrieving forms and folders from the drawers in the office until Mona began to calm down.

Cornetti walked into Pete's office to tell him that his men had completed their tasks and were now leaving the scene.

For the killer it had started like the other crimes. He had worked himself into a rage because his love was planning to leave him. The more he thought about it the angrier he became until he decided he would do it one more time. He'd send a message that couldn't be missed. No way would they be able to ignore it. It would be chancy, the risk of being caught tonight was great but it was worth it.

The shots the doctors were giving him were beginning to have an effect. He was leaving. He'd be changing his entire life, with or without the approval of this so-called lover who didn't care, who didn't listen. By the end of the week he'd be gone, bag and baggage. This would be the final and explicit message-one they couldn't miss.

He had spent the early evening in Everett at a popular disco club. They knew him there and he danced until almost midnight. He drove directly from the club to North Bend, stopping on the outskirts of town to change his appearance. He pulled his pony tail loose and combed it out. He applied lipstick using the rear view mirror to be sure it was correct. Satisfied with his look, he drove into the small town, cruising the streets, while avoiding any headlights. He was also careful to avoid the walking patrols he knew were out on the streets looking for him. They probably had a description of his truck by now.

He found the boy sneaking up to the back window of a home with no lights. The boy was obviously doing something he shouldn't. That made things easy. He made a big show of catching the boy in the act. The youngster tried to be tough, but he broke down when the blonde lady ordered him into the truck. She was going to take him to his mother.

From that point on the crime became routine. He had done this many times before and the emotional outlet fueled a flood of fantasies for the blonde killer. It felt good to be in control, and to vent his rage. He even came close to sexual satisfaction. His emotions ran wild. Finally he was to fulfill one more emotional need, vengeance. He was getting even and delivering a message to the one who had treated him so wrongfully.

He drove around the neighborhood until there were no cars on the streets. It was now early morning. He stopped at the front door of the police station where he placed the nude body of Bobby Carstairs on the sidewalk face down, left arm under his face. He was busy placing the neatly folded pile of the child's clothing next to the body when the headlights from Gary Durbin's car illuminated the scene. The young killer jumped to his feet, slammed down the canopy door and jumped into the front seat of his gray Toyota. He sped off, turning right to the Falls City road. He planned to drive to Redmond, then to Interstate 405, if he could outrun the sheriff's car. He was losing the race until the place on the Redmond highway where the Bjustroms pulled in front of Deputy Gary Durbin. He had seen the erratic action of the headlights in his rearview mirror. He didn't slow down but took advantage of the time to speed to the interstate. Before pulling onto the highway he stopped. He reached behind the seat to retrieve three magnetic signs for each side of his truck. "JOHNSON'S JANITORIAL, RENTON, WASHINGTON phone 555-9922." One on each front fender. One on each door and one on each side of the pickup box. The signs were large and covered the striping the factory had painted down the side of the sporty truck.

He entered Interstate 405, maintaining the posted speed limit. Several Washington State patrol cars had converged on the area, each looking for the sporty Toyota Pickup. None had thought to stop the janitorial truck. Their target had no signs.

He drove to Renton, then back toward Boeing and on to his apartment where he showered and dropped, exhausted, into bed. Once again, and for a final time, he'd been successful.

Jodi and Nancy Piedmont spent more than a half hour consoling Lois Durbin. She was beginning to calm down when Larry Piedmont knocked on the door. Jodi answered it.

"Hi, Larry."

"Hi, Jodi. How is she doing?" he asked quietly.

"A little better now. I'm grateful your wife is stepping in. Eileen has had about all she can handle in the past few weeks, what with the Campbell family and all." He looked into the pained eyes of his deputy. "Any word on Gary?"

"I haven't heard anything."

Jodi looked into the living room where the two women were sitting, one crying hard.

"Go ahead and take them to the hospital in Bellevue. Call me as soon as you hear anything. I have to go back to the office and try to sort some of this out."

The two men walked into the living room.

"Come along, Lois. Larry will drive you to the hospital. There isn't any news yet on his condition. Perhaps there will be when you get to the hospital. Nancy, can you sit with her at the hospital for a while? Larry can stay with you for a little while."

"Of course. Jodi. We'll call you as soon as we hear anything. Will you be at the office?"

"Yes. Thanks again." Jodi helped the Piedmonts escort Lois Durbin to the patrol car and made her comfortable inside. He stood on the street and watched as the car pulled out, dreading his return to the office, and thought it was only a matter of time before the news media found out about this death and descended on his office. The new sergeant wondered if the promotion was such a good idea after all.

In his own car he spoke into the radio, reporting that he was en route to the office and gave an ETA of ten minutes.

Back in the office, Jodi stopped first in Pete's cubicle.

Chapter 18

"Tough morning, Jodi?" Pete asked.

"I've had better." "Have you notified the Bjustrom family?"

"Yes, I just got off the phone with Pierce County. They notified the family. They were all waiting for the parents so they could have a family breakfast. It's terrible to think that every time the Bjustrom boy remembers his first day as a pastor, it will be with a sad note that it was the day his grandparents were killed. Life just isn't fair sometimes."

Jodi just shook his head. "Any news about Gary?"

"Not yet."

"See you later. I'm going to try to build a file. Anything else I need to know?"

"Connie is still interviewing Mona Carstairs. They were using your office. Brice is out on the street. He volunteered when he heard about Gary. Other than that I can't think of anything. The notifications are done, so now we just have to do the reports."

"I'm sure you realize the reporters will be here before long."

"I've been working on a statement for them. It will be pretty much a rehash of the last ones. I'll get with you later."

In the outer office, Jodi could hear Connie asking questions of the child's mother. He walked to the coffeepot where he lingered for a minute. Miss Emma stepped up to his side.

"You okay. Jodi?"

He had been so deep in thought he was surprised by her voice. "Oh, Emma. Yes, I'm all right. I don't know if I can stand any more of these cases. I think my grandfather must be disappointed with me for not tracking this guy down before now. He taught me to be a hunter and a tracker but I haven't been able to track this one. He just seems to vanish into thin air."

"Be careful not to take this too personally," she cautioned.

They both turned toward his office when they heard Connie and Mona get up to leave. Since Mona had no family and few friends, Connie had called Mary Lafferty to stay with Mona this morning. Connie drove the stricken mother to her home where Mary was waiting. After cautioning her about the reporters, Connie drove back to the office. There was a lot of paperwork to be done.

She was sitting in Jodi's office with a Coke in her hand when Pete came in with a smile on his face.

"Larry just called from the hospital. Gary is out of surgery. They have upgraded him from critical to serious. He has a fractured skull and a lot of cuts and bruises. His seatbelt and the airbag saved his life. They sedated Lois and she is resting now. But the prognosis is good."

At least there would be this little bit of joy in the office today.

CHAPTER 19

Monday morning took up where Sunday had ended. There were reports to be filed and updated. Information was slow in coming. Cornetti had not called with results or photos of his investigation. Those were expected later today. Reporters were asking for information; some calling and some coming into the office for direct contact, and a statement on the latest killing.

Emma Garson was a master at handling pushy reporters. They wanted information, which she could not give them, but there was to be a news conference and an official statement at one o'clock this afternoon. She knew how much they wanted something for their papers and news broadcasts, but she had nothing until then. All their questions would be answered at the press conference. Lieutenant Kaufman would answer all their questions at that time.

Jodi was deeply engrossed in his work when Emma buzzed his intercom.

"Someone on line two says he has some information you wanted. He won't give me his name," she reported.

"Thanks, Emma. I'll take it." He cut her off by punching the button for line two.

"Sergeant Eagle here, can I help you?"

"Sergeant, this is Tom Logan. Remember me?"

"Yes, Channel five, right?"

"Yes. Do you have a minute to talk?"

"Go ahead, I'm alone."

"Your friend from the *World Inquirer*, Jerry Lomax, is in town. He is bragging that he scooped everyone last week and that when this week's edition hits

Chapter 19

the streets we will all be scooped again. He says he has pictures and reports from your office on the Campbell killing. Deputy Eagle, if there is any truth to what he is saying, you guys are going to look pretty bad. His paper hits the streets today."

"Oh, great. Do you have any idea where he is getting this information? Are there any rumors about it?"

"Not a word. That's strange, too. Usually there is something, but not this time. Whoever is giving Lomax his information is in your office, that's all I know."

"Will he be at the press conference today?"

"He said he would." Tom thought for a moment, then added his own comment. "Jodi, this little punk is gloating. He is going to give all of us a bad name. I don't want that to happen. His paper is popular, but most people don't want rumor and speculation, they want facts. The information he has come up with has given him a modicum of credibility. He doesn't deserve any respect either from the public or from the other reporters who are honestly trying to do their job. He is hurting us all. I hope you can stop him before we all get burned by them."

"I'm sure going to try, Tom. I appreciate the information. We are trying to find the leak in the office. I hate to think that I can't trust one of the people I work with. Thanks again."

"I'll let you know if I hear anything else." The line went dead.

Jodi checked the time, 10:35. The distributor would be getting to the store about now.

"Emma, come in here, will you?"

She peered around the edge of the door.

He reached into his pocket for some change. He handed it to her.

"I want you to go to the store and find a copy of this week's *World Inquirer*. I need it right away."

"I'll do it right now."

This week's magazine supply was not yet on the stand but stacked in front of the magazine racks, wrapped in newspaper and tied with plastic bands. She found the manager who quickly cut the band on the stack when he heard it was for the police department.

She bought three copies when she saw the pictures on the front page of the weekly tabloid. The four-column-wide picture was in color. It showed the face-down, nude body of Darren Campbell at the Railroad Park site. Bold type above the picture proclaimed ... **MT. SI KILLINGS CONTINUE,** and underneath, in smaller type, KILLER FOUR, POLICE ZERO. Emma rushed back to the office.

Back in the office she handed a copy to Jodi. "Oh, Jodi, this is awful."

Jodi read the entire article without looking up. It continued from the first page to page three, with more pictures. As he read, Jodi knew that the information came from the official reports locked in the files of this office.

Following the main article there was another shorter one with comments about the killer and the killings. Included in that column was a word-for-word quote of the FBI criminal profile summary. Jodi was astonished to find this classified information staring him in the face. He was furious.

He carried the newspaper to Pete Kaufman's office. "Have you seen this?" He tossed the paper on the lieutenant's desk. It hit the desk and flopped open to the front page, leaving Pete to stare at the color photographs taken at the crime scene.

"Oh, my God!" he said. "When did this come out?" Without looking up he began to read.

"It's hitting the newsstands right now."

"Give me some time to read this. I'll give a warning about this kind of stuff when I have the news conference today."

The same store manager who had helped Emma locate the *World Inquirer* was talking with Loretta Moser. He quietly passed a copy of the tabloid to her and whispered something before leaving the real estate office. Loretta opened the paper to be shocked by the picture centered on the front page. She took several minutes to compose herself before carrying the newspaper into the office where Darren Campbell's mother was working.

"Mrs. Campbell … Linda," she began nervously. "I'm sorry to be the one to have to bring this to you." She held up the folded paper. "I wouldn't show this to you, but I know you will see it anyway. I'm sorry." She laid the newspaper on Linda's desk.

As the paper flopped open in front of her, she started to scream, then choked it off. She clasped her hands over her mouth as tears filled her eyes. It was such a horror to see the picture of her son, dead and humiliated, glaring up from her desk. She began to tremble, her knees became weak and she sagged into her chair. Her shoulders jerked from the heavy sobbing, though she made no sound.

Loretta didn't know what to do; should she leave, should she stay, what should she say?

"Can I get you anything Linda?"

Linda Campbell didn't speak. She only shook her head slowly. Her hands were still covering her mouth, tears running over the backs of her hands. She

Chapter 19

stared at the picture for several minutes while Loretta stood by the door and waited. She finally mustered the strength to speak.

"Please, Loretta. Let me be alone for a little while."

"Are you sure you will be all right?"

"Yes, just close the door. Let me have a few minutes. Thank you."

Loretta closed the door as quietly as she could. When she returned to her own desk, she tried to think of what she should do. Finally she reached for the telephone and dialed.

Emma passed the call to Jodi's desk. "She says it's important."

He picked up line one. "Yes, Loretta?"

"I'm sorry to bother you, Jodi. But I didn't know who else to call. Earl isn't himself and you are their best friend, I just thought I should call you."

"What's the matter Loretta? Has something happened?"

"Not exactly. Have you seen this week's edition of the *World Inquirer*?"

"Yes, they just brought it to me."

"The store manager brought one to the office. I didn't know what else to do except give it to Linda. Someone was bound to ask her about it and I didn't want her to be surprised by it. She is in her office now. She is taking it really hard. Please, Jodi, what should I do?"

"She's going to have to deal with it in her own way. I don't know what I can do except give her some moral support. Just keep an eye on her for now and I'll be over as soon as I can. Call me if you need me before I can get there."

"Thanks, Jodi. I'll see you later."

Jodi hung up the phone, leaned back in his chair and rubbed his face with the palms of his hands. He closed his eyes and gave out a long sigh. "I wonder if this Lomax character knows how much pain he is causing, or if he even cares."

It was just after noon when Jodi dialed the intercom phone to connect with Connie Lupine. She had been in the office all morning, writing the reports and transcribing the interview with Mona Carstairs. She'd been at her desk too long and was getting a king-sized headache.

"Connie, do you have a minute to come to my office?" Jodi asked into the phone.

"Be right there." She welcomed the chance to get away from the typing.

While waiting for Connie, Jodi stepped to Pete's office and asked him to come to his office for a short strategy meeting.

The three deputies crowded into the little office.

"What's on your mind?" Pete asked.

"I want to throw a little scare into Jerry Lomax. I want to threaten him with arrest for obstruction of justice. Interfering with a police investigation, and receiving stolen property. I want to snatch him up right after the press conference at one o'clock."

Connie couldn't hold back the excited grin.

Pete wasn't as enthusiastic about the idea. "We don't have enough evidence to make any of those charges stick," he said. "We don't have any idea who is supplying him with information. If we drag him in here, do you think he will give up his source?"

"I doubt it. But we can't just let him go on thinking he is operating without someone noticing. I want to roust him a little. I want him to know we're watching. I want to make him nervous."

"Don't you think this borders on harassment?"

"Probably. But you and I both know he is guilty of all those things. I just want to question him and to make him nervous. When I get enough rope, I'll hang him. Right now I just want him off balance."

"I am not going to sanction any vigilante action. I want you to keep it strictly within the lines. I agree he needs to be put on notice. I just don't want him to have any grounds for legal action." Pete cautioned.

"I understand. I'll keep it strictly legal."

"What do you want me to do?" Connie asked.

"Pete will be delivering his press release at one. I want you to move around to the rear of the group and keep an eye on Mr. Lomax. As soon as the briefing is finished I want you to invite Lomax into the office for some questions. I'll be watching to back you up if you need it. Just bring him into my office."

"I can handle that."

"I'm going to Linda's office right now, but I'll be back in plenty of time."

Jodi checked the time as he left the office. He would have to hurry in order to be back in time for the press conference. Two minutes later he was parked at the curb in front of the real estate office. Inside Loretta Moser met him. During the years she worked for them she had formed a deep loyalty toward the Campbell's. Her concern for Linda was obvious.

"Hi, Jodi. She's still in her office. I haven't talked to her since I called you."

"I'm glad you called, Loretta. Sorry I couldn't get here sooner."

She watched him walk to the office door and tap gently. A quiet voice inside said, "Come in."

Linda had dried her face and applied fresh makeup to her swollen eyes. Jodi thought she had aged at least ten years in the past week. When she saw him enter her office she stood, stepped from behind her desk and wrapped her arms around the deputy.

"Oh, Jodi, I'm glad to see you." She was trying hard not to cry.

Chapter 19

"I'm really sorry you had to see that newspaper, Linda. There just isn't anything we can do to stop that kind of thing. I know how painful this is to you and to Earl. Is there anything I can do to help you?"

"No. I know we will have to deal with it ourselves. I thought we were through with the emotional attacks. I guess I was wrong. I'll get over it. I won't show this to Earl; I don't think he is ready to deal with any more hurt right now."

"That's probably wise." He held her away from him. Holding her shoulders, he looked into her red and swollen eyes. "Are you sure you are going to be okay?"

"Thank you for asking, Jodi. Yes, I'll be all right. I have a lot of work here in the office to keep my mind occupied. In fact I have a meeting with Lloyd Bemis in a half hour. There are some rather large decisions to be made in the next few days. I wish Earl was here to make them, but that's not going to happen, so I guess it's up to me."

"I wish there was more I could do to help. Eileen and I share your grief and sadness. We want to help take the load off you but there just isn't any way we can do that. Just remember we are there if you need us."

"Thanks, Jodi."

"I have to get back to the office now, but you call me if there is anything you need." He started for the door, then turned back. "Do you think Earl would be up to going out for dinner tonight? You know, take the kids for burgers or pizza?"

"I don't know. I'll call you later to let you know."

He checked the time to find he was again going to have to hurry again to make it to the press conference on time. As he turned the corner near headquarters he could see the crowd of reporters and their various cars and trucks blocking the street. Connie was in her car behind the crowd. He parked across the street and walked to the office doorway where Pete was about to start his statement.

Jodi listened to the short press release. It sounded like a recording of all the previous statements. The reporters were getting tired of the same information being passed out each time. They would be digging to find new information, especially since the release of the summary of the psychological profile by the *World Inquirer*. Jodi saw the Channel 5 news-team and knew the brown sport coat would be among the first to ask questions regarding the *World Inquirer* article.

A young man wearing a polo shirt and blue jeans stood at the back of the throng. He didn't seem particularly interested in the press release or even the questions being asked by the other reporters. Connie Lupine was out of her car and standing a short distance behind young Lomax. As the press conference came to a close she stepped up to him. Jodi watched intently, ready to run to her assistance if she needed him. It proved unnecessary as the young reporter walked to the office with her, and was, in fact, a little cocky about it.

Inside she led him to Jodi's office. Lomax sat in one of the two chairs in front of the desk. He crossed his legs, leaned back and clasped his hands behind his head. Connie parked in the other chair while Jodi stepped behind the desk. He pulled a file from his drawer and opened it on his desktop. It was all for effect; the file had nothing at all to do with this case. Jodi pretended to read the file for several minutes, making the reporter wait for him to open the conversation. A few seconds was all it took for the young man to begin to squirm in his chair. It took less than three minutes for the ploy to work.

His face had become red and his eyes darted from Jodi to Connie and back again. Finally he could take it no longer. He nervously jerked his hands from behind his head and put both feet flat on the floor. He leaned forward in his chair in an attempt to get Jodi's attention.

"I don't have the time to sit here all day while you read some file. I have things to do. I have a deadline to meet. If you don't have anything to say I'm out of here."

Jodi didn't look up; his control amazed Connie Lupine. "Shut up and sit still. I'll be with you in a minute," he continued to read.

The young reporter became more agitated. He stood up to leave.

"I'm not staying here for this" he said.

"Sit down and shut up."

Connie stood and stepped back behind her chair, blocking the entry. Lomax started to move toward her, then changed his mind and returned to his chair.

"What do you want from me?" Lomax asked.

Jodi closed the file. He looked up at the young reporter and smiled.

"Nothing. I don't want anything from you. I just wanted to tell you how much I enjoyed your writing. It's a nice piece of creative journalism. Funny thing though. I don't remember any of the information in that article being released today or in the last press releases. Do you want to tell me where you got your information?"

"I don't have to account to you for anything, especially about my sources. I only have to be certain they're accurate with their information." Lomax was prepared for that one.

"Well young man, I just wanted to be the one to tell you that the grizzly is on your trail. While you were tracking the bear, he walked in a circle and is coming up behind you. He is about to bite you and you are too dumb to know he is there."

"What the hell does that mean? I heard you were Indian, but I don't understand your mumbo-jumbo."

"It means you are in over your head. You had better start swimming or you will have to drink a lot of water in order to survive."

"Can't you just say what you mean? I don't know what you're talking about."

"It means that by releasing privileged information you interfered with a criminal investigation. You are obstructing justice. By obtaining this unauthorized information you have received stolen property. What I am saying, in words even you can understand, is that before long I am going to arrest you. I am going to put you in jail for being such a great creative journalist."

"You can't do that. My paper has many attorneys just waiting for some hick deputy to come along and arrest one of its reporters. You will be in court before you can say Clarence Darrow."

"Just remember what I said; keep looking over your shoulder because the bear is quickly closing in on your trail. Now get out of here. You know where to reach me if you decide to tell me how you got this information." Jodi opened the file again.

The *World Inquirer* reporter started to say something but changed his mind. He stormed from the office, nearly tripping over the small gate in the rail by Emma's desk. Connie watched him as he strode from the office into the street. She could not see his car but heard it as the tires screeched when he pulled away. She snickered to herself as she stepped back into Jodi's office.

The departing reporter had nearly knocked down Brice Roman at the door.

"What was all that about?" he asked Emma Garson.

"I don't think he liked what the sergeant just told him," she replied.

Brice saw the fat envelope on Miss Emma's desk. It was addressed to Jodi and was from MCU, Seattle. This was the report from Cornetti with information and pictures from the Carstairs killing. Brice knew it represented his bonus from the *World Inquirer* and his associate Jerry Lomax. He would have to be careful though. Jodi was on to Lomax. They would have to meet in a new place this time. The restaurant at Snoqualmie Lodge, on top of the pass, yes, that would be a good place.

CHAPTER 20

Lloyd Bemis entered the offices of the North Bend Real Estate Company carrying a battered old leather brief case in his left hand. The case was heavy with papers, so heavy in fact that the elderly lawyer leaned to the right to compensate for the weight of the case. He stopped at the desk of Loretta Moser and asked to be announced.

Linda opened the door to her office and invited him inside. She had done her best to cover up the signs of crying, and had her distress under control for now. The one thing she didn't need right now was to have to explain her tears. A Kleenex in her hand, she sat at her desk, wiped her nose and dabbed at her eyes. She took a deep breath, broken by a small sob, before she spoke.

"Well, Lloyd, how does it look to you?"

"Everything I have here seems almost too good to be true. They have made you a nice offer. It looks legitimate. If you accept this offer you will be a rich lady."

"Do you think they would be amenable to an offer with twice as much property?"

He thought before speaking. "Everyone would make more money if there were more land to develop. Quite a lot of the permit costs and the costs for utilities as well as the development cost being amortized over a greater number of lots would cut the cost a great deal."

"I was hoping you would say that," she said. "I have asked Mary Alice Jade to come over. She owns the lots on either side of ours. If we can persuade the investors to include her property in the deal, it should be a better deal for everyone. It would also ease my responsibilities. I am afraid that, with Earl the way he is I may not be able to handle it alone. Loretta is a wonder, but I need someone who understands real estate and can make decisions, someone I can trust. I think Mary Alice is right for that. What do you think, Lloyd?"

"I think I don't want to play poker with you. You're a lot more savvy than I have given you credit for. With or without Earl you are going to do just fine in the business world. Heh, heh," he chuckled. "Yessir. You're going to do just fine."

"Thank you, Lloyd. Coming from you that is quite a compliment." She stood up and smiled.

"Would you like some coffee or something, Lloyd?"

"No, thanks. I just finished lunch."

She turned to Loretta, who had been called to the office. "Mary Alice will be here shortly. Please show her in as soon as she arrives. And would you bring me a soda, please."

"Right away, Mrs. Campbell," she said, rushing from the office.

She turned back to Bemis. "If Mary Alice agrees to join in this venture, would you do the legal work for us? These contracts will have to be amended and the percentages changed. Once we talk with her, we can call John Aderle and set up a meeting to discuss the final numbers. I will need to know who his participants are. I don't want to be in business with someone with a shady background. I will have to leave it up to you to investigate that aspect of this agreement. Do you want to go ahead with this?"

"I'd be happy to do it."

The intercom buzzed. "Miss Jade is here."

"Ah, Mary Alice." Linda greeted the new arrival. "Would you like something to drink?"

"A Coke maybe." She dropped her purse on the small couch next to the entry.

"I believe you know Lloyd Bemis. He has been our lawyer and adviser for many years. If you have no objections I would like for him to handle this arrangement. Are you still interested?"

"Hello, Lloyd. Good to see you again." She turned back to Linda. "Yes, I'm still interested. In fact, I'm a little excited by the offer. How soon will I be able to hear the details?"

By the end of the afternoon, Bemis had filled an entire yellow legal pad with notes. Costs were estimated, percentages worked out and a hundred details were questioned. By 5 p.m. the lawyer had all he needed to get started. He agreed to contact Aderle to set up a meeting.

Linda stepped into the late afternoon air outside her office. She locked the door and was walking to her car when Eileen stopped her station wagon beside her.

"Jodi wanted me to ask if you and Earl would like to bring Matthew with our boys and have dinner somewhere this evening."

"Could we go to Bellevue? I don't want to have everyone looking at me. That terrible newspaper article ruined my day. I thought I had my emotions under control until I read it." Tears began to form in her eyes again. "Yes, I think it would be a good idea. Something to take my mind off what has happened. It would be good for Matthew too. I can only hope no one asks him about the article."

"We'll pick you up at seven."

Jodi had been busy all afternoon, and had scarcely noticed the time. He had talked with Brice, who said he would cover the night shift in place of the injured Gary Durbin. Larry Piedmont had spent the day at the hospital with his wife and Lois Durbin. They had spent the night in the waiting room at the hospital waiting for some word. It was after two in the afternoon when the doctor finally came out to tell the wife and friends that the injured deputy was regaining consciousness, and the prognosis had been upgraded to good. A full recovery was expected, although there would be a long period of rehabilitation. The pressure had been relieved within his head; however, further X-rays had shown a cracked pelvis. This would require he stay immobile for an extended period of time. He might have some loss of mobility in his legs after the injury and would have to undergo some intensive therapy.

The news was both a relief and a letdown. There was relief knowing that Gary would be all right, yet the adrenaline that had kept them awake all night was gone and fatigue was overtaking the group. Gary was asleep now, sedated. The doctor advised the four to go home now, get some rest. They could come back later and would be able to see Gary then.

After hearing the news, Larry found a telephone. He dialed the office to report the good news to Sergeant Eagle. It was the high point of Jodi's day.

"That's great news, Larry," Jodi said. "Have you had any sleep?"

"Not much. Just a catnap on the couch here at the hospital. I'm going home now to get some sleep. I'll be on duty tonight. Do you have someone to cover Gary's area?"

"Yes. Brice will be moving to nights with you. Are you sure you will be rested enough to come in tonight?"

"I'll be fine. Just knowing Gary will be okay is like getting a night's sleep."

"How is Lois?"

"I was worried about her last night, but when the doctor told us about Gary she seemed to light right up. She'll be okay. Nancy is staying with her today."

When Jodi came in with the good news Pete was busy cleaning out his desk.

He had been the sergeant here for a long time and this was a task fraught with nostalgia. Each little item taken from the desk drawer had some memory to be savored. The pictures, diplomas, certificates and awards were taken from the walls. The final job of cleaning out the desk he had saved for last.

"I just got a call from Larry at the hospital. Gary is going to be all right. The doctors said he regained consciousness. They have him sedated, but he is going to be okay. Isn't that great?"

"Oh, that's really good news. How is Lois doing?"

"Nancy Piedmont is with her. Larry says she's fine since she heard about Gary."

"Good, I'm glad. You know, this entire headache is going to be yours after tomorrow. We need to sit down tomorrow and discuss the transition. You're familiar with most of the goals I set for the detachment. Now you are going to have to set your own. Anyway, tomorrow afternoon this will be your office. Good luck with it."

Jodi stepped back out of the office to let Pete continue what he had started. He stopped at Emma's desk to ask her to post a notice that Gary was improving. All the duty officers would be interested in knowing his condition.

Eileen called at five-thirty. Jodi gave her a short report on Gary's condition.

"I told Linda we'd pick them up at seven. Are you going to be able to make it on time?"

"Yes, I'm almost finished here. Pete has gone home for the day and the new schedule is posted. I'll be leaving here as soon as I can lock up the files. Where are we going to eat?"

"Linda wanted to go to Bellevue to get away from people. She said if we ate here everyone would be staring at her."

"Good. We'll go to Bellevue then. I would like to stop by the hospital just to look in on Gary. It won't take long."

"I thought you might. See you soon. I love you."

Jodi finished reading the report on his desk before gathering the file, placing it on the top of the stack beside his desk, then carrying the whole pile to the file cabinet behind Emma Garson's desk. He meticulously filed each file in its proper place before closing and locking the cabinet. It had been a long day. He was glad to have a few minutes to drink a cup of Emma's fresh coffee and reflect on the day.

It was just ten o'clock when the family station wagon returned to North Bend. Jodi dropped the Campbell family at their home before swinging the car back toward town and the office. The mid shift was going off duty and the graveyard shift was checking in. The family waited in the car while the sergeant went inside to talk with his men before they went on duty. Ten minutes later he was back in the car driving toward home.

It was eleven twenty-five by the clock above the filing cabinet behind Miss Emma's desk. Brice Roman sorted through his keys to find the one that unlocked the files. He was the only officer in the building. The others had gone on the road as soon as possible after Jodi left the office. The thick envelope from Lewis Cornetti was filed in the center of the Carstairs file. He slipped the file from the drawer. It took a couple of minutes for the copy machine to warm up, which gave him time to sort out the pages he wished to copy. He also found several duplicate photographs in the fat envelope. He sorted through the stack of photos and selected five clear shots of the body lying on the sidewalk in front of the police station. The READY light on the copier turned green. Brice efficiently copied the sheets and returned the originals to the file. When he had finished he returned the file to the drawer and placed it in its original position. He was finished. He found a large manila envelope and placed the photos and the warm copies inside.

Lomax would be waiting for his call. He waited until midnight, then placed his call from a pay phone at the truck stop on Edgewick road.

"Meet me in an hour. I have the file. This one is going to cost you, Lomax. I want five grand for this one. No more bargains. If you want to do business with me, bring the cash. Five grand."

"I can't get my hands on that kind of money this time of night even if I was willing to pay your price." Lomax was trying to regain control of his stooge. "I told you that if the stuff was good I would get you a bonus. Don't get greedy on me, Deputy."

"I have a lot to lose in this deal. You're not getting off cheap any longer. I know you can get the money. Call your editor. If you want to stay on the front page, you'll pay. Snoqualmie Lodge, one hour."

Jerry Lomax knew Brice Roman was serious by the tone of his voice. He also knew he had bought the other files at a bargain price. He had the money and was authorized to pay the price because of the front page status of his story. By now he had captured the attention of the readers as well as that of his editors and publishers. No sense letting the story get away from him now. There wasn't much time to prepare or devise an alternate plan. He took the money from his dresser drawer, counted it and placed it in a white business-size envelope, sealing it with tape. It was going to take him almost an hour to drive to the rendezvous site in the oil-burning old car.

The white Chevrolet with the gold and blue stripes was parked at the far end of the parking lot. Several trucks with trailers were parked in the lot, the

Chapter 20

drivers inside drinking coffee and eating a late dinner. Lomax pulled up with his driver side window next to that of the patrol car. Brice had his window rolled down. The night was warm and the air felt good. He could smell the diesel from the trucks parked on the other end of the lot.

"Did you bring the cash?" Brice inquired.

"I have it, but I'm not paying until I see the file. This was a pretty slick move on your part. Don't try to raise the price again."

"If you get any more files the price will be five thousand, cash." His eyes narrowed. "And, if I do raise the price, what will you do about it? You'll pay if you want to stay on the front page. Now, give me the cash and shut up."

Lomax handed the fat white envelope through the window. "You seem to forget that I still have some leverage here. If you try to raise the price on me again, I'll have your picture on the front page of the next issue. This was supposed to be a cooperative venture with profit for everyone. If you think you are going to shake me down, then think again. It ain't going to happen, old buddy."

Brice tore the end from the white envelope and thumbed through the bills to make sure the pack was genuine. Once he was sure he handed the large manila envelope, which had been resting on the seat beside him, to the outstretched hand of the young tabloid reporter. He opened his envelope, thumbed through the contents, then said, "Be seeing you, Deputy." Blue smoke trailed from his old white car as he sped away.

On his way back into town, Brice stopped at his apartment, where he left the money. He didn't want to carry it around with him the rest of the shift. He did have to go to work. He had duties that needed tending. He began his patrol by checking the back door of Mary Alice Jade's real estate office.

CHAPTER 21

Jodi awakened to confusing sounds. The alarm clock was emitting its electronic birdcall, while at the same time the telephone was ringing. He rolled over to check the time and shut off the alarm. It was five-thirty in the morning, Wednesday. He forced a groggy body into action. Still half asleep he answered the ringing phone.

"Hello." He said in a raspy voice.

"Jodi, are you awake?" It was Pete Kaufman.

"Yeah, Pete. What's up?"

"Get down here, to the office, as soon as you can. I need you right away."

Jodi was instantly wide awake. "Be right there, Pete."

Eileen's sleepy voice came from under the covers. "What's wrong now?"

"I don't know. Pete just said he needs me at the office right away. Go back to sleep. I'll call you later."

Fifteen minutes later Jodi, in full uniform, walked into the office. Pete was waiting by the coffeepot. He handed a steaming cup to the new detachment commander. He was sipping his own cup as he walked back into his office. The tiny office seemed bare and lonely with all the personal items gone from the room.

"Sit down, Jodi. I have something to show you." He turned to the small, thirteen-inch television set on the credenza behind his desk. He flipped the *on* switch and immediately the screen turned bright.

"Do you remember last week when the Telephone Company had a man working here most of the day?" Pete asked.

"Yes, I saw him here." Jodi answered.

Chapter 21

"Well, he wasn't from the phone company. He was from the electronic surveillance unit at MCU. I asked them to install a video camera in the office to see if I could catch the person pilfering our locked files. They put in a split screen image recorder and two cameras; one covering the file cabinets and one covering the copy machine. You're not going to believe what I found on it this morning."

"So that's why you have been in here early every morning this past week. Did you find out who our man is?"

"Watch this." Pete said as he slipped a black video tape cartridge into the machine.

The built-in tape player swallowed the tape, whirred a moment, then the screen came to life. Motion detectors operated the cameras. The pictures were reminiscent of the ones taken by bank or supermarket surveillance cameras. The pictures were in black and white with good focus and good resolution. The first couple of minutes were pictures of the shift change of the night before. Jerky pictures of officers walking through the office, each one clearly in focus and identifiable. The two men sat in the office watching the little set, sipping coffee. Pete sat up straight in his chair, and Jodi knew something was coming.

The scene was that of an all too familiar deputy in front of the filing cabinets, sorting through his keys for the one he would use to unlock the drawers. The officer was Brice Roman.

Jodi could hardly believe his eyes. He watched more intently as the image on the screen walked out of view with a file from the drawer in his hand. Almost immediately he appeared on the other side of the screen. He laid the file on top of the copier, then punched the buttons, which caused the machine to light up and begin the process of warming up the electronics inside. While the machine was warming, the officer sorted out the papers he would copy. He also took several photographs from an envelope, which had been stored inside the file. He made his copies, then disappeared from the right side of the screen again, only to appear on the left side of the screen. He placed the file back in the drawer as he had found it and locked the drawer. He looked around, apparently to see if he had forgotten anything, then walked to the door, stuffing papers in a manila envelope as he went.

Pete turned off the machine. "Do you believe that?"

"No, I can't believe it. Brice?" Jodi was stunned. "Brice is the guy stealing from the files?"

"Its sure looks like it." He reached up to rewind the tape. "Do you want me to play it again?"

"No, not now. I just can't believe it.".

"I called you down here to discuss this with you before Brice comes in to finish out his shift." He checked the clock. "He'll be in here shortly. This is my last day in the detachment, but I would like for you to leave this to me if you have no objection. I want the satisfaction of firing the weasel. I haven't decided whether to prosecute him or not."

"I would like to be here when you interview him. As a witness, if for no other reason. I sure would like to get enough on Lomax to file charges on him."

"I think that's the tack I'll use on him. Perhaps I can threaten him with prosecution if he doesn't roll over on Lomax. It will be interesting to find out why he suddenly decided to pass information. I wonder if Lomax has something on him and is blackmailing him." He thought for a moment, picked up a pencil and wrote some notes on the yellow legal pad on his desk. "I also wonder if he still has the file. Do you suppose he has already passed it to Lomax?"

"It's hard to say without talking to him. Do you want me to have dispatch call him to the office?"

"Yeah, let's do that."

Jodi stepped out of the little office to use the telephone on Emma Garson's desk. Pete Kaufman walked around his desk to move the coat tree from in front of the door so as to be able to close it when the offending officer arrived. It would soon be shift change and the day shift would be in the office. Miss Emma would be sitting outside the door where she could hear everything. He wanted to keep this as private as possible, at least for now. It had been a long time since the door to his office had been closed.

Jodi returned. "He's on his way in now. Is there anything special you want me to do?"

"No, thanks Jodi. This is going to be tough. We have both known Brice a long time. Just have a seat there, as a witness. I don't expect trouble from him, but if we have to arrest him we should get him cuffed up quickly. I don't want him to have too much time to think about it."

The radio speaker crackled as Brice reported to dispatch. "Dispatch. C-11 is 10-7 station."

"C-11 is 10-7 station," Dispatch acknowledged.

"He's here." Jodi relayed.

A short moment later they heard the front door open and someone enter. Brice draped his jacket over the railing by Emma's desk, then walked to the coffeepot.

"Brice, could you come in here a minute?" Lieutenant Kaufman asked.

"Be right there, Pete."

Brice appeared in the open doorway with a cup of coffee in his hand. When he saw the two men he raised his cup in a salute of greeting. "What are you two doing here so early in the morning? You administrative types aren't supposed to be in before eight."

"Come in Brice. Have a seat." He motioned for Brice to sit in one of the chairs in front of his desk. He also motioned for Jodi to close the door of the office.

The smile left Brice's face as he looked at both men. "What's going on?"

"Before we go any further, I want to ask you to place your gun and badge on the desk." Pete spoke with ice in his voice. Jodi was standing slightly behind Brice, watching his movements.

Brice complied with the order without question. Jodi sat in the chair beside him.

"As you know, we are in the midst of an investigation involving a serial killer. The information we generate relates directly to the legal status of the case. Someone in this office has been making copies of those files and passing them to a reporter from the *World Inquirer*. That reporter's name is Jerry Lomax. I have information that you may be the person responsible for passing that information. Do you have anything to say about these allegations?"

Brice's cup stopped halfway to his lips. He looked as though someone had hit him with a baseball bat.

"That's crazy." Brice protested. "Why would anyone say something like that. You've known me a long time, Pete. Have you ever known me to do something like that?"

"That's why you're in here, Brice. I thought it was impossible too." He continued to stare Brice directly in the eyes, doing his best to control his anger and his disappointment. "You're saying that the allegations are not true. Is that correct?"

"Yes, that is correct." Anger sounded in his voice. "Who accused me of this? Was it another officer? I want to face them, right now."

"I think that's fair." The lieutenant offered. He turned around a quarter turn in his chair to reach the VCR/television on the credenza behind his desk. "I have your accuser right here." He had already queued the videotape to start where Brice entered the office.

The television set lit up; there was no sound. Since there were no words spoken Pete had tuned out the background noise. Brice sat, his eyes riveted to the small screen behind the desk. The scenario played before his eyes. The pictures were good. The date and time were displayed at the top right of the screen. No denial was possible. He was his own accuser.

Brice had not spoken from the time the pictures appeared on the screen. Pete turned to stop the machine when the scenes with Brice were finished.

He had given the deputy some time to compose himself before saying a word. Brice set his coffee cup on the edge of his boss's desk.

"Do you still want to confront your accuser?" Pete asked.

"How did you … When was … I didn't know … I … " His mind was racing faster than he could form the words. He wanted to deny his guilt, but was having difficulty forming a defense in view of the evidence he had just witnessed. He fell silent. His eyes, his body language, everything about him reeked of guilt. "I … I don't know what to say."

"Before you decide to say anything I am going to read you your rights. I want this to be done by the book." He took a card from his desk and began to read. "Though you are not yet under arrest, I wish to inform you that anything you say can and will be used against you in a court of law." He read on, completing the information on the Miranda card. Pete looked up from the card and into Brice's eyes. "Do you understand these rights as I have read them to you?"

"Yes, I understand my rights. I don't need an attorney right now."

"Do you want to make a statement?" Pete asked.

Brice was thinking. After a moment his demeanor seemed to change. He looked Pete squarely in the eyes.

"I think you want something from me. I think if you were going to arrest me you would have done that already. What is it? What do you want?"

"All I want is for you to cooperate." Pete said. "Do you still have the copies you made?"

"I'm not saying a thing until I know where this is going. What's in it for me if I cooperate and give you what you want?" Brice had been a cop for a long time and knew a leverage ploy when he heard one. All he wanted was his best deal.

"I am not going to promise you anything. I will say, though, that I will go as easy as I can if you cooperate."

"Without some kind of guarantee, I'm not saying anything." Brice's face was becoming red with fear and anger.

"In that case, Jodi, would you please place Mr. Roman under arrest?" Pete stood.

Jodi was standing again behind Brice. "Put your hands behind your back, please."

Brice complied, but was shocked to be in this position.

Pete spoke again. "As of now, we'll call it the end of your regular shift, you are suspended from duty pending official dismissal from the department by the sheriff."

The handcuffs were in place and locked.

"Take him to Issaquah and book him, Jodi."

Brice was frantic now.

"Okay, okay. What do you want? I can't go to jail, Pete. I'll cooperate, but I can't go to jail. Will you promise me that much?"

"I'll do what I can. I'll talk with the assistant DA. It's up to her now." Pete seemed disinterested.

"Come on Pete," Brice pleaded. "I'll give you a statement. I'll give you Lomax. I hate the guy anyway. I have the money from the papers I sold last night. Come on Pete, help me out. Don't send me to jail."

"Where is the money?" Pete asked.

"At my apartment."

"How much did you get for tonight's work?"

"Five thousand. I only got a thousand for each of the others. Come on Pete. Help me out here."

"Take the cuffs off him, Jodi. But be ready to put them back on if he decides to get uncooperative again."

Jodi removed the handcuffs and motioned for Brice to sit in the chair next to the wall. Jodi positioned himself in the other chair next to the door. The body heat from the three men in the cramped office had raised the temperature in the room several degrees from uncomfortable to almost unbearable. Pete stood to open the high window above the credenza. The sudden wisp of fresh air felt good.

Lieutenant Kaufman pulled a statement form from his desk drawer. He handed the sheet to his ex-deputy. "There's a pen." He pointed to the cup on his desk. "I want a statement from you. I want to know how you and Lomax met in the first place. Why did you decide to betray your oath? I want to know what information you passed to the reporter. I want every detail. I want to know what he said and when he said it. I want to use this statement to arrest him and to convict him." Pete's personal involvement and his anger were apparent in his voice.

"Will you keep me out of jail?" Brice wanted firm assurances.

"I'll do what I can. I have already fired you from the best job you have ever had and cost you your career in law enforcement. I'm not interested in sending you to jail on top of that. I'll call the D.A. and tell her that. I can't do any more than that."

Brice picked a pen from the cup, slid his chair closer to the desk and began to write. Pete motioned for Jodi to step out of the office with him, leaving Brice alone with his writing and his thoughts.

Emma Garson was in the outer office when the two stepped from the room. She had made fresh coffee and was busy with a stack of papers on her desk.

"Good morning lieutenant. Good morning sergeant."

"Good morning Emma." Pete answered.

The two men poured fresh coffee and entered Jodi's office. Jodi sat behind the desk this time.

"I'll take a look at the statement, and if it looks good, I'll take it to the D.A.. You take Brice home and get the money," said Pete. "You will have to stay until he changes his uniform. I want all his gear in the office as soon as possible. I don't want him to have anything that belongs to the department." Frustration was again creeping into his voice. "I feel responsible for this situation. I should have been on top of this before it got this far."

"Don't blame yourself, Pete." Jodi consoled him. "Nobody could have seen this one coming."

They both sat quietly waiting for Brice to finish writing. They sipped their coffee; both relieved that the leak had been stopped.

CHAPTER 22

Pete reviewed the statement given by Brice Roman, and read it through twice. Brice knew what questions would be asked and had attempted to answer them all in his statement. He had been honest about needing the money and about how Lomax had approached him, and didn't try to make excuses for any of his actions. the statement was straightforward, the wording in the suggesting that he didn't care much for the reporter or his newspaper.

Pete finished the second reading, then handed the sheaf of papers back to Roman for signing.

"If you think of anything else I want you to contact me so I can include it in this official statement. You know, of course, this is going to require you to appear in court to testify against the reporter and his newspaper?"

"Yes, I know. I'll testify. I'm not proud of what I've done. I knew the risks when I agreed to participate. It's my own fault." He was slumped in the chair. "For what it's worth, I'm sorry, Pete. I let everyone down and I'm sorry."

"It's a little late for that now, Brice." Pete chided. "We have a job of repairing fences now. You damaged the reputation of this detachment and the entire department with this. That rag of a newspaper painted us as a bunch of country bumpkin, Keystone Cops. It's going to take a long time to rebuild our image with the public after this. You hurt a lot of hard-working officers who trusted you. One of them is now lying in the hospital. This department didn't deserve what you have done to it. And I wish you'd been there to see Linda Campbell and her son's face when they opened that paper."

Jodi was at the office door. "If you're done here, I'll take you home, Brice."

"Don't forget to pick up his property and the money." Pete said.

Jodi and Brice left the office together. Brice left his jacket lying over the railing in front of Miss Emma's desk. They climbed into Jodi's car to slowly make the drive across town. It was a silent trip. Jodi parked in front of the townhouse and the two men went inside. It took only a few minutes for the two to gather the property owned by the department. Brice reached into a dresser drawer and retrieved the envelope containing five thousand dollars; the payment for his last delivery. Jodi left the apartment without saying anything to his ex-colleague.

"Get the Assistant District Attorney on the phone for me." Pete commanded Miss Emma, then returned to his office.

Connie Lupine came to the front office with several file folders in her hands. She filed part of the stack, put part of it in Miss Emma's IN basket. The remainder would be placed on Jodi Eagle's desk for review.

"What is all the fuss out here this morning, Emma?" Connie inquired

"I'm afraid you'll have to ask the lieutenant that question," Emma replied.

Connie knew better than to press Miss Emma any further. Instead she carried the files remaining in her hands to Jodi's office, put them on his desk, and returned to her own desk to continue her report writing. She checked her watch; it was about time to patrol her area.

Emma buzzed Pete on the intercom. "I have Barbara Canter on line one."

"Thanks Emma." Pete said before punching the flashing button on line one.

"Good morning Barb. You're in the office early. I thought lawyers all slept until noon."

"Only the ones with large retainers, Pete. I have court this morning. What can I do for you?"

"I need an arrest warrant for a reporter named Jerry Lomax. That's Jerry with a J, L-o-m-a-x. He's a reporter for the *World Inquirer*. I'm working on the complaint now. We can amend the charges when we book him, but for now I need him charged with Conspiracy to Felony Theft, three counts; Obstruction of Justice, three counts; and Bribery, three counts. I have all the particulars and the corroborating statements here on my desk. If you can start the paperwork down at the courthouse I'll bring everything to you right away. What time is your court this morning?"

"Holy Smokes, Pete!" the surprised D.A. exclaimed. "What have you been doing there?"

"We caught up with the officer passing information to this reporter. I'll talk with you about it when I get there, but for now I want to start the ball rolling on that warrant. I want this guy in jail. I want him in jail today." He felt the anger welling up inside him.

Barb Canter recognized the anxiety in his voice, even on the telephone. "I'll get it started, Pete. What time are you coming to Issaquah?"

Chapter 22

"What time is your court?" Pete asked again. "I can meet you at the courthouse if you want."

"Let's see. It's almost nine-thirty. I have court at ten-fifteen. Meet me at Judge Mortimer's office at eleven."

"I'll be there."

"Who was the leak? Can you tell me?" Her curiosity had gotten the best of her.

"Brice."

"Brice! I can't believe it. Brice?"

"I know. I could hardly believe it myself. But I have his statement and video of him taking the files. We have him cold. He gave us a full statement about his involvement and how Lomax paid him. By the way, if you can get an injunction to stop the *World Inquirer* from publishing what they have, and to return the files and pictures, it would sure make me happy. Do you think you can get the judge to go for that one too?"

"I might. I'll give it a try. I'll see you at the courthouse at eleven."

"Thanks Barb. See you at eleven."

Jodi walked through the front door from the street carrying a box and a large paper sack. He dropped his bundle next to the rail by Emma's desk and picked up the jacket draped over it. He tossed the jacket on top of the uniforms and effects he had brought from Brice's home, he poured a cup of coffee and walked into Pete's office where he dropped into the chair with a thump.

"If being sergeant means I'm going to have days like this on a regular basis, I don't think I want the job." He tossed the fat envelope full of money onto Pete's desk.

"I hope you never have another day like this one. How did it go at Brice's place?"

"He never said a word. I think the shame is catching up with him. The rooster can pretend to be a weasel, but the hawk knows the difference. When the hawk strikes the rooster, it is not the weasel who is hurt."

"Sometimes your thinking scares me, Jodi."

"What's the word on the warrant?"

Barb is meeting me in the Judge's office at eleven. It looks like we have it."

"Pete, I want a favor. I owe one of the reporters some information. I'd like to give him first shot at the Lomax arrest and the information about Brice. Do you have any problem with that?"

Pete thought a moment. "I guess not. We'll pick up Lomax today and, I hope serve an injunction on that scandal sheet he works for. Your guy can't put this out to the public before six. That will give us time to serve Lomax and his paper."

"No problem. He'll agree to that. Thanks, Pete. I just want to keep the score sheet clean."

Brice Roman was sitting on his couch, drinking a Coke. He was trying to weigh his options, which seemed limited at this point. He was through in the field of law enforcement. No department in the country would hire him now. His credibility was gone. He wouldn't be prosecuted for his part in the theft of the files, but it had cost him dearly. He didn't know how he was going to make his payments on the townhouse and on the Buick. He would still have to eat and pay for lights, heat, water and the other necessities of life. He could sell some of his personal things to help cover him for a little while but the long term was hopeless. Brice thought about how nice it would be to be able to go to his lover and discuss his problems. That, too, was out of the question now. He was alone. He picked up the stainless steel 9MM Smith and Wesson he had brought from the nightstand by the bed. He had always kept it hidden there for protection. It was fully loaded, with one in the chamber, ready for action on a moment's notice. He thumbed the safety off, pointed it at a picture on the wall and aligned the sights. He lowered the gun, laying it in his lap while he thought. He picked it up again, pointing the barrel toward his face. He hooked his thumb inside the trigger guard and stared down the black hole of the barrel. It seemed to represent his life at this particular moment in time. He tried to pull the trigger, but could not force himself to press the trigger with the necessary two pounds of pull. He began to shake. He began to cry. He began to scream. He couldn't even do this properly.

Jodi's next call was to Torval Laxo. This day would need a sweat at its end. After his call to Torval he contacted Miss Emma on the intercom.

"Emma, do you have the number for the hospital in Bellevue?"

"Yes, I'll dial it for you."

"No, wait. On second thought, I think I'll go there. If Gary is awake I want him to know we are thinking about him. If he isn't I need to give my regards to Lois. Thanks anyway, Emma."

He came out of his office and went into that of the lieutenant. Pete was just getting ready to leave for the courthouse to meet with the D.A. and Judge.

"I think I am going to drive to Bellevue to visit with Gary. Is there anything on our agenda before noon?" Jodi asked.

"Nothing I know of. I should have the warrants in hand by then. Who do you want to send to serve them?"

"Connie," Jodi said without hesitation.

"You can have this office this afternoon. I'll be gone from here as soon as I get back from court. If I don't see you before I leave, I want you to know that I am sure you are the right man for the job. I have enjoyed working with you for all these years, Jodi. Thanks for everything."

Chapter 22

"I'm the one who should be thanking you. Good luck in your new job. We're going to miss you around here." Jodi turned to leave the office, then turned back again. "I have written a memo to be posted on the bulletin board concerning Brice. I thought an official statement would stop the rumors that are bound to start."

"Good thinking. I have been so busy with this end of it I almost forgot the rest of my job. It must be time for me to move on. Thanks again, Jodi."

Jodi took his time driving to Bellevue. He needed time alone to settle his thoughts. Things had moved so rapidly this morning that it would be easy to make mistakes. A review of the morning's activities seemed to be in correct order. He went over them again.

In the hospital parking lot he found a space close to the front entrance. He backed his car into the space in case he had to leave in a hurry. The sun was warm as he walked to the front door. Inside he checked with the desk to make sure Gary was in the same room. He had been moved. He was no longer in the Intensive Care Unit, but in a single bed room on the fourth floor, the Orthopedics ward.

Lois sat in a chair by the bed, reading. She looked up as the sergeant quietly slipped into the room.

"Hi, Jodi," she whispered.

"Hi, Lois. How is he this morning?"

"Much better. He is still in a lot of pain, but he is much better."

"Has he been awake?"

"Oh, yes. And really grumpy. He gave the nurses all kinds of trouble when they came in to change his bed and bathe him this morning."

"What are the doctors saying? Is Gary going to have a full recovery?"

"They seem to be confident about that. They say he will have to have a lot of therapy for his broken hip. But his head injury won't leave any scars or permanent damage. He was really lucky there. The doctors say his airbag saved him. It kept the force from driving him into the steering wheel and dashboard. They say the seatbelt would have slowed him down, but he would likely have come out of it because of the violence of the crash. They say that he hit his head on the top of the door when it caved in as the car rolled over. He was very, very lucky."

"It really says something about our job when you consider a fractured skull, a broken pelvis, broken ribs and cuts and bruises, lucky."

"Gary knows the risks. He wouldn't do anything else. I worry all the time, but he tells me not to. It's in his blood. He loves his job."

"We'll get him back on the job as soon as we can. Until he can go back full time or to regular duty we'll find something for him. You let me know if there is anything I can do to help you."

"Thank you, Jodi. I know Gary will appreciate that."

The patient in the bed began to stir. He was in a body cast from the waist to his knees. His chest area was wrapped with an elastic bandage to prevent any movement of his broken ribs. His head was bandaged where the surgeons had operated on his broken skull. Gary Durbin was a broken mess.

"That you Sarge?" It came from the bandages in the bed.

"Yes, it's me, Gary. Sorry, I didn't mean to wake you."

"I'm glad you're here. They keep me doped up for the pain. I don't visit much."

"I know this is a dumb question, but how are you feeling?" Jodi asked, embarrassed.

"I feel pretty good, actually. My ribs hurt the worst."

"Everyone at the office wants to know how you are doing. I thought I should come down here and get a first-hand report."

"The doctors have talked to Lois more than to me. I have been out of it most of the time. She tells me I will be off work for quite a while. The doctor said this morning that I might go home in a week. They want my ribs and my pelvis to mend a little before they move me out of here. The head is okay. They say the worst thing about my head now is infection. I guess all in all I'm doing pretty good."

"Those black eyes aren't too becoming." Gary tried to grin at his sergeant, but couldn't manage it.

"Is there anything you want or need? Can we bring you anything?"

"No. I have everything here. Lois takes good care of me. Thanks for the offer though."

"I won't tire you any more. I just wanted to see you for myself. Let me know if we can do anything. Lois, if you need a break, just call Eileen. I know Nancy has been good about helping, but if there is anything you need, just ask."

"Thank you, Jodi. We appreciate that."

Jodi found his way back to the parking lot and his patrol car. As he pulled out of the hospital parking lot he thought that this had turned out to be a good day after all. The leak was plugged at the office and his injured officer was on the mend, though he was still in a great deal of pain.

The sweat lodge would feel good tonight.

CHAPTER 23

By one o'clock Jodi was back in the office. Pete came back from the court in Issaquah at ten minutes after the hour, Jodi followed him into his office. Pete was standing behind his desk, surveying the room that had been his office for so many years.

"Did you get the warrants?" Jodi inquired.

"Right here." The lieutenant said, pointing to the desktop. He continued to look around the office, attempting to remember how it used to be in here. He wanted to be sure he had taken everything belonging to him.

"It's going to be strange without you here," Jodi commented.

"I am sure going to miss this place and all the people here. We have had some good times, haven't we Jodi?"

"We sure have." Jodi thought for a moment, then offered, "I know people always say they will stay in touch, but they never do. I don't want that to happen to our friendship, Pete. I want you to come to dinner from time to time and to drop by when you are on this side of the county. My whole family is going to miss you."

"Thanks, Jodi. I'm going to miss them too. I have coached Little league and been a part of the town for a long time. I really will miss it. And I'll make it a point to come visit you and your family." He reached across the desk to shake hands.

"Are these warrants ready to serve?" Jodi asked.

"Yes. I got them issued for three felony counts. If we add anything to that, then we will amend the charges at grand jury. Right now I just want to get this guy behind bars." Pete thumbed through the stack papers on his desk, picking out the injunction orders. "I'm going into town right now. As soon as I check in with the sheriff, I'll personally serve this at the office of the *World Inquirer*." He bent to pick up the box resting on the floor behind his desk. "Good luck, Jodi. I'll be in touch, and you know how to get hold of me."

Pete carried the box from the office. He made a quick stop at the desk of his old friend Miss Emma Garson.

"Good-bye, Emma. I am going to miss you."

"I'll miss you too, lieutenant." She had a little tear in her eyes as he left the office for the last time as its commander.

"Connie, can you come up here?" Jodi called from beside Emma's desk.

She appeared from the back room. "Yes. What do you need?"

"Help me move my stuff into the front office, then you can move into my old office. You are now the chief investigator here."

"Really?" she asked with a huge grin.

"Yes, really. Don't look so happy about it. It will mean twice the work and the same pay. The good news is that you will have to work more hours to get the job done. Congratulations on your promotion, it's almost as good as a raise."

The two began to move files and pictures to the new office. Miss Emma made fresh coffee. When it was brewed she brought three cups to the sergeant's office, gave each of the occupants a cup and proposed a toast. "Here's to happier days ahead."

The move took only about ten minutes. When it was complete the two officers sat in the new front office. "I want you to call dispatch and have them put out a *wants* on Lomax. As soon as he is stopped I want you to serve them personally. I think he will be in town today. If you patrol close in, you may see him during your patrol. Let's bust him today."

"It will be my pleasure." She grinned as she stood with the warrants in her hand. Just for this she'd spend extra time on patrol today.

Jodi was alone in his new office for the first time. He flipped the Rolodex, picked out a number, dialed Channel 5, and asked for Tom Logan. The Muzak playing in his ear was somehow soothing.

"Hello, Tom Logan here. Who am I talking to?"

"Hi, Tom. Jodi Eagle."

"Oh, Jodi. Good to hear from you. What can I do for you?"

"It's the other way around this time, Tom. I have some information for you, but you can't use it before the six o'clock news. And you can't use my name."

"I can live with that. What do you have?"

"Several things, all of them related. First, I saw Gary Durbin this morning.

Chapter 23

He is going to be okay. He will be off work for a long time and have to undergo a lot of therapy, but he will have a full recovery."

"That's good news."

"Second, we found our information leak. It was Brice Roman. He has given us a full statement. He has been suspended pending termination action by the sheriff."

"More good news." Logan was writing while he listened.

"Third, a warrant has been issued for the arrest of Jerry Lomax, the reporter for the *World Inquirer*. The warrant is for three felony counts. I expect him to be in town this afternoon, at which time we will arrest him. That is the reason for delaying the release of any of this information before six o'clock this evening."

"All right!"

"One final thing, there has been an injunction issued to bar the *World Inquirer* from using any of the information or pictures acquired through Brice or Lomax. Pete Kaufman is serving that paperwork this afternoon."

"Wow! You folks have been really busy up there in the valley."

"We're trying. I'm sorry I can't give you any specifics, but the warrants and injunction haven't been served yet. I told you I owed you one. I haven't given this to anyone else. It's all yours. That's why I don't want you to use my name."

"I really appreciate the information. This is big, Jodi. Thanks. If there is ever anything I can do for you, just let me know."

"I will. I'll be talking with you later. Thanks again, Tom."

Jodi hung up the phone and checked the time. He picked his jacket from the coat tree and told Miss Emma he was going to the North Bend Real Estate office.

Loretta Moser greeted him when he entered. "Hello, Sergeant Eagle. You became the boss today, I understand."

"Today's the day. Is Linda in?"

"Yes, just a moment and I'll announce you." She picked up the phone, stabbed one of the buttons, then said, "Mrs. Campbell, Deputy Eagle to see you."

"You can go right in," she said, returning her gaze to Jodi.

Jodi tapped lightly on the heavy oak door before opening it. He could see she was busy with papers scattered over the entire top of her desk. She looked tired.

She looked up as he entered. "Hi, Jodi."

"Hello, Linda. How are you?"

"Busy. Earl isn't able to come to the office and there is so much going on I don't know if I can keep up."

"You'll do just fine." He smiled. "How would you like to hear some good news?"

"I would love it."

"We found out who was giving information to that reporter. It was Brice. He's been fired. We have issued a warrant for the reporter's arrest and have an injunction against his paper barring them from publishing any more pictures or stories they got from Brice. We hope to arrest Lomax this afternoon."

"That is good news."

"I wanted you to know. I know how hard those articles are for you to face. Just keep this information to yourself until we arrest Lomax."

"I will, Jodi. Thank you for telling me."

"What is making you so busy these days?"

"I'll give you some confidential information. Just keep it under your hat." she requested. "I am in a big merger deal with some people from Bellevue and with Mary Alice Jade. We have some property they want to develop. We're forming a corporation called Emerald Empire Investments. We plan to develop that property on the south side of the highway. If everything goes as planned, we should make quite a lot of money off this venture, and the town will see a lot of new citizens."

"Well, I'll get out of here and let you get back to work."

Jodi was driving back to his office when a call came for him on the radio. It was dispatch. "C-1, C-4 requests backup at exit 31. Felony stop. Warrant arrest."

"Ten-four, ETA two minutes."

Jodi hit the switches for siren and lights as he made a U-turn in the middle of North Bend Way. He accelerated toward the exit on the west end of town. He was still two blocks away when he saw the flashing lights of the patrol car behind the old white station wagon. Connie Lupine had things well in hand by the time he arrived. The reporter was bent over the hood of his own car. Connie was locking the handcuffs on his wrists as Jodi pulled to a stop in front of the reporter's car.

"Is everything all right?"

"Yes, fine." Connie answered. "He didn't give me any trouble. I am about to read him his rights and serve the warrants."

"Go ahead. I'll stay here until we impound his car, then follow you to Issaquah and help with the booking." He helped his deputy search the prisoner and load him into the back seat of her patrol car. He couldn't help smiling as he called on the radio for a wrecker to come take the old Chevy away.

By the time he returned from the jail, it was almost five. Miss Emma was closing the files, preparing to go home for the day.

"Pete called to say he'd served the injunction," she told him.

"Thanks, Emma. Is there anything else I need to know today?"

"I think you have taken care of everything," she said, picking up her sweater and lunch bag. "I'm going home now. You've had a successful first day." She smiled and left the office.

Jodi's tenure as commander of the North Bend Detachment began with a bang, but things soon became routine. The month of August was hot but uneventful. There had been no new abductions or murders. He was grateful for that.

Toward the end of the month, the new school year was about to begin. The chamber of commerce members came to talk with Jodi about ending their daily patrols. He hated to see them stop, but could not give a good reason for them to continue. He knew that the killings could start again without notice, but he also knew that these men had lives and businesses of their own that required their attention. He agreed to stop the patrols as soon as school opened on the third day of September.

Eileen was still apprehensive about letting the boys out of her sight. She had spent the summer at the school helping to monitor the kids. Tensions in the small town were generally lower since it had been a month since the last killing. When school started she would have more time to herself. She could relax and be responsible for only her own children.

Gary Durbin was out of the hospital. He would have to go to therapy every other day for the next two months. Lois was good at taking care of her injured husband. The Piedmonts helped her as much as their time would allow.

By the end of August, Gary was walking with crutches. The swelling in his face and his blackened eyes had healed. His ribs were still hurting which made it difficult to walk any great distance on his crutches. His pelvis was mending and the therapist said he should be able to walk without crutches in about a month. The body cast would come off in two weeks. It was going to be some time before he could return to full duty, but he was promised he could return to the office and light duty before Thanksgiving.

There were no new clues to the killer. The FBI was slow to send anything back from Washington. Cornetti kept prodding them, but it didn't help.

Jodi found it more and more difficult to talk with Earl, to answer his questions. Earl was losing weight and becoming less sociable. The more frail he became the more obsessive his behavior. He was consumed with hate for the person who had murdered his son.

CHAPTER 24

Captain Jodi Eagle looked into the rear-view mirror at the image of his own aging face. Had it really been eight years since the last young boy was killed? July twenty-seventh. He had been busy with present-day problems when Tom Logan called this afternoon to remind him of the anniversary. Tom had made it a custom to do an editorial, on the Channel 5 six o'clock news, each year on this date. The reminder wasn't necessary. There hadn't been a day since the first killing that Jodi hadn't thought about it. Over the years, Tom had become a good friend. It was painful to read the editorial each year. Tom had hoped that one of these programs would spark some memory in a witness and bring him forward to solve the case. So far it had only served to remind those who had been involved just how long the pain and suffering would last or how strong the hurt would be after all these years.

His home was still in North Bend, but his office was now in Issaquah. Since his promotion to captain, two years ago, he had commuted to and from work daily. It was a short drive that took only about ten minutes if traffic wasn't bad. Today white fluffy clouds were visible above the mountains ahead of him. The warm, moist coastal air was condensing in the cool dry air above the Cascade mountain peaks. Jodi enjoyed the drive home after work each day. It gave him time to relax and to set his mind in order, to lose the tenseness and stress of his job.

His promotion from sergeant to captain meant that he was now in charge of the entire King County Police Department on the east side of King County. It was a giant step in his career. It had taken him further from real police work and deeper into the realm of administration. He spent less time reviewing criminal files and more time checking statistical data, which affected his budget. He had a lieutenant, Steve Burnside, who was in charge of the daily operation and personnel assigned through the Issaquah office.

It was five forty-five when Jodi parked his unmarked brown Chevrolet in the driveway. Eileen met him at the open door with a hug and a kiss. Jodi looked at her and wondered why she had not aged as much as he had. He slapped her gently on the rear as they went into the house, he dropped his duty belt on the coffee table and turned on the television.

"How about some iced tea?" Eileen called from the kitchen.

"That would be great," he called back as he changed to channel 5.

"Are you going to watch the news before dinner?"

"Yes. Tom Logan is doing his annual editorial on the Mount Si Killer tonight. He called me to be sure I watched."

"Oh, I'm sorry, Jodi. I had forgotten that today was the twenty-seventh."

Jodi tried not to think about it. "Well, what did you do today?"

"I spent the day here, working in the yard. The flowerbeds are in terrible shape. I got them weeded, but we are going to have to do something about the slugs in the lawn."

"Come here and sit with me."

Eileen sat on the couch beside her husband. She cuddled up under his arm. Jodi turned the sound low while the two enjoyed just sitting, being close. They sipped iced tea and relaxed until the screen lit up with huge letters. "Editorial by Tom Logan." Jodi picked up the remote and turned up the sound.

"Good evening." Tom began, "especially to those fine people who live in North Bend. Tonight's editorial is done with you in mind. We're hoping that it will spark some memory that would help bring a closure to the terrible events of the summer of 1991.

"For those of our audience, who are new to the Emerald Empire, that was a summer filled with sorrow, tragedy and despair for five families of that small town. That summer, in a period of less than two and a half months, five young children were abducted and murdered. The killer has never been apprehended.

"The first victim was Toby Stevens, 10 years old. His father has since moved the family to Oregon where he works as a logger. The second victim was little Aaron Wilson. His father is the manager of a local grocery store. His mother is suffering from cancer and spends much of her time in the hospital taking treatment for her disease. The third victim was the only female victim of the group. She was Shirley Ng, a bright young freshman in high school. Her father quit his job with Boeing to take his ailing wife back to California where she could be near her family. Victim number four was the son of a prominent businessman in North Bend. Darren Campbell played Little league ball and had hit his first home run the day before he was brutally murdered. His parents, too, have suffered great pain since their son's death, and his father has not worked at his business since that day in 1991. Number five, and the last victim, was Bobby Carstairs. His mother was a single parent who could not live with the pain and died of an overdose of sleeping pills just one year after her son was killed.

"That summer, in 1991, saw a town band together to protect itself from an unknown assailant. It started a neighborhood watch program. Citizens patrolled the streets every day, all day and all night. The school board opened a summer program for the city's children to give them supervised activities. It was a united community.

"A King County police officer, Gary Durbin, was seriously injured and an elderly local couple, Nels and Hilma Bjustrom, were killed in a collision while the deputy was chasing the killer on Highway 202, the Fall City/Redmond road. Gary Durbin is back on duty with the Department and has recovered from his injuries.

"This case has been the one black spot on the record of the King County Sheriff's Department. It has been seven long years since the last crime was committed. This case is not closed. There are officers who want nothing more in their career than to close this case; to bring this killer to justice. These officers want closure, not for themselves, but for the families who have waited for so long to know that, the killer of their children is finally brought to justice.

"If you have any information that would lead to the capture of this killer, please, call Channel 5 or the North Bend office of the King County Police, 555-1234.

"Thank you and good night."

Eileen was wiping a tear from her cheek and spoke with a slight crackle in her voice. "That was a nice editorial. It was kind of a memorial to the children."

"Yes, he did a fine job." He didn't want to think about it any more right now. "How about some dinner?"

Jodi was about to put his fork into his salad when the phone rang.

"Hi, Jodi. It's Linda." The sweet voice said on the other end. "Did you see the editorial on Channel 5 tonight?"

"Yes, we saw it. I thought Tom did a good job of bringing out the details without adding to the trauma everyone here has suffered. Are you okay?"

"Yes, I'm fine. I wish Earl were home. It's been a week now and I haven't heard from him."

"You know how he is. He does this periodically. He just disappears for a week and then one day comes he home like he was never gone. He won't say

Chapter 24

where he has been or what he was doing. My guess is that he'll be home in the next day or two. Would you like to come and have dinner with us?"

"Thanks Jodi. I'm just sitting down to some hot soup. I just wanted to call and see if you had seen Tom Logan's program. I won't bother you any more."

"You're never a bother, Linda. You're a part of our family."

"Thanks, Jodi. Good night."

"She saw the program?" Eileen asked, after Jodi hung up the telephone.

"Yes. She seems to be all right with it, though. Earl is gone and she doesn't know where he is … again. I wish all this would end, somehow."

"It will, Honey. It will."

They ate dinner in silence.

Jodi read the paper while Eileen did the dishes. When they were done the couple went into the backyard to look at slugs. Slimy little creatures, they had infested the yard and flower beds and seemed to be everywhere. They walked around the yard, hand in hand, looking here, looking there.

"Aren't they terrible?" Eileen asked.

"I didn't realize they were this bad. Why don't you call one of the exterminators tomorrow? Have them come out and spray." They headed back toward the house as the telephone again began to ring.

Eileen answered it this time. It was Philip calling from Moscow, Idaho where he was preparing for law school. He had a summer job as a law clerk for one of the local law firms. He was three years away from the bar exam but the boss had offered him a position with the firm once he finished school and passed the bar exam.

"Hi, Mom. How is everything at home?"

"Just fine. Hold on a minute and I'll have your father get on the other line." She nodded her head and motioned for Jodi to take the phone in the living room.

"Hello, son. How are things?"

"Great, Dad. I just got home from work. The firm is involved in a big lawsuit against PetroChem. A group of wheat farmers are suing for big bucks over their chemical fertilizer poisoning their grain. Lots of work."

"That's why lawyers can afford to drive big Mercedes Benz limousines."

"I'm just a clerk, Dad. I have trouble affording my old Ford."

"Are you taking care of yourself?" his mother asked.

"Mom, I'm 20 years old. I know how to take care of myself."

"I'm your mother and I have the God-given right to worry about you."

"Have you heard from your brother?" Jodi asked.

"No. The little rat never writes."

"Don't talk about your brother like that." Eileen scolded.

"Ah, Mom. You should hear what he calls me."

"I'm glad you called tonight, Philip. It's good to hear from you."

"I didn't have anything special in mind. It's just that I hadn't talked with you and Mom for a while and I thought it was time for me to call."

"Have you got a girlfriend yet?" his mother inquired.

"You ask me that every time, mom. No, I don't have a steady girlfriend. I don't have time. Between school and work I don't have time."

"You'll let me know when you get a steady girl, won't you?"

"Yes mom. Listen, I have to go. Some guys are coming to pick me up to go for pizza and beer. I have to change clothes. I don't want to get pizza sauce on this suit. I'll call you again soon."

"Thanks for calling, son."

"You take care of yourself and don't drink too much beer." His mother warned.

"Okay, mom. Gotta go. Bye." The phone clicked and her son was gone again.

"I hope he's taking care of himself." she said again, this time to Jodi.

Jodi went upstairs to take a shower and to call it a day.

CHAPTER 25

The next morning Jodi left home early for the drive to work. He wanted to make a stop. Instead of driving straight ahead to the freeway ramp, he turned right on North Bend Way and drove the short distance to where Torval Laxo would be sitting on the porch with a cup of hot coffee.

Torval had lost his devoted wife to cancer last year. It broke his heart. The twins came home for the funeral and spent almost a month with their father. Since that time he had adapted fairly well to the single life of a widower. The boys called regularly to check on their father.

Both boys had graduated from high school and gone to college. Both had studied accounting at Pullman, and graduated from Washington State University as Certified Public Accountants. They each had a degree in business. Their parents were proud that both their sons had gone on to college and done so well.

After college, they decided to join the Navy. They signed up together and went to boot camp together. During this time they expressed interest in learning to fly and in being pilots. Both boys had passed the tests and were accepted at flight school. They became great rivals and their mischief continued. They were nearly kicked out of flight school for romping through the air in their Navy trainers, engaging in mock dogfights every chance they had.

The Navy had a different view of their fun, censuring the twins, making them toe the line with threats of dismissal. The two had been the subject of several squadron meetings, but in the end it was decided that the two were outstanding pilots and had the potential to be good Navy officers. The boys took all the disciplinary actions in stride and laughed about it quite often.

Einer once told Aino, "Wouldn't Jodi give us the devil if he knew we were in trouble all the time?"

The Navy had a solution to the problem. Upon completion of initial flight training, the Laxo twins were separated, for the first time in their lives. It was traumatic for each of them, but they made the best of it.

Einer was sent to Alameda Naval Air Station in California for advance flight training in F-14 Tomcats, Aino to Whidbey Naval Air Station where he trained in A-6 Avengers. Both young men set new standards for their respective classes. They were outstanding pilots and each was soon assigned to duty in active flight squadrons. Aino was assigned to the Lexington which was cruising in the Indian Ocean. Einer was sent to Florida to fly from dry land.

The twins were happy in the Navy, but missed their family terribly. They both kept close contact with their folks by telephone and by letter. They called each other regularly too, just to laugh and to see which one was to be promoted first.

The death of their mother had brought them home. They each had a life and a career now, but it was difficult to leave their father in his sorrow. Duty called.

Torval was proud of his boys, and rightly so. They must go and live their own lives. "Us old folks are content to stay here and watch how they build the new world," he would say.

Torval lost interest in the towing business, so when Northwest Towing and Parts Company came to him with an offer, he sold the business. They hauled away all the parts in the warehouse and took the truck and trailer frames and chassis away on flatbed trailers. Torval was saddened and at the same time relieved to see the business he had worked most of his life to build hauled away piece by greasy piece. The buyer didn't want the wreckers. They had equipment newer and larger than that owned by Torval. A young truck driver from Wyoming stopped one day to talk to Torval about what he was going to do with his wreckers. Torval said they were for sale and for the right price the young man could own them. It took some negotiation and some creative financing but in the end he bought the equipment.

Out of the inventory Torval kept a small Caterpillar tractor and used it to clean up the yard. He worked hard to level the land and to seed it into lawn and trees. Since his beloved wife had passed away he spent more time with the plants and flowers on the place. The sauna had a fresh coat of stain and a new walk up to the front step. His next project was to change the front gate, to make it look more like a home than a junkyard, he said.

Jodi eased his car into the drive. Torval was there, sipping coffee. Before

Jodi could get out of the car, the older man disappeared into the house only to reappear almost immediately with a coffee cup in his hand.

"Mornin', Torval," Jodi said, as he stepped up onto the porch.

"Good morning, captain deputy." Torval handed Jodi the steaming cup.

"How are things out here?" Jodi asked, sipping the hot coffee.

"T'ings, they go good, eh. I don't have all those people bothering me for parts any more. It is peaceful here now."

"I am on my way to work, but I thought I should come by and say hello. I'm sorry I don't get out here more than I do."

"You are a good friend, Jodi. I understand. We know each other a long time, eh?"

"We sure have, Torval. I miss Ma and the boys."

"The boys have a good life now. They like to fly airplanes. They are half a world apart and still they compete with each other. I am proud of my boys. So was their Ma. T'ings change, Jodi. T'ings change."

Jodi finished his coffee and set the cup on the small table. "I have to get to work now, but I just wanted to come by and say hello. Good to see you again Torval."

"You take care Jodi, you hear?"

In his car, driving back through town, he thought how it used to be. This small town with its small-town closeness was changing. The new townhouses and the big subdivisions were crowding people into the valley at an unbelievable rate. As he drove down the main street he didn't see one person he recognized. He looked into the window of the Mar-T Cafe as he drove by. Ester Parks was still serving customers in the old cafe. She was still the prime source for rumors, if any were being spread.

He turned left, past the new factory outlet stores; there was a new Safeway across the street. Gas stations and fine restaurants were springing up, changing the complexion of this small town that once seemed to be so far away from the city and all its hustle. The sun was warm and bright as he sped up the ramp to Interstate 90, going west to Issaquah.

It was just 8 a.m. when he sat down to review the stack of morning reports he must review. It was just past ten when he finished. He met with the lieutenant regarding a letter of reprimand to be placed in the file of one of the new officers. Jodi had told the lieutenant that the kid seemed to be "badge-heavy." It was up to the lieutenant to keep a paper trail in case his heavy-handed methods continued.

Back at his desk, he was wondering which pile of paperwork to attack first. He was sorting through the stack of files when the intercom line buzzed. He stabbed the blinking button and answered; it was his secretary.

"Captain, I have a call for you from a Captain Mike Masters of the Alaska State Troopers in Palmer, Alaska."

"What's it about, do you know?"

"No, but he said it was important and he needed to talk with you right away."

"Okay, Joan. I'll take it."

"Line three."

Jodi switched to line three. "Captain Eagle here."

"Captain Eagle. This is Captain Mike Masters, AST. I'm in Palmer, Alaska. Please call me Mike."

"Okay Mike, what can I do for you? And, where is Palmer, Alaska? Is it close to Anchorage?"

"Yeah, Palmer is only forty miles east of Anchorage," the friendly voice explained. "The reason I'm calling you is that one of my men put a set of prints into the computer and came up with a hit. We couldn't find any prints matching this body anywhere, so we tried the computer. We came up with a set of prints on a case from seven years ago. The case refers to you as the investigating officer. I'll fax you the information we have, but I was wondering if the old case is still open. The name on the case is Shirley Ng."

Jodi felt as if he had been struck by lightning. "You what?" he shouted into the phone.

"Yeah, then you know the case? Is it still an open case?" the Alaska State Trooper wanted to know.

"Are you sure about this?" Jodi couldn't believe his ears. "You have a body matching the prints in the computer from the Shirley Ng case?"

The trooper must be beginning to wonder what kind of a person he had on the other end of the line. "Yeah, that's what I said. Is there some kind of a problem with that?"

"How long can you hold the body?"

"I don't know. For a while I suppose. Why?"

"I'll call you later today and let you know when I will be in Anchorage. Is it possible for you to have someone pick me up at the airport?" Jodi sounded excited.

"I'll pick you up myself. Just let me know what time and I'll be there. I'm assuming by all this interest that your case is still active."

"You have no idea. Mike, I have to impose, but I'll bring the files on this case with me. We can talk then. If you will indulge me until I can get there I'll explain. I need to make arrangements and to get the files here before I leave. I'll call you as soon as I have the flight arranged."

"Okay, captain. I'll be waiting for your call."

"Mike."

Chapter 25

"Yes?"

"You have earned the right to call me Jodi. You don't know how good this news is for me."

"Glad I could help. I'll talk with you later."

Jodi hung up the phone and immediately called Joan into the office. He dialed the North Bend Detachment with the speed dialer, while waiting for her to come into the office.

"King County Police, North Bend office. Can I help you?"

"Emma, Jodi Eagle. Let me talk to Connie, right away."

"Of course, Jodi. Please hold. Nice to hear from you."

The line was put on hold for only about fifteen seconds when Sergeant Connie Lupine answered the phone.

"Hi, Jodi. What's up?"

"Connie, I want you to get me all the files on the Mount Si killings. I need them right away. Put them in a briefcase and bring them to my house. I'm going there now to pack a bag. I need it all, Connie and I need it right away."

"You'll have it by the time you get home. Can I ask why?"

"I'll tell you as soon as I can, but right now I don't have time." Jodi was bursting to tell her anyway. "I can tell you that maybe the killer is dead. They have a body in Alaska that matches the prints in the Shirley Ng case."

"You're kidding. Really?" Connie was as shocked as Jodi had been. "I can't believe it. After all this time."

"Gotta go, Connie. Get that stuff to the house for me. Right away. Thanks."

As he hung up the phone, he turned to the confused young secretary, who had no idea what was happening or why.

"Joan, I want a reservation on the first flight I can get to Anchorage, Alaska. Call Alaska Airlines and get me a seat. Tell them it's official business and that it's an emergency. I'm going home to pack a bag. You can reach me there. I'll pick up the tickets at the Alaska Airlines counter. Do it now."

She scurried from the office. She had never seen her captain in such a hurry for anything.

Next he called the lieutenant to his office.

Steve Burnside was as confused as the secretary had been.

"Steve, I want you to be in charge of the office while I'm gone. I don't know how long I'll be out of the office, but if you need anything just call the main office downtown. The sheriff will know where I am and he will have someone give you advice if you need it. You can handle it. You do most of the work around here anyway."

Next on his list of things to do was a call to the sheriff. He explained what was happening and that he was going to Alaska to check it out personally. It was too important to have someone else check it out. The sheriff reluctantly agreed to let him go.

It was almost impossible to control his excitement. He had the urge to push the accelerator to the floor on the drive home. He wanted everything to speed up. He wanted to get to Palmer, Alaska where he could see with his own eyes, the person who had been the focus of his professional life for the past seven years.

Joan called to tell him that he had a flight at two-thirty. He checked the time. He would just make it. Connie was downstairs waiting when he finished packing. She had a smile on her face that would light the entire east side of the county.

He kissed his wife. "I'll be back as soon as I can. I hope you understand that this is important to me and that I can't let anyone else do this." She smiled, she knew. "Connie, do you have time to take me to the airport? I have a two-thirty flight out of SeaTac."

"I'll take the time, Jodi." She turned to Eileen, "Would you like to ride along? I would sure like to have your company on the ride back."

"I don't think so, Connie. You two will have all that official conversation and I wouldn't have a chance to visit with Jodi anyway. Thanks, though."

Jodi turned to his beautiful wife. He looked deeply into her black eyes. He hugged her tightly, then gave her a long kiss. Eileen was surprised because it wasn't his custom to show his affection when anyone else was present.

"I'll miss you, honey. I'll call you."

"See you when you get back. Now get out of here before you miss your plane."

CHAPTER 26

Jodi looked out the window of the airliner into the bright sun. During the ride from the runway to the gate the stewardess made her announcements and welcomed everyone to Anchorage. He set his watch back an hour; it was seven after five here. By five fifteen he was at the baggage carousel. He waited impatiently for his lone bag to appear on the moving conveyer belt that snaked through the baggage claim area. He picked up the worn old suitcase and began to scan the crowd for the trooper who'd said he would pick him up.

As he made his way around the enclosure of the baggage claim area, a tall, thin man in a blue blazer strode purposefully through the automatic doors. He scanned the crowd until he made eye contact with Jodi. There was instant recognition, though the two had never met.

As he approached he asked, "Hello, are you Jodi Eagle?"

"Yes." He put out his hand. "I'm Jodi Eagle, and you must be Captain Masters."

"Call me Mike." Masters had a firm handshake and a friendly smile. "My car is just outside the door. Is that all your luggage?"

"Yes. I didn't plan to stay long." They reached the car and Jodi tossed his black suitcase on the back seat. "I haven't made hotel reservations. Can you recommend a place to stay? I can drop my bag and then we can tend to business. I'm anxious to see the body." He adjusted the large briefcase between his feet.

"I have plenty of room at my place, in Palmer. I thought you could stay with us while you're here." The trooper merged into traffic on International Airport Way. "Summertime is a tough time to get a room without reservations. The prices double and the rooms are filled with tourists." He changed lanes. "I've got a big place and there is just my wife and me. You can stay with us and, since it will be daylight almost all night, we should have some time to do some sightseeing. Does that sound all right to you?"

"Sure, but won't your wife mind having me just show up without any warning?"

"Hey, this is Alaska. We get used to that. In the summertime there is always someone dropping in for a few days. Besides, she'll want to go out for dinner. She'll take any excuse not to have to cook." Mike laughed. He turned left on Minnesota Drive, maneuvering to the right lane. "How was your flight?"

"It was fine. On the plane, I looked over our old files." He pointed to the old leather briefcase between his legs.

Masters checked his rear-view mirror, and then signaled for a right turn to Tudor Road.

"I thought we should go to the crime lab first. If you want to see the body before the autopsy, we need do that right away. The pathologist is waiting for you before he begins."

"I've waited more than seven years to have something turn up on this guy. He killed five little kids in our little town."

"Wait a minute. You're looking for a guy?" Mike asked, surprised.

"Yeah. Why?" Jodi looked at him. "I thought you knew that."

"No, I didn't. We may not have the right body. This body is a female. I'd say she was in her early thirties. She was in good physical condition and a real looker. Blond and built really well." Mike explained.

"Oh no." Jodi said with disappointment. "I thought the prints were a match."

"I thought they were, too." He glanced into the back seat. "Grab that file folder there, on the back seat."

Jodi retrieved the folder, placed it on his lap and opened it. He was met with pictures of the corpse. The pictures showed, what was once a pretty girl. He flipped up the pictures and searched the file for the fingerprint card he knew was there somewhere.

"How did she die?"

"Murdered." Masters glanced at the file. "The prints are at the bottom of that pile. The computer prints and the ones taken from the body should both be there." He slowed the car for a traffic light. "Someone tied her to a buried log and let the tide come in on her. She drowned."

"Where?"

"At the mouth of the Knik River. I'll show you the spot on the way home."

Jodi studied the copies of the fingerprint cards. "They look like a match to me, but I can't believe it could be the same person."

"It doesn't sound right to me either."

The trooper captain slowed again, this time to turn into the fenced yard of

Chapter 26

the Alaska State Trooper headquarters. A large complex of buildings, the crime lab was to one side of the main building. Mike parked the car near the door.

"I see Doc's car there."

Inside the two men walked halfway down the hall to an office where two men waited. Mike Masters made the introductions.

"Jodi Eagle, this is Lieutenant Burton." The two men shook hands.

"And this ghoul is Doc Colburn, our pathologist."

"Pleased to meet you, Deputy Eagle. I've been waiting. As soon as you're finished I'll start the autopsy."

"I just wanted to see the body before the autopsy. How long will the exam take?"

"I've already done the external stuff. Fingernails, blood, hair, cursory external exam. I have taken vaginal samples to test for sexual activity or rape. It doesn't appear she was raped or had sex with her assailant. There is one big surprise, though." He said with a wide grin.

"What is it?" Mike asked.

"You would never guess." The doctor chuckled.

"Come on Doc. Are you going to tell us or not?" Mike wanted to know.

"Okay, Mike. You sure have a short fuse anymore. Well, it seems our lady started life as a gent."

Jodi was shocked. "You mean she has had a sex change?"

"You got it." The pathologist was shaking his head and smiling. "This is the first time I've seen it in a murder victim. I was really surprised when I saw the work. Good job too. Probably more than five years ago. This lady worked hard to become what she was."

"Can I see the body now?" Jodi asked.

Lieutenant Burton answered. "Follow me."

The group walked to the end of the hall to enter the exam room. It was a sterile place with a strong antiseptic smell. There was a body on the metal table in the center of the room, covered with a white sheet. Doctor Colburn reached up to turn on the bright medical exam light over the table. He pulled down the sheet to reveal the body of what was once a attractive woman. She was now just a stiff, bleached body; about to be cut open and her organs examined. It was a degrading procedure, required by law but it sometimes gave clues to who had committed the crime.

"Do you have pictures I can take with me?" Jodi asked.

"Yes, we do." Burton said.

"And I would like to have an original set of prints, if that's not too much trouble."

"We'll do that right away." Colburn said.

"Anything else?" Mike asked.

"No, I think that's all. I have our files on the killings if you want a copy. How was the body found?"

"You know, that's a strange thing." Mike commented. "Most killers just do their victim and get away as fast as they can. This guy tied her up and waited for the tide to come in and kill her. He waited for the tide to go out and cut the body loose and carried it up on dry ground. A kid riding an ATV found the body and called us. The body was face down, nude. I have pictures of the scene in my office. Her clothing was placed in a neat pile by her side. I've never seen a murder scene quite like it."

"Was the clothing by her left elbow?" Jodi asked. "And her left hand under her face?"

"Yeah, how did you know?" Mike was surprised he knew this fact.

"In 1991 there were five kids killed in North Bend. Four boys and one girl. They were all 10 to 12 years old except for the girl. She looked younger than she was and she had short hair. We think the killer mistook her for a young boy. Anyway, each of the bodies were found that way. They were naked, left hand under their face and their clothing folded neatly and placed by their left elbow. The killings just stopped after the fifth one. He left the last body in front of our office. It was my first day as sergeant in charge of the North Bend detachment. One of my deputies saw him with the body and chased him. In the car chase he collided with an elderly couple. They were killed and my deputy was badly injured. It took him almost a year to get back to normal." Thinking about the case had brought sadness back into his voice. "I wanted to see this guy with my own eyes."

There was silence in the room. Mike was the first to speak.

"Is there anything else you want here, Jodi?" he asked. "If not, let's get out of here and let Doc do his work."

"Good idea. I want to thank you guys for your help." He looked across the table at the lieutenant and the doctor. "I know this has cost you a lot of time, but you have answered a lot of questions that have bothered me for a long, long time. Thanks."

"I'll have the autopsy report for you tomorrow afternoon. If you leave those files here for me, I'll copy what we need and give them back to you tomorrow when you come in." The trooper lieutenant was trying to be helpful.

"Okay, I'll leave my briefcase here. Copy what you need. Thanks. See you tomorrow." He started to walk toward the door then turned to ask, "Do you have an I.D. on the body yet?"

"Not yet."

The two men walked from the building into the bright afternoon sun. It was downright hot. Jodi had not expected it to be this warm.

Chapter 26

"Let's go home." Mike said in a cheery tone. "I'll show you where we found the body as we drive to Palmer." They were back on Tudor Road, driving toward the Glenn Highway.

Jodi was fascinated with the scenery. He was used to seeing mountains, but these were breathtaking. The craggy peaks rose from sea level to more than seven thousand feet. White glaciers dotted the bare tops of the mountains. The lower elevations were densely covered with birch, aspen, alder and spruce. Willow and other types of brush grew on the hillsides, interspersed with so many different kinds of wildflowers it was difficult to make out individual colors.

Mike knew how he felt. "Beautiful, isn't it? I never get tired of looking at it."

"I expected bigger trees."

"I know. That's what everyone says."

"It's different than I expected."

"We'll go home and get you settled, then go out for some sightseeing. There's a great restaurant about forty miles the other side of Anchorage. We'll go up to Portage Glacier and then to Girdwood for dinner. Judy will like that."

As they crossed the bridge spanning the murky Knik River, Mike pointed downstream toward the salt water.

"See the end of the brush line down there, about a mile? That's where we found the body. You can see this bridge from the spot. There isn't much to see there. The tide took away all the tracks in the sand. Up on the high bank, where the body was found, is all beach rye grass. There weren't any identifiable footprints. You can see where someone parked a car, but there is no way to tell if it was the killer's car. He didn't leave us much to go on."

"I hope you have better luck than I had with my case," Jodi commented.

Jodi continued to enjoy the scenery until the car pulled into the driveway of a large white house with tall columns supporting the porch roof. The grass was green and well kept. Flowers bordered the lawn and the front of the home. Again, Jodi thought, he had not expected so many flowers.

Jodi took the bag from the back seat of the car before Mike pulled into the garage. The door was closing and the two were looking at the view of the mountains from the front porch when another car pulled into the drive. It was Judy Masters.

"Leave the car out, honey." Mike called to his wife.

As she climbed from the car, Jodi could see she too was tall, thin and pretty. Her dark hair, was pulled back in a ponytail. She wore colorful slacks and a plaid shirt. Jodi stepped off the porch to meet her.

"You must be Jodi Eagle, from Washington State," she said. "I'm Judy."

"Pleased to meet you, Judy. Mike says you are a tolerant lady and won't mind if I stay with you folks." Jodi gently shook her hand.

"I'm used to it. We like the company. And, besides, when we get company like this, I don't have to cook," she laughed.

A half hour later the trio was loaded into the car and headed back toward Anchorage and an evening of sightseeing. It was after midnight when they returned home. The sun was still high in the sky, peeking over the mountaintops to the southwest.

"Holy smokes!" Jodi exclaimed, checking his wristwatch, "It can't be that late."

Mike and Judy both laughed. "No one sleeps in Alaska in the summertime. There isn't much nighttime."

"This would sure take some getting used to," he said, yawning.

"Do you want coffee before you go to bed?" Judy asked.

"Gosh, Judy. I don't know where I would put it. They really feed you well here." He patted his stomach. "If you don't mind, I think I'll take a shower and turn in. It's been a long day."

"You know where your room is. The shower is right across the hall. See you in the morning." Mike liked this man. He seemed instantly at home in this land that was so strange to him. It would be nice to spend some time with this quiet man from North Bend. Tomorrow they would have more time to get better acquainted.

Jodi showered and dropped into bed. Exhaustion overtook him and he was asleep as soon as his head touched the pillow. His final thought of the day was of his wife, so far away. He wished she had come with him. She would like it here.

CHAPTER 27

Wednesday morning a bright sun streaming into his room awakened Jodi. He checked his watch and found it was half past six. He slipped out of bed, shaved and dressed. He was downstairs by seven fifteen. As he reached the bottom of the stairs he could smell the coffee. Someone was up. He made his way to the kitchen to find Judy fixing breakfast.

"How did you sleep?" she asked, with a big smile.

"Great. You run a pretty nice hotel."

"There's a coffee cup in the cupboard above the coffeepot. Mike is in the shower and will be down in a minute."

Jodi poured his coffee. "Do you mind if I use the telephone?"

"You go right ahead. There is a small desk in the office at the top of the stairs, first door on the right. There should be legal pads and pens there, if you need them." She was flipping pancakes and checking the eggs in the pan. "Breakfast is almost ready."

"I won't be long." Jodi said as he took his coffee and disappeared up the stairs.

His first call was to Eileen. He filled her in on the case and the fact that the killer was dead. "I should be home sometime tomorrow."

"I'll be glad to see you. I don't like being here without you." There was a short pause. "Earl came home. He is really sick. Linda called last night and told me. Earl wanted to see you. He said he has something to tell you. He didn't say what it was."

"Okay, tell him I'll be home tomorrow evening sometime. I'll call you to let you know what time my flight will be. Will you come to the airport and pick me up?"

"Just let me know what time and I'll be there. I love you."

"I love you too, honey. I'll call you this evening to let you know the time. Bye."

His next call was to his office. Joan Woods, who had been his executive assistant since he became captain, answered the telephone in his office. She handled administrative duties well, kept meticulous record, and liked to let folks around the office know who was running things.

"Captain Eagle's office, can I help you?"

"Hello, Joan. I am just checking in. Is there anything going on I should know about?"

"Oh, hello captain. Things are pretty much as you left them. There are a few messages, but nothing that can't wait until you get back. Do you know yet when that will be?"

"If things go as planned, I'll be home tomorrow night. I can't say for sure right now. You can reach me through the State Troopers in Palmer, if you need to contact me. I'll be with Captain Masters all day."

He was just hanging the telephone back on the stand when he heard the cheery voice in the kitchen calling.

"Breakfast is ready."

Mike was in the kitchen when Jodi returned. "Good morning. Ready for another fun-filled day?"

"I'm still trying to recover from yesterday. Did the sun ever go down?"

"Not for long." Judy commented, while pouring Jodi a fresh cup of coffee.

"I have to go to the office first thing this morning. There are some reports I have to sign. It shouldn't take more than an hour. Once I finish there we can go to town and see what the autopsy found." Mike was piling pancakes on his plate. "Is there anything special you want to do today, anything you want to see?"

"I would like to get all this business about the body out of the way as soon as I can and make an arrangement for my trip back to Washington. It's not that I don't like your hospitality, but I have a lot to do when I return." Jodi took a stack of pancakes from the plate. "I want to take the two of you to dinner tonight. You have shown me a lot of hospitality, and it's my turn. Besides, Judy cooked breakfast; I should cook dinner. You will have to tell me where you want to go, because I don't have any idea."

"Do you like beef?" Mike asked.

"It's my favorite."

Mike turned to Judy. "Would you like to go to the Club Paris?"

"Ooh, I'd love it," she replied.

"Okay, make reservations for us, will you, Judy?"

Chapter 23

The group ate breakfast and chatted about this and that. The two lawmen left the house and drove to the detachment office. Jodi was introduced around the office and given his own AST coffee cup.

Mike gave Jodi the cook's tour of the headquarters building. He introduced the deputy to troopers as they passed in the halls. He showed off the dispatch center and the locked evidence storage safe. The building was an efficient and modern structure, not unlike others in the state.

Walking down another hall, Captain Masters detoured into a large office with conference tables and chairs. On the walls were maps of Alaska, and a map of Palmer. Masters guided Jodi to a large map with red lines drawn at varying angles.

"Everything inside that red outline is my responsibility." He gave a sweeping gesture with his arm. "Here's Palmer," he pointed. "This line running north from Palmer is just over 200 miles long. You can see it then runs east, then back toward the south and zigzags back to Palmer. The area is roughly equal to western Washington from the Cascade Mountains to the beach. And from Canada to Oregon. One of my greatest problems is logistics. It is just so blamed far from one place to another; it's difficult to manage. The good news is that there aren't many people in the entire area. There are some villages, but no large towns. In this detachment, the largest concentration of population is right here, Palmer, Wasilla, Big Lake and the surrounding area. You have twice as many people in Bellevue as we have in the entire state, so population is not the problem, isolation and distance are."

"Hmm. I don't know how your troopers cope. It seems to me they would be out of contact with this office and without backup a good deal of the time."

"That's true. We try to hire special people to handle the job. The stress levels are pretty high. An officer can be fifty miles from a telephone, in an area without radio contact. He may be 150 miles from his nearest back up. He may be in mosquitoes and white sox, our quarter-inch fly with four inch teeth, being eaten alive. He may be out there in minus sixty-degree weather. My men patrol that area, winter and summer. Sometimes by air, sometimes by boat, sometimes by car. In the winter they travel by any means that will get them to a scene; be it snow machine, dog sled or snowshoes. Sometimes the weather is so bad that it is impossible to get to where they need to be. Most people think this is an easy job, sitting in a nice new patrol car, writing speeding tickets. They don't see what these officers must go through just to do the job, and our job is protecting our citizens."

"I thought I had a large area. I'm responsible for eastern King County. I don't know if I could handle your job."

"You could do it. It would take some getting used to, but you could do it." Mike laughed. "If you can deal with the population you have in Western Washington, this would be a snap."

Mike showed his guest the coffee room. "Have a seat and gab with the troops. I have a few minutes' work to do, then we'll go into town."

A half hour later, Mike came to get him. "Sorry it took so long, but I may have some good news. I just got a call from Anchorage Police Department. They have a missing person's report on a topless dancer. She meets the description of the body we have at the lab. The club manager won't be in until noon, so we have some time to see the kill sight and to stop at the Crime Lab."

"If I could, I would like to wrap this up today and make a reservation to return home. I have a lot of work to do. I want to close this case after all these years." Jodi seemed apologetic. "Don't get me wrong, I'm enjoying my time with you and your lovely wife, and I hope you will invite me back. And, God knows, I don't want to come all this way and miss something, but I have to get back. I'm like you, I have a lot of other responsibilities."

"I understand. We'll try to get everything done so you can get on the late flight tonight."

The two men drove toward the city of Anchorage. As the car neared the Knik River, Mike turned off the highway. He followed a narrow, bumpy path through the willow and alder thickets to the rye grass flats near the mouth of the river. He drove on several hundred more yards until he came to a spot overlooking the flowing water of the river. The tide was out and there was a large sandy beach below them extending more than a hundred yards to the river. Jodi noticed the river was thick with silt and mud.

"Is there a flood somewhere? What's making the water so muddy?"

"That's glacier silt. The glaciers grind up the rocks and as they melt they bring that rock downstream with the water. All this sand you see is silt deposit. It's dangerous out here. People have walked out there and been trapped in the silt. They can't get out and are covered by the tide. It happens quite often."

The two men climbed over the sand bluff to the lower level of the beach. They walked downstream a few yards to an old log, half buried in the silt of the riverbank.

"This is where he killed her." Mike pointed to the log. "See that line someone drew with a felt tip pen?"

Jodi nodded.

"The killer must have planned this ahead and set a trap. He had a short piece of cable with an eye on each end. He buried it under the log, directly under that line on the log. He put plastic cable ties through the eyes in the cable. When he got her out here, he pulled the cable ties up on her ankles and tightened them. She couldn't get away. We think he sat up there on the grass and watched while the tide came in and covered her up. I'll bet that when we see the autopsy report, we'll find she drowned, but was suffering from hypothermia. She would have passed out before the water came up over her."

"You say you found her up there on the grass, though. Her clothing, was it wet?"

"No. We think that he talked her into taking off her clothes. We, of course, don't know how he did that. Maybe he said he wanted sex, who knows. The thing is , though, there are no signs of a struggle before she was tied up. She came here willingly, and as near as we can tell, took her clothes off willingly."

"I don't understand that." Jodi commented.

"If you think that's strange, think about this. He sat here for up to five hours, watching her drown. He had to tie her to the log before the tide came in and then waited for the tide to go out before cutting her loose. Then he carried her body up onto the grass and posed her." Mike was mopping sweat from his face. "Most killers, even crazy ones, have their fun before the act of killing. After they kill, they just want to get away from the scene before they are discovered. This guy was just the opposite. He made sure it took a long time for his victim to die. He watched her the entire time. He stayed here long enough to cut her loose and to carry her up on the bank. I don't think he cared if he was caught. Everything points to vengeance as a motive."

Jodi surveyed the area. He walked around, looking in the grass, back and forth, back and forth. He found nothing.

"Is there anything else you want to see here?"

"I think we have seen it all." Jodi answered. "You know, this case has been like this since the beginning. The killer, it was this woman before she was a woman, was so careful not to be caught. Yet, every body was dropped in an area where it was sure to be found. Every body was posed like this one. It was like the killer was delivering a message that we never were able to understand."

"Nobody ever said police work would be easy." Mike Masters commented as the two men returned to the car. Inside, he started the engine and turned on the air conditioning unit.

In Anchorage, Lieutenant Burton waited in the crime lab. He was in his office when the two men arrived. Jodi saw his briefcase resting in a chair by the door inside the office.

"Have you heard that APD has a missing persons report on a topless dancer that matches the description of the body we have?"

"Yes, they called me this morning. We are going to go to the club to interview the manager, but he won't be in until noon." He looked at the time. "We'll go there as soon as we finish here."

Burton turned to Jodi. "I have the report right here. Cause of death drowning. She suffered severe hypothermia in the process. The only body trauma we found was where the assailant tied her ankles to the log. The ankles were bruised and there were cuts from the plastic straps. She had abrasions inside her legs from rubbing on the log. There were no other bruises or cuts. Her larynx suffered some damage; all internal. It appears she did a lot of screaming before she passed out from the cold water."

"Do you have a name?" Masters asked.

"We have a name from the missing persons report. She was a topless dancer, so, without confirmation, we don't know if it is her real name or just the name she goes by as a dancer." He thumbed down a few pages in the papers in front of him. "The name we have on the report is Dava Bennett. Are either of you familiar with the name?"

Both Jodi and Mike shook their heads.

"Would it be possible for me to get a copy of the entire report for my files?" Jodi asked Burton.

"I have already made copies and they are in your briefcase along with all the original files you had in there. I made copies of what I needed out of your files. Thanks for letting me have the information."

"Happy to oblige."

"Listen lieutenant, Jodi wants to try to make a flight out of here tonight. If we have everything, I think we'll go to the club. I'll talk with you later. Thanks for everything."

"Do you want lunch before we interview that club manager?"

"Gosh, no. I couldn't eat a thing. Your wife made me eat too much this morning. She is a great cook."

"Yeah, I like her." Mike laughed.

Riding down Tudor Road, Jodi wondered if this case was winding down or just taking another strange turn. It had been a long time coming, but this killer was never again going to hurt another child. As brutal as this death had been, Jodi found no compassion in his thoughts, only relief.

CHAPTER 28

The Great Alaska Bush Company II was a large wood structure with a front resembling that of an old west saloon. A large veranda adorned the front of the plain-looking building. Cars had already begun to assemble in the parking lot. The doors were wide open.

"Check the license plates on the cars. A large percentage of them are rentals. High rollers come here and fish all morning, going out at three or four in the morning. By noon they're back and ready to party. They serve a good drink here. The music is so loud you can't possibly carry on a conversation, but conversation isn't what most of these guys have in mind. They run a good place here. There is seldom any trouble on the premises. The owners protect the girls and the patrons get a good show."

"I take it this is an old, established business," Jodi commented.

"The same family has owned it for a long time." Mike said as the two men entered the bar.

Inside, there was an open expanse, a sort of amphitheater, balconies terraced off from the walls down to the rail around the dance floor. The dance floor was in a pit; a staircase led from the floor level to a balcony, high above the audience. Dressing rooms and offices filled the upstairs rooms.

Along the right wall, as they entered the front door, were the bar and restrooms. Three bartenders worked the regular shift. The manager and one of the bartenders were inventorying the liquor when the two officers entered. A security man was posted at the door, but had left his post to talk with someone at the end of the bar. Mike seemed to know the hulk of a man who stressed the buttons on his blue blazer.

"Hi, Tony. How are things?" Mike asked.

"Things are good, Mike. How are you?" The security man inquired. "I haven't seen you in a while."

"You know how it goes, Tony. I took a desk job and never get to see my old friends any more." Mike reached into his pocket and retrieved his notebook. "Tony, is Albert Zeller in?"

"Yeah, that's him down there counting the liquor. Do you want to see him?"

"Please, when he has a minute." Mike was friendly to the security man.

Tony walked down the bar to talk with Zeller. "I've known Tony a long time. I kept him from going to the big house for manslaughter once. Some guys jumped him in the parking lot. He put them all down, I think there were four of them, but he killed one of them. The guy hit his head on a car bumper during the fight. All the witnesses swore Tony hit him with a club. I handled the investigation. The evidence didn't show that Tony was guilty, so I said that in court. Tony has been my friend since that time."

Tony returned with Zeller. Zeller was behind the bar, leaning on its top. His shoelace necktie and sleeve garter made him look like an old-time bartender.

"Al, this is Mike Masters of the troopers." Tony introduced them. "I'm sorry I don't know this gentleman."

Mike introduced Jodi to the club manager and to Tony.

A girl, wearing a sheer robe, had been working on the sound equipment at the edge of the dance floor. As Mike finished the introduction there was a blaring sound, roughly equated to music, making it impossible to talk.

"Can we go outside to talk?" Mike asked.

"Sure, meet me out front." He walked to the other end of the bar while Jodi and Mike stepped out the front door. It was only a minute until the manager appeared.

"Sorry about that, but that's our business and the customers are impatient."

"I understand. This will be fine. How about stepping to the front of our car?"

The three men stepped from the porch. Mike tossed his notebook on the hood and pulled a pen from his shirt pocket.

"Are you the one that filed the missing persons report on Dava Bennett?"

"Yes, she hasn't been to work for a couple of days. That's not like Dava. She never misses work. She is one of those rare girls that dance for the love of it. She is really popular with the patrons. She puts on a good show." Albert Zeller explained. "Have you found her?"

"I'm afraid I have some bad news for you." Mike looked directly into Zeller's eyes. "We found the body of a murder victim. She meets the description on the missing person's report. That's why I'm here, to check it out." Mike saw the shock on the club manager's face.

Chapter 28

"Oh, no. What happened? How was she killed?"

"I'll tell you she was drowned, but I can't tell you any more right now. The investigation is still going on."

"Do you know who killed her?"

"Not yet. That's why we're here." He showed a picture of the dead girl to her boss. "Is this Dava Bennett?"

Albert Zeller was choked up. "Yes," he said quietly. "That's her."

"Can you give us any details about when she was last seen or if she was seen with anyone?" Mike asked.

"I'm sorry. This is quite a shock to me. We don't often have trouble here." Zeller said, clearing his throat. "As club manager, I filed the missing persons report with the Anchorage Police Department. I had all the employment information they needed for the report. The truth is that I didn't even know she was missing. Her friend Candy said she was missing and asked me to file the report."

"This Candy. Is that her real name?"

"I doubt it. She dances under the name of Candy Cane. I have her real ID in my files; I'll get it for you. She and Dava were friends. They came here together. Candy said they had worked together for a long time ... about three years, I think."

"Was Dava seeing anyone on a regular basis?" Mike was asking.

"I'm sorry. I just don't know. We have some rules for working here. The girls don't confide in me about that sort of thing. They don't want me to know."

A taxi pulled up to the front door. The three men watched as four pretty girls exited the cab. The last one out was a red-head carrying a plastic bag that looked as though it had just come from the dry cleaners.

Mike had stopped talking when the girls arrived, not wanting to be overheard.

"Candy, come here a minute, will you?" Zeller called to the red-headed girl.

She gave her bag of clothing to one of the other girls, said something to them and giggled. The other three went inside as Candy Cane walked to the three men.

"Hi, Al. What's up?" she asked, eyeing the other two men.

"Candy, this is Captain Mike Masters of the Alaska State Troopers and Captain Jodi Eagle of the King County Sheriff's Department." Mike said hello while Jodi nodded recognition.

"Hi, fellas. I didn't do it, whatever it is," she joked.

Mike gave her a weak smile. "Ma'am, would you give me your real name?"

"If you promise not to tell." She was still in a joking mood. "It's Cary, Cary Kincaid."

Mike made notes. "How long have you worked here, at the Bush Company?"

"A little more than a year, why?" She was curious now.

"I understand you are a friend of Dava Bennett. Is that correct?"

"Yes, I'm her friend. Is that what this is about? Have you found her?"

"Yes," Mike said, "We've found her. I'm sorry to have to tell you this, but your friend is dead. We think she was murdered."

Cary put her hands over her mouth as though to stifle a scream. Tears formed in her eyes. "Oh, no. Not Dava, please not Dava."

"The two of you were good friends?" Jodi spoke for the first time.

"Yes," she said through the tears. "We worked together for three years."

"Where did the two of you work before you came here?" Mike asked.

"We worked in Fairbanks about four months. Neither of us liked it there. The weather is horrible. It was Dava's idea to come to Anchorage, I wanted to go back to Portland."

"Is that where you came from, before Fairbanks? Portland?" Again it was Mike's question.

"Yes. That's where I met her. She was so nice. She had been sick and was working hard to recover from some accident she'd had, but would never tell me what it was. She was having trouble moving. Dava worked so hard. At first, before she got her strength back, she just sort of hopped around the stage. You guys know she was really good-looking, so most of the customers didn't care. They just wanted to look at her. It took her almost six months of hard work to get back to where she could move like she wanted. And could she move. That girl was one of the best dancers I've ever seen in this business." Candy Cane wiped her eyes.

"Did you associate with her away from work?"

"Sometimes. She was a private person. She seldom dated. Sometimes we would go out to dinner or a movie. The truth is that we lived pretty dull lives away from the club. Some of the girls are into drugs and other things, but Dava and I made enough money to live on and weren't into it. Neither of us wanted that life, that's why we stayed such good friends."

"Was she dating anyone recently?"

"Not really. There was this guy she had been seeing for the last week. But they weren't into sex or anything like that. He just wanted company and he paid her to be his tour guide. She liked him. They went out and saw the sights during the day and she worked here at night. He didn't come to the club after that first couple of nights and she started traveling with him. I met him a couple of times. He seemed like a nice guy, kind of sad, but a nice guy."

"Do you know his name?" Mike asked, writing furiously.

"He said his name was Earl."

"What did he look like? Can you describe him?"

"He was older, about fifty, I'd say. A black guy. He was a little more than six feet tall with salt and pepper hair. He was quiet. Not the usual customer you get in here."

"Did he ever give a last name?"

"I can't remember if he did."

Jodi was chewing on his lip. He was trying not to say anything.

"Do you know where he was staying?" Mike continued the questioning.

"No. They always met at Elmer's Restaurant for breakfast. I never had breakfast with them, but that's what she told me. She said they just drove around and saw the sights. Once, they went to the Matanuska Glacier for the day." Cary began to cry again.

"I have a lot more questions to ask you, Cary." He closed his notebook. "I know this is difficult for you, but we don't know much about your friend and if we are to catch her killer, we need your statement. Will you come to my office tomorrow to make a full statement? I'll have my assistant type it up and you can sign it. It will take most of the day, so if you want me to, I'll talk with the club manager and have him give you the day off."

"Okay. I'll be there." She said.

"My office is in Palmer. Here is my card. If you think of anything else, please call me. I'll see you tomorrow."

"Captain Masters?" She turned back to talk to him again.

"Yes?"

"Thank you for treating Dava like a real person. Most people think we are all hookers, and a lot of dancers are. But some, like me and Dava, just dance. That's our profession."

Mike waved and smiled at her. "See you tomorrow."

Mike stepped to the door and motioned for Zeller to join them again.

When he came out the door, Mike met him. "The autopsy is finished and as far as we can determine, she doesn't have any relatives. Do you and the girl want to make arrangements for the body?"

Zeller thought a moment. "Yeah, I think that would be a good idea. These girls usually don't have any money. They spend everything they make. Yeah, Dava was a good girl. I'll make sure the club takes care of her. And, trooper?"

"Yes?" Mike replied.

"Thanks for treating Candy so well. She's a good kid."

"I'll need your official statement. Can you come to my office today or tomorrow? I'll have one of my officers take your statement and you can read it before you sign it. It won't take long."

"Be happy to do it. Thanks again." Zeller disappeared back inside.

"How about some lunch now?" Mike asked, as he turned the car back onto International Airport Road.

"Something light, maybe. I'm still full from that breakfast."

"Let's go to Elmer's. Give you a chance to see where they met." He hesitated a second. "Do you know something about the killer?"

Jodi's head snapped around. "Why do you ask?"

"Nothing specific, I just saw the way you looked when Candy described the guy Dava was dating. Do you know someone who looks like that?"

Jodi didn't want to lie to his new friend, but didn't want to implicate his old friend either. Besides it may not be him. "I'd rather not say, at this time. I need some time to talk with someone. I don't mean to leave you out in the cold on this, but I can't say right now." Jodi didn't feel good about not sharing the truth; it wasn't his way.

"If that's the way you want it." Mike replied, his voice a little cold.

"I promise you this, Mike. I don't want anything covered up. As soon as I talk to this guy, I'll call you. I'll call you first."

"I guess I can live with that. Just don't jerk me around, Jodi. I have a murder on my hands. If you know anything, I want it. I'll give you some time, but I want it."

"That's fair enough. I promise I'll give it to you. Do we have anything else to deal with today?" Jodi asked.

"I don't think so. We will be heading back to Palmer as soon as we finish lunch."

"I'll make a call to Alaska Airlines, then. I'll make a reservation for late tonight."

"I might be able to help you there. Do you have your tickets with you?"

"No, I don't."

Mike picked up the microphone for the radio. "Dispatch, patch me through to my office." A short pause, "Yes, captain. What can I do for you?" His assistant asked over the speaker.

"Will you call Alaska Airlines and make a reservation for Jodi Eagle on the redeye tonight? He has a ticket; he just needs a seat. Tell them it's official."

"Will do. Do you want me to call you back with the information?"

"No, we'll be in the office in a couple of hours."

The two men had a pleasant lunch. Jodi did his best to mend his fences. Mike seemed to understand. They talked about the investigation. Mike assured him he would have all the statements and reports copied and sent to Jodi in Issaquah. Back in the office, Jodi retrieved the cup he had been given. He would pack it carefully. His seat had been confirmed for the redeye flight tonight. That allowed for a pleasant dinner at the Club Paris with Mike Masters and his wife Judy. They drove to Beluga Point to watch the evening sun and the tide change. The whales were swimming past the big rocks, making a postcard setting for Jodi's last evening in Alaska.

On the plane ride home, Jodi could hear his grandfather's words. "Be honest," his grandfather had said, "But do not hurt others with your honesty."

"Sometimes," Jodi thought, "it is difficult to be true to your beliefs."

Jodi was glad to be going home. Eileen would meet him at SeaTac Airport.

CHAPTER 29

As the Alaska Airline jet descended, clouds obscured the Seattle area. It had been raining and as the jet broke through the cloud layer Jodi saw how the rain had made the world look green and lush. When he stepped off the airplane the fresh, clean air greeted him. Even the smell of jet fuel had been washed from the scents of the morning.

Eileen met him at the baggage carousel. He spotted her as he rode down the escalator. She was beautiful. She never seemed to age, only matured. He was nearly at the bottom level when his wife noticed him. She waved and smiled, he smiled back. Their eyes locked onto each other until they touched. He kissed her lightly on the cheek.

"It's good to be home," he said.

"I'm glad you're home, too," she replied. "I missed you. I can't remember the last time we were apart this long."

He hugged her around the waist as the two waited for the luggage to spill down the stainless steel slide.

"Is everything okay at home?"

"Yes, there weren't any great mishaps while you were gone," she answered. "I told you that Earl wants to see you, didn't I?"

"Yes. When did he get home?"

"Let's see. Hmm. I think it was the day you left for Alaska. Yes, it was. I remember. Linda called that evening and asked if you could come and see Earl. She said he was really sick and wanted to talk with you. He's still sick. Doctor Dennison has been there every day to see him."

"I'm sorry to hear that." Jodi hesitated. "Did Earl say where he had been?"

"I haven't talked directly to him, but Linda didn't say." She looked at him curiously. "Why?"

"I'd rather not say until I talk to Earl," he said. His bag came down the ramp and he released his wife long enough to retrieve it.

Eileen drove back to North Bend. Jodi offered to buy her breakfast on the way home but she refused. She said she would fix something for them at home. She told him that the boys had each called to check on their mother. They were both anxious for the new college year to start. They were fine and working hard, of course.

Jodi was silent most of the trip home, thinking about Earl and how he would go about asking where he had been. He hated the fact that his friend seemed to be the one responsible for the death of the person who had murdered his son. First he'd see Earl, and then he would stop to see Connie Lupine. Better call the office to let them know he would be late getting in this morning.

As the car approached the mountains and home, the sun broke through the clouds to light up the greenery in bright round patches like spotlights illuminating reflective gems in the trees. Once again the earth had been baptized and cleansed. Jodi's thoughts came back to Earl as the car slowed to make the stop at the foot of the exit ramp. He looked at his watch to check the time.

"Let's go to Linda and Earl's place before we go home. I need to see Earl and Linda probably hasn't left for the office yet. Do you mind stopping?"

"Of course not." She glanced at him. "Are you sure you're all right?"

"Yes, I'm fine. I just have some things on my mind right now."

Eileen stopped the car in front of the Campbell home. The couple walked up to the door. Linda answered with a broad smile. She motioned them into the house as she disappeared into the kitchen, followed by Eileen.

"Where's Earl?" Jodi called after them.

"He's upstairs in bed, he isn't feeling well. I'm worried about him." Linda called back to him. "Go on up. He's awake."

Jodi slowly climbed the stairs; this was not going to be a pleasant visit. At the top of the stairs he opened the door to Earl's room. He was shocked to see how terrible his friend looked. His eyes were red and only half open. His skin sagged about his face, which gave him the appearance of death. As Jodi opened the door, Earl waved his hand without lifting his arm from the bed. Jodi's old friend smiled.

"Hi, Jodi," he whispered weakly. "Come here and sit on the bed. I have a story to tell you."

"You look awful, Earl. What does the doctor say?"

He looked past Jodi, to the door. It was closed.

"Doc Dennison says I'm about to die. Something has gone wrong with my heart. He couldn't find out what it is, but he can't cure it either." He looked his best friend in the eyes. "Jodi, I need to tell you something. I'm about to die, I'm ready, but there are some things I want you to know before I do. Do you have your little recorder with you?"

"Sure." He reached into his coat pocket to bring out the micro cassette recorder. "Are you sure you want me to record this?"

"Yes, it's important." He seemed more frail than before. Jodi nodded and turned on the machine.

Jodi spoke into the recorder. "It is July twenty ninth, 0944 hours. I am in the bedroom of Earl Campbell. Mr. Campbell is ill and unable to get out of bed. The following statement is given voluntarily. Mr. Campbell, at this time I want to advise you of your rights." He read them from the card. "Do you still want to continue with this statement without your lawyer present?"

"Yes." Earl answered.

"Go ahead, Earl." Jodi laid the recorder on the sick man's chest.

"Seven years ago this month my youngest son was killed by some unknown person. They picked him up off the street, strangled him, and abused him. They left him on the side of the road like some dead animal. My little boy was only ten years old." Tears formed in Earl's eyes as he paused to catch his breath. "I have looked for that killer since that time. I made trips all over the United States. Every time I heard of a similar case, I would get on an airplane and go there to see if it was the same as my boy. I've been doing this for seven years. It's the only thing that has kept me alive.

"I traveled all over the country. But, none of the killings I investigated turned out to be the same. Still, every time I heard of one that was similar, I went.

"Then about ten days ago I got a tip. I met with someone who had some answers for me. I thought about calling you, Jodi, but I knew he would get a lawyer and get off. So, I found him myself, and I killed him." Again he rested to regain his strength. "I did it to avenge the death of my son and for the other four parents that have suffered for the past seven years. I killed him and I have no remorse. I'm glad I did it." He began to cry.

"Don't talk, Earl. Just rest a minute. Do you want some coffee?" Jodi asked.

"Thanks, Jodi. I would drink a cup." Earl struggled to wipe his eyes.

Jodi walked down to the kitchen where the two women were talking. "Can I get a couple of cups of coffee to take upstairs?"

"Sure. Do you want something to eat, Jodi?" Linda asked.

"No, thanks. But … Linda … " Jodi didn't know how to say it. "Don't go to work today, Linda. Earl is going to need you. And you had better call your lawyer to come over."

"Why, Jodi? What's happening?" Linda was beginning to panic.

"Earl is making a statement to me now. I'm afraid he's in a lot of trouble. I'll tell you more when Earl is finished with his statement." Jodi hated treating his old and dear friend like this. He took the coffee cups and walked back up the stairs to where Earl lay. He closed the door behind him when he entered the bedroom.

Earl didn't have the strength to pull himself into a sitting position. Jodi helped him sit up and propped him up with pillows. The two men sipped their coffee in silence.

Finally, Jodi took the cup from Earl's hand and asked if he was ready to go on. His old friend nodded. Jodi turned the recorder on again.

"Continuing with your statement now, Mr. Campbell, you said you had a tip as to where the killer was. Who gave you the tip?"

"It was Brice Roman. It seems that Brice is gay. He had a lover in South Seattle by the name of David Bennett. They had a long and, I guess, loving relationship. Brice said they got along fine until his partner started to talk about having a sex change. Brice didn't want him to have it. The two of them fought all the time after that. Brice said he tried to work it out with this Bennett guy, but he was adamant about having the operation. He kept asking Brice for money and Brice kept giving it to him. When he had nearly enough money for the operation, Brice realized he couldn't talk him out of it. He began to see less of this Bennett guy. Bennett got jealous and began to kill children in the North Bend area. He left them in obvious places so they would be found. He thought he would bring some kind of pressures to Brice. The trouble was that no one knew Brice was gay or that these killings had anything to do with him. Brice said he didn't know it until my son was killed. He figured it out then. He had been stealing information from your office and selling it to some reporter, but you caught him and fired him. Brice said he never saw Bennett again." Earl gave a sigh; this was taxing his strength.

He continued. "One day, about a month ago, Brice got a letter from Bennett. Bennett wanted to know if Brice would reconsider his feelings and the two of them might get back together again. He told Brice he had had the operation and that he was now a woman. He said he was dancing in a club in Anchorage, Alaska. Brice was still furious over getting fired from the sheriff's department and blamed Bennett."

"He hated Bennett for everything he'd put him through. Pressing him constantly for money. And then Bennett turned around and left him anyway, and used *his* money to get the sex change. That's what he'd lost everything for; his job, his money, his reputation." Earl was tiring.

"About ten days ago, Brice came to me. He told me who had killed my son and where he was. He told me about the sex change operation and about his involvement with Bennett. He told me that David Bennett was a topless dancer in Anchorage, using the name Dava Bennett. I don't know how Brice knew I was looking for the killer on my own, but he knew. He kept calling me about it and telling me I shouldn't let the guy get away with it. He wrote me a letter with the same stuff in it. The letter is there, on the nightstand. Finally I couldn't stand it any longer and went to Alaska.

"I found Bennett, who was now a good looking blond *woman*. At first I didn't know what I was going to do. I wanted to find out all I could about her, so I hired her as a sort of tour guide. She worked nights, so had all day to show me around. She knew a lot about the area. She is the one that told me about the tides and how high and fast they are. One day she showed me that spot at the mouth of the Knik River. I saw a big log there. I went to the hardware store and had a piece of cable made. Two feet long with a thimble in each end. I bought some plastic cable ties. I dug under the log and slid the cable under it. I put one cable tie on each end and started the end in the slot, making a loop. I buried it all in the sand." Earl was weak now, barely audible.

"The next morning we went for a ride. I told her I wanted to go to the mouth of the Knik River and take some pictures. When I got there I talked her into taking off her clothes. She was afraid I was going to rape her, but I assured her that all I wanted was pictures. After she took off her clothes, I pretended to pose her on the log. I reached down and slipped the cable tie over her foot and pulled it snug. I did the same thing with the other one. For a while she didn't realize she was tied. She just talked and laughed and posed for the pictures I was taking.

"I kept taking pictures for a long time. After a while she tried to get up and found she couldn't. By then the tide had begun to come in. She wanted me to untie her. I just kept asking her about the kids she had killed and about my son, Darren. She was crying and admitted she had done it. She said she was sorry. She said she did it to get even with her lover, Brice.

"She screamed and begged and cried and screamed some more. As the tide came in she tried to pull the plastic straps from her ankles. Those things are really strong and she couldn't do it. I sat on the riverbank and watched the entire time. I watched the water flow in and keep rising up her body. She kept screaming. Then, when the water was about up to her ribs, she began to get weak. She wasn't screaming as loud. She began to fall over, then sit back up and try to scream again. I think the cold water must have made her unconscious, because she just bent over, face first in the water, and never came up again. The water was so murky, I couldn't see her in there for a long time. Then as the water went back out, she became visible again. She was covered with silt from the river. After the tide was out, I took a pair of diagonal cutters I had bought from the hardware store, and cut her loose." He rested once more before continuing.

"I wiped her body off and put her up on the grass. I folded her clothes like she did Darren's and put them by her left arm. I tried to make her look like she made my boy look.

"The sun was shining and it was a beautiful day. I looked at the body and thought I should feel bad for her, but I didn't. I didn't feel anything. I didn't feel bad, and I didn't feel good. I just felt like my job was done."

"You know, Jodi?" Earl's sad eyes looked up at his friend. "If Brice hadn't kept calling me and goading me, I probably wouldn't have gone up there and killed her. I'm not sorry I did it, but I wouldn't have done it, if it weren't for Brice."

He was gasping for air now. "Anyway, after I killed her, and cut her loose, I turned in my rented Jeep Grand Cherokee at the Hertz counter and got on an airplane and came home. I think the strain has been too much, though. My heart is giving out on me. The doc says I don't have much time left. Linda is doing well with the real estate office and Matthew is in college. I'm ready. My job is done. I just wanted to make sure you had the real story on what took place. You and I have been friends for a long time and I wanted to be the one to tell this to you."

Jodi was in shock. He found it almost impossible to believe what he had just heard

"Have you told Linda?" Jodi asked.

"No, I'll do that as soon as you leave. Thank you, Jodi. Thank you for being there for us all those years. You are the best friend I have ever had."

Jodi turned off the recorder. "Don't you think you should rest a little while?"

"I will, Jodi. I want to talk with Linda first. Would you call her for me?"

"Sure."

"And would you stay? Would you wait until I finish talking with Linda? She is going to need a friend when I finish. She's going to think that I have let her down."

"Sure, I'll wait." Jodi got up from the bed. He was dazed from this revelation. He knew he should have arrested his friend, but he just couldn't do it. He walked down the stairs to get Linda. This would be even harder on her.

CHAPTER 30

The city of North Bend had changed during the past seven years. It had grown from a sleepy rural community into a suburban city. Every little valley had become home to families wishing to escape the urban life. The subdivision south of Interstate 90, started by the Emerald Empire Investment Corporation, was now a reality. Large and expensive homes had begun to spring up on roads carved into the hillside. As the new roads were established, so too, were the new neighborhoods. Each home represented a new family added to the community.

Linda Campbell and her partners had done well. They built homes, not just houses. Linda brokered most of the properties sold while Mary Alice Jade handled sales. Though the investors were not visible, their contractor was. He swiftly built large and well-designed homes on the hillside. Each home was situated so as to allow a view of the mountains rising up at the end of the valley. It was an orderly expansion. Seattle and Bellevue had lots of families willing to make the drive to town in exchange for the quiet rural life offered by this North Bend community.

Linda called Loretta Moser to tell her she would be late getting to the office. Loretta was now Linda's personal assistant. She had kept the office running smoothly for many years. As the business grew Loretta had become more indispensable; anyone wishing to see Linda must first pass through Loretta's gauntlet of questions. Loretta agreed to supervise the morning sales meeting and to assign any new projects to the staff.

Jodi had not told Linda any of the story her husband had just related; she'd have to learn it, firsthand, from Earl. Jodi felt sorry for the woman as she climbed the stairs. She was about to learn that her husband, as ill as he was, was a murderer. Her feelings and emotions for her murdered son were about to be brought back. All the hurt and sadness she had experienced, those many years ago, would again be fresh wounds in her soul.

Linda Campbell opened the door to her husband's room and went inside. She walked quietly to the bed. She sat on its edge and bent down to kiss Earl. He smiled, but seemed weaker than he had been earlier in the morning.

"Hi, sweetheart," she said. "You wanted to tell me something?"

"Yes." His voice was weak and strained. "I want you to listen. Please don't interrupt, I don't have the strength to go through this more than once."

Linda sat quietly on the edge of the bed, listening to the story. He told her of the calls from Brice and of the trip to Alaska. He told of the girl that he had hired to show him around. Finally he told his wife who the girl had been. About her sordid affair with Brice and how Brice had jilted him because he wanted a sex change. He told his disbelieving wife all the details. He told her about tying the woman to the log and allowing the tide to come in over her, killing her. He told her he had extracted an eye for an eye. A life for a life. He had killed the one responsible for the death of their son Darren.

Linda Campbell sat on the edge of the bed, in total shock. She found the story her husband told incredible. It wasn't possible for him to do those things. She wanted to scream, and she wanted to run. Most of all she didn't want any of this to be happening. Her life had suffered enough death and misery. Horrified, she found herself gasping for breath.

For several minutes Linda stood in shock, wringing her hands, not knowing what to say. Earl could see the bulging, Y-shaped vein above her eyes, distorting her forehead. She began to cry, then to sob. She sat back down on the bed, wiping tears from her eyes, but they continued to flow. Each time she tried to speak she only sobbed. Her face was distorted in a horrified, disbelieving expression.

Earl tried to reach her hand but didn't have the strength. "I love you very much." he said. "I'm not sorry I did it. I did it for Darren. I did it for us. I guess I just want you to understand that." After a moment of silence he tried to explain. "When she died, I felt relief. I felt like my job was done."

She was still crying. "I don't know what to say, Earl. No matter what happens, I love you. I wish you had talked with me about this before you went to Alaska. I don't know what to do."

"I just wanted you to hear the story from me. Jodi will have to arrest me and take me to jail. I have told him everything. He recorded my confession. I don't know what's going to happen now, but I have done my work.

It doesn't matter now. I love you, remember that. I loved you with all my heart and being."

Linda took his hand, crying even harder now. "I love you too, no matter what, I love you."

Earl Campbell took one last long deep breath, closed his eyes and smiled. One more time he opened his eyes to look at his beautiful wife. He gave a long sigh, closed his eyes and was gone.

Linda sat there on the edge of the bed, holding onto Earl's hand, for a long time. She thought of nothing in particular and yet her mind raced a million miles an hour. What would the community think when they found out Earl had killed someone? What would Matthew think of his father? How would she tell her son? What would Jodi do now? The more questions she asked herself the fewer answers came to her. It took several minutes for her emotions to subside enough for her to go down the stairs to the kitchen where her friends were waiting.

Jodi watched the old family friend walk down the stairs. He could tell something was wrong, but that was to be expected. Earl would have told her about killing Bennett. She showed no anger or remorse, only sadness.

When she reached the kitchen door, Jodi asked, "Are you all right, Linda?"

"I'll be fine." She said, then looked into Jodi's eyes. Tears filled her own eyes. "He's gone, Jodi."

"What do you mean, he's gone?"

"He's gone. He passed away. He told me he loved me, and then he was gone."

Eileen clutched her mouth to stifle a shriek.

"Are you sure?" Jodi asked.

"Yes. I should call Doctor Dennison to come, just to be sure, but he's gone," she sobbed.

"I'll call him for you." Jodi said before going up the stairs to check for himself.

Eileen had said nothing. But she held Linda around the shoulders consoling her. This family had suffered so much tragedy, she thought. Would this be the end of it?

Jodi used the telephone in the bedroom to call the doctor. After hanging up he called the police station where he was greeted by the friendly voice of his old secretary and friend, Miss Emma. He asked to speak with Connie Lupine.

"Hi, Captain. Glad you're back. How was the trip?" Connie's voice was warm

"Hi, Connie. The trip was fine; I'll fill you in later. Right now I have some other business. I need an officer at Earl Campbell's house. He has just died. I've called the doctor for an official pronouncement, but I've seen the body and he is dead. There will have to be an unattended death investigation. Call the Coroner to pick up the body."

Chapter 30

"I'm sorry Jodi. I know how close you and Earl were. I'll have someone there right away. Is there anything special you want me to do?"

"No. Let's just handle this as quietly as possible. I have some information for you, and as soon as I can get away from here, I'll be there to pass this along to you."

"I'll be here."

"Thanks, Connie. By the way, will you call Joan at my office and let her know I won't be in today?"

"Of course I will," the police sergeant said. "If you need anything else, just ask."

Jodi stayed to direct the police and the coroner. He answered their questions about how the death occurred. He hadn't decided how much to tell about Earl's story of the killing in Alaska. For right now, he didn't mention it. There would be plenty of newsprint about it when it was confirmed that he was the one that killed the dancer in Alaska. Jodi was certain that there would be little mention of the grief this father had suffered from the death of his son.

All the public officials had departed. The coroner had removed the body. The house was quiet once again. Eileen and Linda had spent most of the morning in the den, avoiding, as much as possible, contact with the people investigating the death. It was all routine. The law required that the police must investigate any death not attended by a physician and an autopsy must be performed by the coroner. With these steps set into motion, Jodi sat at the kitchen table, sipping hot coffee.

Earl could be at peace now, Jodi thought. His spirit had been lost in the shadow land for many years. It was bound to happen, he thought. A man cannot live without his spirit. Darren could now meet him and lead him from the land of the shadows. Yes, Earl could now be at peace.

The two women emerging from the den interrupted his thoughts. Both had eyes that were swollen and red. Each had dried their eyes now and applied fresh makeup to their puffy faces.

Linda was the first to speak. "I will have to call Matthew right away. And the office, I'll have to call the office."

"Our boys will want to come home too," Eileen commented.

"If you ladies can do without me, I have some things to do," Jodi said.

"Of course, Jodi. You have duties, I know. Please, we'll be all right here. You go and do what you have to do."

Jodi told his wife he would be at the North Bend Police Department if she needed anything. He walked out to his car to get the briefcase from the back seat, and walked the few blocks to his own home where he started his official car. The walk home was good. He was able to stretch his legs and enjoy the fresh air of the late morning. There were some high clouds, but the sun was quickly burning them off. He reached into his inside pocket to pull out a picture of Earl he had taken from the man's desk. "Good-bye old friend," he thought. "Good luck on your new journey."

In Connie's office he filled her in on his trip to Alaska. He told her about the death of the dancer and the confession made by Earl. Together they composed a cover letter about Earl's death. They sent the letter and the photograph of Earl, by fax, to Captain Mike Masters of the Alaska State Troopers, Palmer office.

With the fax in the machine, Jodi pulled a card from his wallet and dialed the trooper's number. The two men talked for a long time. Mike received the fax and promised to show the picture to Candy Cane for positive identification. The trooper said his men had found the car rented by Earl. It was a Jeep Grand Cherokee, owned by Hertz. The Hertz lot boys had been too efficient, though. The inside of the car had been checked for fingerprints, but none were found. The carpet, on the other hand, had retained several grains of glacier silt, presumably from the Knik River bank.

Alaska would now be able to close the file on the death of Dava Bennett. That would make Captain Masters happy. The phone call also solidified the trust and friendship between the two officers. Mike had stuck his neck out for Jodi by not demanding to know whom he suspected of the killing. Jodi had promised to give the trooper information as soon as it was confirmed and had done just that. The two men would remain friends from this day on.

"I guess this closes our file, too." Connie said.

"Not quite. I want to talk with the D.A. and see if we can arrest Brice on a conspiracy to commit charge. Earl said Brice had called him several times and needled him until he finally agreed to go after Bennett. Brice had to know that Earl was unstable and had been looking for his son's murderer. I think Brice played on that, and therefore, knowingly incited Earl to commit murder."

Connie grinned. "You get the warrant and I'll personally serve it."

"I know this warning isn't necessary, but don't let word of this out of the office. I don't want Brice skipping."

"You don't have to worry, Jodi."

"I know. Is Brice still working for that security company?"

"Yes, Merchants Security. He's still driving that blue Buick and lives at the same townhouse. I don't think he makes much money, just enough to make his payments on the townhouse and to meet monthly expenses. You never see him in town, anywhere."

Chapter 30

"Let's see if we can help him out. Perhaps we can get him some rent-free lodging for the next few years." Jodi wasn't joking.

He had returned all the files to Connie, who returned them to their proper cabinet. They made a copy of the confession given by Earl. A few loose ends were satisfied, taking up most of the afternoon. Late in the day the two sat in the sergeant's office drinking coffee. It seemed a little like the old days.

"Do you remember Jerry Lomax, Brice's reporter friend from the *World Inquirer*?" Connie asked.

"Yeah, I remember him. Where is he now, still in jail?"

"No, he works in Oregon as a laborer," she said. "I got a call the other day from some construction company that wanted to do a background check. He had listed his prison career on his job application. His new employer wanted to know about him and if he was dangerous. I looked him up. He did four years for his deals with Brice. He had a couple of years probation, but he is done with that now. Jerry Lomax is a free man."

"I was in the store a few days ago," Jodi told her. "The store manager told me that they don't carry the *World Inquirer*, even today."

Jodi called his office to check in and to tell Joan he would be in the early tomorrow. She said there was nothing important awaiting him; Lieutenant Burnside had done a good job in Jodi's absence.

Before hanging up, Jodi had one more request. "Call the D.A.'s office and see if I can get an appointment for nine tomorrow morning with Barbara Cantor. Tell her it's important and that the meeting will take more than an hour. See you in the morning, Joan."

Jodi said, "See you later," to Connie and Emma. It was time to go back to helping his wife care for Linda. He planned to take them out to dinner. Somewhere quiet. Somewhere where no one would recognize them. He made a patrol around the streets of North Bend before returning to the Campbell home. There had been many changes in the little town.

CHAPTER 31

One of the great innovations in communications is the cell phone. Jodi picked his up from the seat and punched the speed dial. After a series of beeps a telephone rang. The voice on the other end of the line was that of his wife, Eileen.

"Hi, honey. How is everything there?" he asked.

"We're doing fine. How about you?"

"I think I have finished for the day. How would you and Linda like to go to dinner? I'll bet she hasn't eaten all day."

"You're right, she hasn't. Yes, I think that would be a good idea."

"Okay. I'll take my car home and change clothes. Pick me up there."

It was almost six when the three began the drive to Bellevue. Eileen sat in the back seat while Linda sat up front with Jodi.

"Can I ask you a very personal question, Jodi?" she asked.

"I guess so. What's the question?" he asked, curiosity digging at his nature.

"I have been thinking about it all day. I've tried to attend church regularly. I took Matthew and Darren when he was alive. I still go as often as I can, but with Earl being sick and the business demanding so much time, I don't go often. The church demands that we accept and follow certain doctrines, and if you follow them throughout your lifetime, you will be judged good by God and be admitted to heaven. The past several years, since the death of our boy, Earl has left the church." She spoke of him as though he were still alive. "I guess my question is, do you think God will judge Earl by the way he was or by the way he became?"

Eileen was interested in how Jodi would answer this question. He had studied in the Lutheran church with her, but had always followed his Dakota way.

"You are asking a difficult question, Linda. Judging is God's bailiwick, not mine. I can only tell you, for certain, about the way I believe. That will be different from the way you believe."

"I think that's what I want to know," she said.

"It is difficult to explain. Have you ever heard of the Medicine Wheel?"

"I don't think I have."

"The Plains People believe in the Medicine Wheel. It is the basis for all things. Imagine, if you will, a circle of stones. There will be a stone at each of the four directions, north, east, west and south. Between these stones other stones are placed. The people sit around the wheel, one at each of the stones. If we stand an eagle feather in the ground at the center of the wheel and ask each of the people to describe it, each of the people will describe it in a different way. They all see the same feather, but they see it from a different perspective. Each of the people would see the feather from a different angle around the wheel. Each would describe it from his viewpoint, using his own life experiences to explain what he sees." Jodi looked at her. She was listening intently.

"Imagine, now," he continued, "that, at the center of the Medicine Wheel, an idea is suspended, not an Eagle feather. How much more difficult would it be to describe an idea than a feather? Since it is not a tangible item and cannot be seen, you could only be able to describe it from your past experiences and knowledge. Since each person learns from different experiences and environments, each would perceive it in a different way. And when listening to the others describe what they see, each would interpret what he heard based on his own experience and knowledge." He looked at her again "Do you understand what I am trying to explain?"

"I think so, but I'm not quite sure." she replied.

"Let me tell you what my grandfather taught me," Jodi continued.

This was the most Eileen had ever heard Jodi speak about the subject. She was fascinated.

"My grandfather was a wise man. He taught me that there are many trails across the shadow land. If one loses his way in the shadow land, he must search until he finds the trail again and continue his journey. Some trails are wide and distinct. Some are winding and hard to see. Some, like the one described in the Holy Bible, are straight and narrow. Each path becomes what it is by the way we are taught. All the paths go to the same place at the other side of the shadow land. Sometimes the paths cross, but one path does not block another; they only cross. In the shadow land you should follow the path you know, remembering all the while, that it is not the journey that is important, but the destination. Your goal is to come to the great encampment in the sun on the far side of the shadow land."

Jodi could see that his student was puzzled. "Let me put it another way. The Holy Bible is used by more than a hundred religions in this country, but they each have different methods of worship. Each teach that you should worship only the one true God and have no others. How many people do you know who revere and worship the church and not their God? The church is the path, not the destination. All churches say their God is merciful. The Lutherans, Eileen's church, say that your salvation is given as a promise, not earned by deed. You and I cannot judge Earl, Linda. That is the job of the Great Wakan. Leave it up to him."

There were tears in Linda's eyes again. "Thank you Jodi. Earl always said you had a different way of looking at things, a fresh perspective. He was right, thank you."

It was after ten when the three friends returned home. Eileen decided to spend the night with Linda while Jodi went home. He would have to go into the office early to prepare for his meeting with District Attorney Barbara Cantor. His talk with Linda had helped him to resolve some of his own feelings. He felt more relaxed now. He had taken a lock of hair from his departed friend before the Coroner arrived and would, on Saturday, hike to the top of Mount Si to ask his grandfather to help Earl across the shadow land where his spirit had dwelled for so long. Jodi was satisfied that Earl would now complete his journey.

Jodi was in his office a few minutes before 7:00 a.m. His desk had accumulated a tall stack of files for review and a basket full of new reports for him to review. He had sorted through the stacks when the door to his office opened and Joan, carrying a cup of fresh coffee, entered. She was smiling.

"It's good to have you back, Captain. The place just isn't the same without you."

"Thanks, Joan. I don't see anything really pressing in this stack. Do you have any urgent items for me this morning?"

"You have an appointment with the D.A. She said she could come here if you want her to do that. She said she was going to be by here on her way to court. I am to call her if you want her to come here."

Jodi sipped his coffee. "That would work better for me." He reached into his briefcase and pulled out a new white coffee cup with the Alaska State Trooper emblem on the side. He reached into the case again and came out with a micro-cassette recorder. "Copy this tape for me. It's a confession; I don't want it damaged. When you finish, I want the original logged into evidence. Give me the two copies you make. I'll give one of them to Barbara and keep the other."

Chapter 31

"I'll take care of it personally," she said. "And I'll call Ms. Cantor and have her come here." She turned on her heels and quickly set about her tasks.

Jodi busied himself with the stacks of papers on his desk. He had forgotten about time when his intercom buzzed. It was Joan.

"The D.A. called and will be here in ten minutes." She said.

"Thanks, Joan." He replied, looking at the clock on his wall.

He flipped the wheel on his Rolodex until he came to the number for Tom Logan. Tom was now news director at the Channel 5 station. He continued to do some news broadcasts and editorials, but mostly he selected news stories and directed the large staff of news people.

"Jodi, good to hear from you," The reporter said. "What's on your mind?"

"How would you like me to buy you dinner tonight?"

"I'd like that. Where would you like to go?"

"Salty's," Jodi said.

"This must be important. I don't get to go to Salty's that often."

"Is seven o'clock okay for you?" the captain asked.

"See you then."

As Jodi hung up the telephone, Joan opened the office door and announced the arrival of District Attorney Barbara Cantor. While the D.A. found a chair in front of the captain's desk, Joan placed the copies of the cassette tape on his desk, then exited the room, closing the door behind her.

"I wanted you to be the one to hear this, Barb. You have been with me on this case since the beginning. It seemed only fair that you be in on it at the end."

"Does this have to do with the Mount Si murders?" she asked.

"Yes." He dropped one of the copies into his desk drawer and put the other in tape player on his desk. "Before I tell you what I want, you have to hear this tape. I recorded this yesterday. It's a conversation with my friend Earl Campbell. It's his dying statement. He passed away about a half hour after he made this statement."

"Earl is dead?" she asked with surprise.

"Yes," he said sadly, watching her take a yellow legal pad from her briefcase.

"I'm sorry, I now how close you two were."

"Thanks, Barbara. I appreciate it. I want you to hear this tape. It explains everything. I want to know if you have the same reaction as I had when he told me the story."

It took several minutes for the tape to play from start to finish. Barbara Cantor listened intently, making notes on her yellow legal pad as she listened. When the tape finished, she scribbled another note. She was shaking her head when she looked up at Jodi, her face filled with an incredulous expression.

"Earl killed David or Dava Bennett?" she asked.

"Yes. I just came back from Alaska where I witnessed the interviews with the witnesses who saw him with the topless dancer. I have sent a picture of Earl to the captain of the troopers in Palmer for verification. With this statement backing up the other evidence, I don't think there's any doubt."

"Did you catch what he said about Brice? How he repeatedly called him to get him to do something crazy?"

"That's what I wanted to hear from you. I wanted to be sure my personal involvement wasn't coloring my judgment about Brice. I think there is enough on the tape to get an indictment for conspiracy to murder. Earl never said Brice asked him to kill Bennett, but Brice was aware of how unstable Earl had become. He knew that Earl had been traveling and looking for his son's killer for seven years. I think we can make a case. The question is, do you think you can get a conviction?"

"I'm about 80 percent certain. You have already mentioned a couple of things the defense is going to pursue." She wrote some more notes. "Let me run this by Glickman. If she will issue the warrant, I'll take it to the Grand Jury. If they return a True Bill, I'll set aside everything else until Brice is convicted. If we convict, his minimum sentence would be twenty years to serve before he is eligible for parole." She gave the detachment commander a wide grin. "I say let's go for it."

"Okay." Jodi said, a little excitement in his words. "Let me know, as soon as possible, how you make out with the judge." He stood as she put her notes into her briefcase.

She reached out to shake his hand. "It's been a long time coming, Jodi."

"Yes, it has."

The Assistant District Attorney went directly from King County Police Headquarters in Issaquah to the new regional courthouse. Armed with a copy of the cassette tape confession given by Earl Campbell and the notes taken in Captain Eagle's office, she strode confidently into Judge Miriam Glickman's chambers.

Burnside was in Jodi's office, reassuring himself, asking if he had handled this properly or that correctly. He related what had transpired in the office during the captain's absence. Jodi chastised himself for not previously delegating more responsibility to his lieutenant, a situation he would immediately change.

"You did a fine job, Steve," Jodi congratulated him. "I think I have been remiss in not taking advantage of your talents. Starting today, you are in charge of the daily operation of the detachment. All these reports and files on my desk now belong to you. I'll be here if you need assistance, but use your own judgement. You did it while I was gone, and you did it well. Just keep

Chapter 31

doing it." Jodi was trying to bolster the young lieutenant's confidence. "You're a good man Steve. I'm sorry I haven't given you more authority in the office. Next week we'll sit down and talk about areas of responsibility. I want some input, because the job we are about to change is yours."

"Thanks, Captain. I'll try not to let you down."

"I am going to be out of the office quite a bit in the next week or so. I am going to have to help make funeral arrangements and meet with Earl Campbell's lawyer. Linda told me I was his executor. I'm going to finish a couple of things here, in the office, then take the rest of the day off. I have a meeting in Seattle tonight."

The intercom rang.

"Ms. Cantor on line two for you, captain."

"That will be all for now, Steve," Eagle said as he jabbed the button for line two.

Burnside waved, picked up the two stacks of paper and carried them from the office. He was a happy man.

"Barb, what have you found out? Did you get the warrant?"

"The least you could do is say hello."

"Sorry. I got carried away with the anticipation."

"We got it. It will take until Monday to have it typed and signed, but we got it. The judge agreed that there are a couple of questions that are going to be hard to get past the reasonable doubt rule, but she thinks there is enough to get an indictment. She gave us the warrant."

"How soon can we serve it?"

"Monday afternoon," she replied.

"Do you have everything you need for your end? I plan to be out of the office the rest of the day."

"Yes, I think so." He heard the excitement in her voice too.

"Joan has my cell phone number, in case you need me."

He hung up the telephone, confident for the first time in seven years that things were on the right track. He took the second copy of the tape from his drawer and dropped it into his briefcase. He paged his secretary and was clearing his desktop when she arrived.

"I'm leaving for the day, Joan. I'll have the cell phone if you need me. I'm going to stop at the North Bend office and give Connie a copy of the tape for her files. Is there anything else I should know about before I leave?"

"No, I think we've put out all the fires for today. The lieutenant has a lot of work on his desk that will keep him busy the rest of the day." She thought for a moment. "I think we have it covered."

"Did you log that tape into evidence?"

"All taken care of."

"I'm out of here then," he said, as he picked up his briefcase and walked from the office.

Clouds were once again building against the mountains as he drove to North Bend. He hoped the weather would clear before he made his climb tomorrow morning. The ten-minute drive from Issaquah to North Bend was relaxing. Traffic was light. Jodi stayed in the outside lane, between two eastbound trucks. The one in the rear recognized his car, with red lights inside the rear window and radio antennas, as a police vehicle. Jodi saw him pick up his microphone to call on the CB to the truck ahead. He would be warning the front trucker to watch his speed. They couldn't know that the deputy's thoughts were far from the freeway and the trucks in his lane.

As he drove through town he could see the customers in the Mar-T cafe. Ester Parks was there serving meals and coffee as she had done for so many years. She had gained considerable weight, but still had the happy nature she possessed during all the years of waiting table. A lot of waitress' had worked in the Mar-T cafe over the years, but Ester was the local favorite.

Two deputies were standing by the side the building when their captain stopped at the curb. When they saw the boss's car, they ended their conversation and drove away. "Some things never change," Jodi thought.

Miss Emma came from behind the rail to by her desk to give him a hug when he entered the office. She knew, too, perhaps better than anyone outside the families, just how close Earl and Jodi had been. She had listened to the two men verbally spar with each other each time Earl came in to visit. Emma showed the captain into the sergeant's office. She stepped out for a short moment, then returned with fresh coffee. Jodi thanked her as she returned to her duties at the front desk.

"How are you holding up, Jodi?" Connie wanted to know.

"I'm fine."

"What's on your mind, Captain?"

"Nothing special. I just wanted to give you a copy of this tape." He pulled it from his briefcase and handed it across the desk. "Losing a friend is tough," he said. "But you know, this is the first time since this thing began, seven years ago, that we have more answers than questions."

"I'm glad it's about over," she said.

"Me too. I have a meeting with Tom Logan tonight. I am planning to fill him in on the latest developments. He deserves that. Is there anything you want me to pass along to him?"

"Just tell him hello. He's turned out to be a good friend to this office."

Chapter 31

"I won't be in until Monday. If you need me for anything, call me on the cell phone." He stood to leave.

He drove to the Campbell home to be with his wife and the widow of his friend. They would be awaiting the arrival of the three boys. Jodi hoped the reunion wouldn't be too sad.

He shared his plans with Eileen. She agreed she should stay with Linda and await the arrival of their boys and Matthew. Jodi said he would go to the lawyer's office to arrange for execution of the will, and call Harry Makin to make arrangements for the funeral. He would take the family sedan to his meeting in Seattle this evening; If she needed a car she would have to use Linda's. Eileen drove the car to their home and waited while Jodi showered and changed for his afternoon schedule.

"I'll be hiking up to the top of Mt. Si in the morning," he told her.

"I thought you might. Do you have everything you need?"

"Yes." He kissed her on the forehead. "I love you. You have put up with a lot from me over the years, haven't you?"

"It's been no trouble at all," she said, smiling.

"I should be home by ten this evening. I'll pick you up at Linda's. Matthew will want to spend the evening with her. They need to talk."

"You're right, they need time together. The boys can bring me home. You just go and enjoy your meeting with Tom."

He dropped her at the Campbell home, waved and drove to the office of Glenn Alger. Five years ago Glenn had taken a position with Lloyd Bemis. He was an up and coming young attorney, aggressive and shrewd like Lloyd had been in his younger days. Two years ago, when Lloyd Bemis died, Glenn become the lawyer for the Campbell business as well as the personal attorney for the family. Jodi's meeting with him took only a few minutes. Arrangements were made to start the legal process which would settle the estate of Earl Campbell.

When he left the office, he drove to the east end of town and the home of Torval Laxo. Jodi knocked on the door. Torval must have been napping from the sleepy-eyed look he presented at the door.

"Come in Jodi. I haven't seen you in a while."

"I'm sorry, Torval," Jodi explained, "I have a meeting in Seattle so I don't have time to visit now. I just wanted to ask if I could use the sauna tomorrow afternoon. I am going to the top of the mountain tomorrow and I would like to have a sweat when I come down."

"What time do you want it?" Torval asked, "I will have it ready."

"Thanks, Torval. I should be down around five o'clock. How about joining me?"

"By golly, I t'ink I'll just do that." His wide grin told Jodi how much the old man liked being asked. It was lonely for him in this big house without Ma and the twins.

CHAPTER 32

Rain began to streak across his windshield before he reached Issaquah. It was raining hard by the time he reached Bellevue, and by the floating bridge the wipers would not keep up. Lightning flashed brightly in the sky, but he could only see the light as it reflected on the water on his windshield. Traffic slowed to a crawl as he exited the freeway and made his way through the shipyard area of the city. The rain slowed slightly by the time he passed over the Canal Bridge and turned onto Alkai Beach. It was almost seven when he parked his car in the lot and made the dash to the front door.

Tom Logan was standing inside, awaiting his arrival. The hostess who verified their reservations and showed them to their table near the window facing the water, left them. The view was spectacular. The summer lightning storm was passing the city, but the late afternoon sun was peeking under the clouds, lighting up the buildings in the city across the channel. The sky behind the jagged skyline was black as midnight with shards of lightning escaping here and there, jumping from one cloud to another. The rain had left the city wet and clean. Lights were beginning to turn on as the setting sun reflected off the glass in the tall buildings that now marked the downtown area. To the north, the Space Needle stood like a giant beacon. A picture taken of this scene, now, would surely be the high mark of any photographer's career. It was truly beautiful.

Jodi seldom drank, but joined Tom in a pre-dinner drink. The two men toasted their friendship. The waitress took their orders; they both ordered the halibut. Neither man spoke for several minutes, but instead just enjoyed the view. A tug towed a large barge up the channel as they watched.

The silence was broken when the waitress brought their salads.

"What's on your mind tonight, Jodi?" Tom asked, digging into his lettuce.

"I am about to let you in on the final chapter of the Mount Si Killer story. The trouble is, you can't use it until at least Monday. We will have the final warrant and make the final arrest in the case on Monday afternoon." Jodi crunched a bite of his salad.

"Are you saying you have found the killer?" Tom was deeply interested.

"Yes, we've got him, and I'll tell you the whole story if you promise me you won't use it until we serve the last warrant on Monday."

"Of course you have my word." He was excited now.

Between bites, Jodi related the entire story. He gave the reporter the name of the killer and the facts of his sex change operation. How he had meticulously avoided any chance to have his fingerprints taken during his lifetime. He told about David Bennett becoming Dava Bennett the dancer. He recapped Dava's career for the reporter.

The waitress took the salad plates away. Tom ordered another drink; Jodi ordered coffee. Tom had aged during the seven years of their acquaintance. His hair was flecked with gray, but he still had it all. He had changed from brown tweed blazers to gray, to highlight the gray in his hair for the television cameras. His voice was still smooth and strong, though the character lines on his face were now becoming deep creases.

He listened intently to the captain's tale, alternating the use of his fork and his pen. He filled page after page with notes, not stopping to ask questions, but nibbling at his halibut from time to time.

Jodi had been on the inside of the story for the past several days, but it was still difficult to talk about his friend Earl's involvement in the death of Dava Bennett. But here, and now, the whole story must be told, and he withheld nothing from the reporter. His voice straining with emotion as he told of Earl's death.

The busboy cleaned away the plates. The waitress came back with the coffeepot. She filled Jodi's cup again. Tom pulled his notebook to where his plate had been and ordered coffee. She recommended the fresh strawberry pie. Both men ordered it; they had time, there was more to tell.

Jodi explained the several key points needed to prove conspiracy to a felony. He said it was going to be difficult to convince a jury that Brice intentionally incited Earl to kill his former lover. That job was up to the District Attorney. Barbara Cantor had promised to do her best and believed she could get a conviction. The whole thing hinged on intent.

"The judge was convinced," Jodi noted. "She issued a warrant for Brice

Chapter 32

Roman's arrest. The warrant will be typed and ready for her signature on Monday. That's why I can't let you use the story before then. I'll call you on Monday and let you know what time we plan to arrest him. If you want to send a camera crew out there, I'll see that you get the pictures."

"Oh yeah! I'll be there with my video crew. What time do you expect this to happen?" Tom asked, moving his notepad to make room for the strawberry pie.

"I will call as soon as I have the warrant and know when the officers are available. I'll let Connie Lupine and her men do the arrest. Since he was fired from the department, Brice has worked as a security guard for Merchants Security in Bellevue. He works exclusively on night shift. He never leaves his townhouse before seven in the evening. We will probably do this some time around three. I promise, I'll let you know the time."

"Are there any other questions you want to ask me?"

"I can't think of any. You covered everything pretty well. It's been a long time coming, hasn't it?"

"Too long." Jodi reached for the check.

"You get the tip; I'll get the dinner," the reporter said as he snatched up the bill. "It's worth it. I hope we can have dinner again sometime soon. I would like to take you and your wife to dinner under happier circumstances."

"I'd like that. I'll buy next time." Jodi slid his chair back and looked out the window at the lights of the city. "I want you to know how much I appreciated your keeping this case alive over the years. You have always allowed the families to keep their dignity. In a town as small as North Bend, that has meant a lot. Thanks, Tom. For everything." The two men shook hands and walked from the restaurant.

The streets and highways were wet, but the rain had stopped. Jodi stayed in the right lane on the drive home. He drove slowly, below the speed limit. It was probably unethical to give Tom exclusive access to the arrest on Monday, but he had become a friend to the department over the years. He deserved the story.

Philip's car was in front of the house when he arrived home. He parked in the driveway, next to his patrol car. Philip and Kyle were in the kitchen talking to their mother when their father came home. Kyle hugged his father, but Philip was far too sophisticated for that; the two male adults shook hands.

Eileen slipped her arm around her husband's waist and squeezed. The boys competed for conversation time, each telling what was currently taking place in their lives. Though he had not yet begun his law studies, Philip was clerk for a large law firm where he was getting experience toward his law degree. Kyle would be a sophomore next September. He was currently working in the Moscow, Idaho office of the Washington Waterpower Company. He had not yet made up his mind about a major, but was leaning toward business or accounting.

The Campbell boy, Matthew, was in his fourth year at WSU. He would be a senior in September. He studied business and specialized in real estate. He was a running back on the Cougar football team and had gone to the Rose Bowl in Pasadena. Michigan State won the game in the last three minutes. Jodi had gone with Earl to watch Matthew play.

The chatter went on until after midnight when Jodi said he had to get up early in the morning. He explained to the boys that he would be gone most of the day Saturday, and invited the two of them to join him in the sweat lodge in the afternoon, but both boys had plans.

Upstairs, Jodi found a small silk pouch. Eileen had bought it to keep jewelry in when they traveled. He opened a folded piece of paper he had taken from the dresser drawer. Inside was the lock of hair he had cut from Earl's head. This was placed in the silk pouch on the dresser with the bow and the arrows. From the closet he took his pipe and the beaded bag that went with it. He put these items on the dresser with the others. Everything was ready for morning.

The alarm rang at five a.m. Jodi slipped out of bed, shaved and dressed as quietly as he could. In the kitchen he made coffee that perked while he ate a bowl of cold cereal. He sat alone in the kitchen, sipping his first cup of coffee, reflecting on the meeting, the previous evening, with Tom Logan.

The sky was getting its first hint of daylight as he started his car for the drive to the trailhead at the foot of Mount Si. He slipped the daypack on his shoulders and fastened the strap across his chest. He had been to the top of the mountain many times, but it seemed, with each passing year the trail became longer and steeper. He used a picnic bench as a warm-up and stretching bar, then began the long trek to the top of the beautiful mountain.

It took him two hours to climb to the top, where he pulled the pack from his back and opened it. First out of the bag was a towel. He mopped his face and neck, then reached for a bottle of water. A couple of long drinks replenished the fluids lost on the climb. He began to relax. He stepped to the edge of the knoll to survey the view below him. The sun was bathing the valley in morning light. Yesterday's rain made everything seem fresh and clean, glistening in the sunlight.

Jodi returned to his pack to get his belongings. These objects were sacred to the beliefs of the Dakota people. He laid the pipe atop the beaded bag in which it was kept. His Indian tobacco lay beside it. He placed the bow and arrows on the ground in front of him; they were symbolic, but his grandfather would be pleased to see them. He got a Bic lighter from a side pocket in the pack and placed it beside the tobacco bag. He double-checked the items to see that everything was in place.

Finally he took the small silk pouch from the pack. He made a small tripod of sticks and hung the pouch from its peak. "We are here, old friend, together." He said to the small silk bag.

Jodi had been away from the reservation for a long time and his recollection of the Dakota language was beginning to fail him from lack of use. He tried desperately to remember the words to one of his Native American songs. A word every now and then was all his mind could muster. He hummed what he could remember of the melody anyway, sitting on the ground beside the tripod, humming, rocking to and fro as he stoked the pipe.

When it was full he lit the tobacco, took several long puffs to make sure it was burning properly. He got to his feet and puffed the pipe. He offered the pipe to each of the four directions, as his grandfather had taught him. When he had offered the pipe and his prayers to each of the winds, he again sat beside the tripod of sticks. He let the smoke from the pipe billow up around the small red pouch hanging below its center. He called upon his grandfather to join him. He asked that his grandfather come to talk with him and to meet his friend Earl. He would ask his grandfather to help Earl pass through the shadow land where his spirit had lived for these many years.

As he sat there atop the green mountain, he heard the voice of his grandfather speaking to him.

"It has been a long time since you have smoked the pipe and talked with the Great Wakan. You should do this more often to be sure he will recognize your spirit when the time comes for you to cross the land of the shadows."

"You are right, Grandfather, and I will try to come more often in the future." Jodi puffed the pipe and offered it to his grandfather.

"Why do you care for the spirit of this dead one?" The grandfather asked. "He is neither a relative nor is he even Dakota."

"He is my friend, Grandfather. He has stood by my family and me for many, many years. His spirit was lost in the shadow land when his son was killed seven years ago. He has come now to join his spirit. I would like you to show him the way across the shadow land. He will need help to find his spirit and to be led to the right path. He has been a good man, Grandfather, and I would like you to help him. I would also like for you to take him to the Great Wakan and tell him what I have said. The spirit of his son, Darren will be there, somewhere. Darren was just a small boy when he was taken. Please Grandfather, help them find one another."

"I cannot say what the Great Wakan will do. I will intercede for your friend and help him to find his son. I will tell the Great Wakan what you have said. I believe he will be pleased."

Jodi then puffed the pipe again. "Earl, my old friend. I leave you in the care of my grandfather. He will help you find your spirit and lead you from the shadow land. Don't be afraid. All men must walk through the shadow land; most walk this land alone. You have the help of a good man who was once my grandfather."

"I am proud of you, my grandson. You have been a patient hunter. You have hunted the bear for many years and now his hide warms your lodge." Grandfather spoke. "There is a time when it is best to pass the things you have learned to the young hunters. I think the time will come soon when you will not want to hunt, but sit by the fire and tell of the successful hunts you have experienced. When that time comes, you should think of returning to the Devil's Heart, to go home. There are young hunters who can learn from you. You have much to teach. The young hunters need to learn from the old ones so they do not make so many mistakes."

The afternoon sun was warm and there was a certain peace on the top of the mountain. Jodi spoke to his departed friend and wished him well on his journey. He took the small red silk bag from the sticks. He dug a small hole in the dirt under where the sticks had stood. He buried the bag and said goodbye to his friend Earl as he covered it with soil.

He packed his belongings, took a long drink of water and began the descent from the mountain. He came down the mountain in long determined strides. He felt good knowing that Earl's spirit would now be at rest.

It was four-thirty when Jodi reached his car. He pulled the pack from his back and took another drink of water. He would go to Torval Laxo's house for a sweat and then it would be time to go home to be with his family.

CHAPTER 33

The weekend had been spent with his family, comforting Linda and Matthew Campbell. Harry Makin had called to make arrangements for the funeral. Jodi was obliged to handle the preparations for the family. Harry told Jodi he would not be able to have the funeral on Tuesday as planned. It would have to be done on Wednesday. Earl had purchased several plots for his family and would be interred next to his son, Darren.

"You were his closest friend," the undertaker said. "It would be appropriate for you to say a few words about the man you knew so well."

"I don't know if I can do that," Jodi answered.

"It would mean a lot to the family and his other friends."

"Let me think about it."

"I'll get back with you on Monday."

Jodi had other things on his mind on Monday. He quickly went through the stack of paper, which had accumulated over the weekend. Most of it he referred to Lieutenant Burnside. In his absence Steve had handled the detachment well. It was time to pass more responsibility to the young lieutenant. Joan would help him through the learning process.

Jodi called Sergeant Lupine to be sure everything was ready when the warrant for the arrest of Brice Roman arrived. Everything was in place. She had asked Larry Piedmont and Gary Durbin to serve the warrant; two young officers eager, to participate, were selected to be the backup team. A capable and aggressive young officer, Tim Grissom had been with the department for three years. John Beardsley, the other backup man, had been on the streets for only a year. He was probably the best shot in the detachment ... not that she expected there to be any shooting.

"If you have no other matters pressing you at the moment, come to my office and wait for the warrant," Jodi requested.

"Be there in a half-hour," Connie answered.

The captain had just hung up the receiver when the intercom announced he had a visitor. Joan opened the door to allow Pete Kaufman into the office. She disappeared to bring coffee for the two men.

"Pete! Good to see you. Have a seat." Jodi stood to shake Pete's hand. "What brings you to the outer limits?"

Joan returned with the coffee.

"Thank you, Joan. I'm expecting Sergeant Lupine soon. Let me know when she arrives."

Pete Kaufman watched the assistant leave the room. When the door was closed he turned to Jodi. "I don't want to take up too much of your time. I know you have other things on your mind today. I hope you know how I feel about Earl. He was a good man. Are you going to be able to get the warrant for Brice today?"

"We're waiting for it now. Connie is coming to pick it up as soon as it arrives. I'll wait here and listen to the radio. I would really like to be out there but it would be unfair to Connie to usurp her authority in this case."

"I won't stay too long, Jodi. I really came to see you about some political points I thought would interest you." Pete smiled.

"You know I don't like the political end of the job, Pete."

"Yes, I know. But, I think you'll be interested in what I have to say." He was smiling again, that smile he used when he was about to surprise you. "The sheriff has decided not to run again."

Jodi was surprised. "What made him change his mind?"

"His physical. He found out he has some health problems that are aggravated by the stress of his job. His wife convinced him to quit."

"Wow!" Jodi exclaimed. "There isn't much time before election. Who are they picking to run on the ticket in his place?"

"That's the reason for my visit." Pete had that smile again. "They have asked me to run."

Again Jodi was surprised. "That's great, Pete. Congratulations."

"If you like that idea, you'll love my next one." He laughed.

"What idea is that?"

"I want you to be my chief deputy." Pete announced. "If you stay for the full thirty years, you have eight years left. That would make you my chief deputy for two terms, assuming I get elected. You can run the department and I'll do the political and administrative duties. We worked well together

Chapter 33

in the past and I don't know anyone more qualified. I am really serious about this. Will you consider it?"

Jodi leaned back in his chair. "Do you have any other surprises for me this morning?" He was nearly in shock. "Are you sure you know what you're asking?"

"Yes, I know. I know you have family ties to the North Bend Township. I know how you feel about moving into the city. You would be able to continue to live in North Bend. It would be a long commute, but, if you like, I can arrange to have a car pick you up each day. I really need you, Jodi. I have been in town for seven years now and the one thing I have learned is that you have to keep people around you that you can trust. I need you. In fact, if you turn me down, I may not run for office. It means that much to me to have you on board. Will you think about it?" Pete knew better than to pressure Jodi any more. "Talk with Eileen and get back to me. Call me if you have any questions. Will you do that?"

"This isn't a decision I can make lightly, Pete. I am going to have to think about it. How soon do you need an answer?"

"By Friday, if possible." Pete stood, ready to leave. "Give it some serious consideration, Jodi. I'll be waiting for your call."

"I'll have an answer for you by Friday. And thanks for the offer, Pete."

As Pete left the office, Jodi could see Connie Lupine at Joan Wood's desk. "Come on in, Connie."

As she came into the office, the telephone rang. It was Barbara Cantor.

"Judge Glickman just signed the warrant. I'll be by your office in five minutes." Deputy District Attorney Cantor took great pride in her work, and rightly so. She did her job well.

"Connie's here waiting for it now."

Connie stood, smiling, in anticipation of this arrest.

Barb Cantor entered the open office door with deliberate steps. She had the official documents in her hand. She handed them to Connie and grinned. "Good luck."

"Keep me up to speed by radio. I want to know what's going on out there."

"Will do," she said, waving the warrant as she departed. She looked at her watch. It was late, two p.m. She picked up her cell phone, hit the green turbo-dialer and waited for the office phone to ring.

Miss Emma answered. She was instructed to have the arrest team meet her at Brice's townhouse, quietly. She would be there in ten minutes.

Two patrol cars were in the parking lot when she arrived. She quickly appointed Piedmont and Durbin to take the front door and to announce the serving of the warrant. She instructed the two rookies to cover the back door, in case Brice decided to run for it when they knocked on the front door. Connie stayed in her patrol car, close to the radio, during the initial approach.

The two young officers went around to the back of the townhouse. It was an end unit with no windows on the east end where the officers must walk. As they approached the rear corner of the building, they waved a signal to the officers assigned to the front door.

Gary Durbin, now fully recovered from his injuries, held the warrant. Larry Piedmont knocked on the front door. There would be personal satisfaction in this arrest for both these men

Brice worked nights and was just starting his day at two in the afternoon when someone knocked on his front door. He was drinking his first Coca-Cola of the day. Through the narrow side window he could see uniformed officers at the door. His patio door was open, making for a quick and easy exit. As he was deciding whether or not to use it, the officers knocked again.

"Police officers, Mr. Roman. Please open the door, sir. We have a warrant."

Brice didn't know what the warrant was for, but he knew he wasn't in the mood to be arrested. He grabbed a shirt from the back of a living room chair and turned to exit through the patio door. As he turned, an officer, weapon drawn, stepped through the door and moved to his left. As he did so, another young officer stepped into the doorway, crouched, weapon in hand.

Brice instinctively slapped at the weapon in the hand of the officer closest to him. He knocked the automatic from his hand. As the officer turned to watch his gun fly through the air, a chopping blow to the throat struck him. The impact of the blow was absorbed, and partially blocked, by the muscles in his neck. The young officer's throat and voice box were damaged, making it impossible to breathe. He fell to the floor gasping and holding his throat.

His inexperienced partner watched the action and saw his partner fall. Before he could react, he caught a foot squarely in the groin, immediately rendering him unconscious.

Brice saw the key to the patrol car tucked behind the buckle of the first officer's duty belt. He pulled the key from the belt and read the number stamped on it. He had been a police officer a long time and knew the number on the key would match the one on the front fender of the car. He would be able to find the right car quickly. He ran from the apartment, key in hand, as a foot began to slam hard into the front door.

Brice ran around the end of the townhouse, using the same path the officers had used to approach the building. Near the front corner he could see the car he needed. It was parked in the center of the parking lot with the nose of the

Chapter 33

car pointing toward the street. The officers who had been forcing his front door were now inside. He made a dash for the patrol car. The key opened the door. He jumped into the driver's seat, slipping the key into the slot and giving it a twist as he sat. The car roared to life. He pulled it into gear and raced from the parking lot. At the street he turned right, heading east on the old highway. He would get on the freeway at Edgewick Road. He had to think; which way from there, east or west, which way should he run?

He was speeding past Torval Laxo's home when he heard Connie Lupine on the radio. She reported she was in pursuit of the suspect in a sheriff's car, and notified dispatch to call the highway patrol for assistance. They were now approaching Edgewick Road.

Brice thought he stood a better chance on the open highway than he would by heading back toward the city. He crossed the overpass on Edgewick Road and sped down the ramp to the eastbound lanes of Interstate 90, trying to estimate how long it would be before the highway patrol would have a roadblock set up. He weighed his options. There were several forest service roads into the mountains, but this was not a good car for backwoods travel. He would never make it to Ellensburg, he guessed. Maybe as far as Cle Ellum, but where from there? What then? He was speeding up Snoqualmie Pass at breakneck speed. Traffic was heavy, especially truck and motor home traffic. His options were dwindling.

The top of the pass, he thought he could make a U-turn at the top of the pass and go back toward the city. Once he reached the Bellevue area, there were a lot of roads he could take. Once he reached a populated area, he could ditch this marked car and find other transportation.

He had been so intent on his driving and preparing to make his return down the other side of the pass that he didn't notice just how close Connie Lupine had come. He was further distracted when he saw the red lights of a Highway Patrolman waiting at the top of the pass. He slowed to turn back to the westbound lane. Connie anticipated his move when she saw the trooper ahead. She turned her car alongside his, forcing him to the outside edge of the road and into the concrete retaining wall. She fought the wheel to regain control of her vehicle after the impact. Metal and plastic parts flew from both cars. The Highway Patrolman was now moving in their direction.

The two battered cars came to a stop about ten yards apart, dust obscuring the vision of both drivers. Connie jumped from her car the instant it stopped. She used the car as a shield, drew her weapon and rested it across the hood of her car. She could see Brice inside the other car, moving around. The door of his car was jammed from the impact. He slid across the seat, slipping the shotgun from its locked restraint as he went. He kicked the passenger door and, he too, was now outside his car.

"Out in front of the car, NOW. Down on the ground, face first, Brice. Do it now," Connie ordered.

The Highway Patrolman was now stopped behind Connie's car, and heard Connie give Brice orders. He walked between the cars, toward where Brice was crouched and hiding.

"Come on Mister. Get your butt out in front of that car. There's no place for you to go. Get out there."

Brice didn't take time to think about it. He swung the 12-gauge Remington shotgun over the hood and fired at the Highway Patrolman, who had never drawn his weapon, but had his hand on the butt of his gun. All nine pellets from the 00-Buckshot round stuck him squarely in the chest. Connie watched in horror as the cop's body flew backward, then crumpled to the ground. She instantly fired two rounds, and Brice disappeared behind his car. Had she hit him? It was impossible to tell from here. She slipped back to the door of her car and reached for the microphone on her radio.

"Dispatch, I have an officer down. Repeat, officer down. Send and ambulance and I need backup." She kept her eye on the other car, looking for the man hiding behind it.

"Backup is on the way. They report an ETA of less than two minutes."

Just then Connie caught a glimpse of the top of Brice's head moving behind the hood of the car.

"You're not helping yourself, Brice." She called. "Throw out the shotgun. Come out and lie down in front of the car." She waited. Nothing.

"Come on Brice. You can't win. Backup is coming." Again she waited. Again nothing.

She could hear the sirens of the approaching cars now. It gave her great comfort to know she wouldn't be here alone much longer. "They're coming, Brice. Throw out the shotgun and come out."

Brice stole a peek over the hood of the wreck. The Patrolman's car was behind Connie's with the engine still running. If he could make it to the car he might have a chance. He moved to the rear of his own car, trying to see where Connie was hiding. She had her head down. He held the shotgun over the rear of the car and fired twice, his spent cartridges clattering on the pavement. He still couldn't see the deputy. The sirens were getting close; he would have to make his move.

Brice sprinted toward the Highway Patrolman's car, firing his shotgun as he went. He had reached the open door of the car when two more Highway Patrolmen made the U-turn and skidded to a stop at the scene. The first officer opened his door as Brice turned the shotgun on his car. The pellets struck the door and the officer dived back into the seat.

The door of the second patrol car was opening and Brice swung the barrel of his weapon toward the new menace. Connie was in the open, behind Brice now.

"Brice, drop it," she commanded, her weapon trained on the fugitive.

He fired a shot at the second officer, then turned to face Connie. He jacked a new round into the shotgun as he turned. He never got the chance to fire it. Connie fired two quick shots. One struck Brice in the left hand, the other caught him at the base of the throat. As the second shot went off, the second officer fired over the top of the door of his car, striking Brice twice in the back before he fell to the ground.

It was over. Sergeant Lupine checked the man she had just shot. He was dead. She went to the side of the road and threw up.

More officers and deputies were now arriving. An ambulance was slowing to a stop near the downed officer. Three paramedics raced from the rescue vehicle carrying red boxes. One of the medics checked the officer, then shook his head. He then checked Brice. The bullets had done their work. He, too, was dead.

A medic asked Connie if she was okay, and she nodded. He offered her a bottle of water. She took it, rinsed her mouth, then took a long drink. It was warm, but it tasted good.

She walked back to her car, retrieved the mike and reported what had taken place.

Captain Jodi Eagle picked up the radio. "I'm glad you're okay. I'll have someone else stay with the cars until they are removed. Get the measurements and have one of the Highway Patrolmen drive you back to the office. I'll meet you at your office. Good job, sergeant." He concluded. He was glad it was over.

CHAPTER 34

The balance of the day, Monday, was given to writing the reports on serving the warrant on Brice Roman. Could things have been done differently? A patrolman was dead. The gunman was dead. Could it have been avoided? The dead patrolman, Vincent Newly, was a family man. He had a wife, a schoolteacher in Bellevue, and three children ranging in age from seven to ten, all in school. Why had Brice fired on the officer? It didn't make any sense. There was no way he could have known what the warrant was for, but he must have guessed. He must have made up his mind not to go to jail, under any circumstances.

Tim Grissom and John Beardsley were taken to the hospital for a checkup and both were released. The pain would remain with each of them for several days, but both would recover from their injuries. It would take much longer for the humiliation to heal. In their youthful exuberance they had made mistakes. Those mistakes could have, and nearly did cost them their lives. It was a lesson each man would carry with him for the rest of his career.

Gary Durbin had stayed with the injured officers until the ambulance arrived to take them away. He contacted the building maintenance man, an aging Tom Dillard, and asked him to secure the broken door on Brice's townhouse. By the time these details were attended to the fracas at the top of Snoqualmie Pass was over. Gary finished sealing the townhouse and returned to the office to await the return of the other officers.

Larry Piedmont had burst into the apartment with Durbin. He helped check the downed officers, found them to be without life-threatening injuries, and left the scene, leaving Durbin in charge there. He scrambled into

Chapter 34

his patrol car and followed Connie Lupine up the pass to the summit. By the time he arrived, Brice lay in the road, covered with blood, four bullets in his body. Paramedics were checking Vince Newly, but he was already dead. It was a shocking scene. It was impossible for Larry Piedmont to comprehend; he couldn't have been more than three minutes behind his sergeant. It had all happened so quickly. He remembered the night Gary Durbin's car struck that of the Bjustroms. He shook his head, then looked for his sergeant.

Connie leaned against the concrete pillar of the overpass, weak and shaking as the adrenaline passed through her body. She saw Larry approaching and took another drink from the water bottle in her hand. She made an attempt at composure before the officer spoke to her.

"Are you all right, Sarge?" he asked.

"I'll be okay," she replied, weakly. "I've never shot anyone before."

A highway patrolman took the initial statements. Names, times and badge numbers were taken. Connie stayed to give information to the investigator. A highway patrol supervisor was on the way to the scene; it was mandatory when there was a shooting. Connie told the on-scene trooper where she would be and left Larry Piedmont in charge of the scene for the sheriff's department. She rode, in silence, back to the office where Jodi was waiting. She didn't stop in the office, but went directly to the restroom where she washed her face and rinsed her mouth. She washed her hands twice and yet they still felt dirty. She looked into the mirror, deciding she looked terrible, took several deep breaths and walked back to her office.

"Are you going to be all right?" Were Jodi's first words.

The two talked for almost two hours. They discussed what had happened and why. Connie blamed herself for sending the two rookies around the back of the townhouse. She should have sent one of the seasoned officers, Piedmont or Durbin, with one of the young officers. She should never have allowed two inexperienced officers to cover the back.

"This whole thing is my fault," she said. "My stupidity got two of my officers hurt and Vince Newly killed."

"Don't be so hard on yourself." Jodi cautioned. "This could have happened to any one of us. No one could have predicted the way Brice reacted. He must have had some idea what he was being arrested for; I don't know how, but he must have figured it out. I don't know why Brice held so much hate for his ex-lover that he kept after Earl until he was sure Earl would do his dirty work. Brice had become lonely and bitter. He'd failed at life, so he overreacted and people got hurt. It's tough, but that happens in our business."

"Have you ever had to shoot anyone?"

"No, I've been lucky," he admitted.

"I don't know if I can live with this. This could happen again. I don't ever want to have to do this again." She was sobbing again.

"I know this is tough on you. You'll live through it. In the end you will be a stronger person. Don't try to justify anything now. And don't try to make decisions right now. It's not the right time. Take the rest of the day and write your report. The highway patrol captain will be in here after a while to interview you. Just try to have everything ready for him. We'll talk about the rest later. If you want a few days off, I'll arrange it. Do you want me to stay until the captain finishes his interview?"

"No, I'll be all right. Just feeling sorry for myself, I guess. I'll call you if I need you." She dried her eyes and stood up. "Thanks for being here for me, Jodi."

Jodi went back to his office to call the sheriff. He would want to be kept abreast of all the details; the press would be relentless.

His next call was to Tom Logan. He apologized for failing to call him before the arrest warrant was served, and gave the reporter a run-down on the activities of the afternoon. He didn't know the names of Vincent Newly's wife or children. There would be an investigation by the Highway Patrol, but at this point it was being considered a justified shooting. Connie Lupine had performed admirably under dire and stressful circumstances. The news came just in time for the six o'clock edition.

It was a little before seven when he finished with Captain Aaron Donlevey. The two men knew each other professionally and often talked on the telephone. They seldom met face to face. Donlevey assured Captain Eagle that the shooting was justified and that he believed Sergeant Lupine had acted with good judgment and with a great deal of courage. One of the surviving Highway Patrol officers told his captain that he would be dead if it weren't for Connie Lupine. Captain Donlevey was going to submit her name to the governor for a commendation for bravery.

By the time Jodi reached home, he was exhausted. He answered all the questions his wife and boys could ask. He ate dinner, showered and collapsed into bed.

Tuesday promised to be a continuation of Monday. The press was either in his office or on the telephone most of the day. The governor's office had called, asking about Connie Lupine. He referred that call to Joan Woods. By late afternoon he wished the calls would just stop.

A call came from Harry Makin, the funeral director. Harry asked if Jodi would deliver some kind of message or eulogy at the funeral tomorrow. Jodi said he would. The funeral had been moved from the Funeral Chapel to the

Chapter 34

Elementary school auditorium. The chapel would not accommodate the kind of crowd that promised to assemble for this funeral. Jodi would, of course, be one of the pallbearers.

A surprise call came late in the afternoon. One of the two men involved in the Emerald Empire Investment Corporation was calling. Jodi had met a few millionaires in his time, but this was the first time he had ever talked with a billionaire.

"Do you know who I am, Captain Eagle?" The man on the other end of the line asked.

"Yes, I know who you are. What can I do for you?"

"As you may or may not know, my partner and I are investors, with Linda Campbell, in a land development company. I am calling you because I understand that you are a close friend of the family. Is that true?" the soft voice inquired.

"Yes, Earl was my best friend. His family is like my own."

"I'm sorry, I never met Earl. All our dealings have been with Linda. My partner and I are fond of her. She has been a good business partner."

"What is it that I can do for you?" Jodi wanted to get to the point of the call.

"We'll be at the funeral tomorrow. However, we want to do something for the family. It will be impossible to talk with Linda tomorrow, and we didn't want to bother her during her time of grief." There was a slight pause. "We would like for you to tell Linda that we are setting up a scholarship in Earl's name. I am faxing you the details now. We would like for you to tell her and her son that we are praying for them in their time of grief."

"I'll do that."

"We would also like you to give her the details of the scholarship we have set up."

"The family will appreciate that. Thank you for being their friend."

"I wish there were something more personal we could do, but time doesn't allow us to indulge in many human niceties. We hope our presence won't cause any publicity problems for her and her son. Thank you for your help, Captain Eagle. It has been a pleasure talking with you."

"My pleasure, any time." Jodi said, hanging up the telephone.

Joan was coming into the office with a stack of papers from the fax.

"These are all addressed to you." She handed them to her boss. "Do you see who they are from?"

"Yes, I see. He told me he was sending me a fax. Thanks, Joan. Bring me some three-by-five cards, will you?"

She left the office, disappointed that she was not included.

His final act of the day was to call Lieutenant Burnside into the office to be sure he was ready for tomorrow. The funeral would take all day. Jodi would not be in.

Jodi was just locking his desk when Eileen called. She wanted to know what time he was coming home. Linda and Matthew were coming for dinner.

Mount Si was clear of clouds and the sun reflected off the dark green trees. Jodi wished he had time to go to Torval Laxo's for a sweat, but that was out of the question. He would spend the evening with his family and his friends. Life was changing in the valley, he thought. Maybe it's time to do something else. For the first time he gave some thought to the offer his old friend, Pete Kaufman, had made. If he took the job, and if Pete was elected, would he be happy? He would be farther away from the action. He would have that long commute to work every day. His duties would be drastically changed. He didn't want to have to think about it tonight.

CHAPTER 35

Early Wednesday morning Matthew drove his mother to the Eagle home where the two families were to have breakfast together. Eileen had bacon frying in the pan and an electric griddle was steaming with six plump pancakes. The boys had volunteered to set the table. Jodi was in the living room drinking his fourth cup of coffee and reading the morning edition of the *Seattle Post Intelligencer*.

The front door was open to the warm summer morning. Linda called through the screen door.

"Good morning. Anyone awake in there?"

Jodi put his newspaper down on the coffee table. "Come on in. Breakfast is almost ready."

Matthew said good morning to Jodi, then deserted the older folks to find Philip and Kyle.

Jodi hugged Linda. "How about some coffee?"

"I'd like that," she said. She looked at Jodi with sad eyes. "I wish today was over."

"Me too, Linda. Me too."

In the kitchen Eileen directed traffic and told everyone where to sit. She offered juice and coffee to all. A large platter of pancakes was set in the center of the table. She pulled a platter of crisp bacon from the oven, where it had been warming. Waving the spatula in her hand, like a bandleader with a baton, she inventoried the items on the table. Satisfied everything was in place she joined the others at the table. There had been many mornings like this when Earl was alive and well. It was good to have both families together again.

The funeral was scheduled for one p.m. At eleven-thirty Matthew ushered his mother to the car, taking her home to prepare. It was only a three-block drive from home to the school where the ceremony would take place. The funeral director would pick up the family at ten minutes before the hour. Jodi drove his family to the school in the family sedan. Everyone was dressed in suits and ties. Eileen wore a black dress with black shoes and a single strand of pearls. A brightly colored, beaded belt wrapped her middle and was tied at her left hip. After all these years Jodi was still thrilled by her beauty.

Eileen and the two boys were seated in the family section. Jodi was escorted to the pallbearers' row by Harry Makin's assistant who, upon giving them their instructions, promptly left them to escort other mourners to their seats.

Jodi turned in his seat to watch the crowd assemble. He was surprised to see not only the number of mourners, but also the variety of dignitaries attending. The crowd grew as the minutes passed. The mood was somber. Jodi watched as people who had not seen each other for some time, met and shook hands in the foyer. All the folding chairs on the gym floor filled and the crowd overflowed into the bleachers. At five minutes before the hour, Linda and Matthew were escorted to their seats. The soft organ music played by Mary Lafferty settled the whispering throng. *Rock of Ages* was Earl's favorite.

The entire school gymnasium was filled with flowers. Wreaths and garlands, bouquets and baskets, potted live plants and artificial flowers, the sweet aroma of the flowers was almost overpowering. Harry Makin walked down the aisle, checking every detail before the start of the ceremony. As he passed the row of pallbearers Jodi stopped him.

"Listen, Harry," Jodi began. "It's going to be impossible to take all these flowers to the grave site. Why don't you have your guys take what they can and send the rest to the senior center, the visitor center and the churches. If any businesses want some, let them have them. It would be a shame to waste all those flowers, but there are too many. Can you do that for us?"

"Of course, Mr. Eagle. That's a nice gesture." And he turned to walk back up the aisle.

The minister walked slowly to the podium, the music became more audible, and he gestured with his outstretched arms for the assembly to stand. The text of *Rock of Ages* was printed in the pamphlet handed out at the door. Everyone joined in. A prayer was given. The religious rite lasted a half hour. The words were a comfort to the wife and son of the man lying in the box in front of the dais. Jodi joined nearly everyone in the auditorium with his tears. Eileen put an arm around Linda as she sobbed deeply. Another prayer and it was Jodi's turn to speak.

He took a small stack of three-by-five cards from his breast pocket and placed them on the stand, and adjusted the height of the microphone, which whistled momentarily, then quieted.

He looked out over the crowd. "We are gathered here to honor a friend." He paused, trying to control the quiver in his voice. "We are here to honor a man who, in some way, has touched the lives of everyone in this room. I have known Earl Campbell for most of my adult life. In college, we played football together. By accident we lived in the same town, as neighbors, for more than twenty years.

"Earl Campbell typified what America is all about. When we think about Earl, we don't think of him as a successful black man. We think of him as a successful man. He refused to be treated in any other manner. He never asked for anything special, but what he gave was special. He came to town as a young real estate salesman. He became the owner of a successful real estate business. His untiring efforts have beautified this town. He fought to improve access to the city. He organized volunteers to build playgrounds for the children in the city. He persuaded the city to give up a parcel of land it owned and, with volunteer labor and equipment, turned it into the little league park, with two diamonds, two practice fields and concession stands.

"He led the crusade to raise money for the renovation of the city swimming pool. This fine auditorium is the result of Earl Campbell's efforts. He organized summer sports for kids, and encouraged them to study, to assure themselves a better future.

"Earlier I saw Curtis Heagman in the room. Curtis, would you please stand up?" A boy of maybe eighteen years stood up. "I don't want to embarrass you Curtis, but, I want to tell the people about you." He turned his eyes back to the audience. "Two years ago Curtis was on a path of self-destruction. He was the poster child for juvenile delinquency. He was smoking pot, committing thefts, dropped out of school and his future was in doubt. Earl took this young man under his wing. He helped the boy stop using drugs. He got the young man a job. He persuaded the school board to let him use a tutor to catch up on his studies. In September, Curtis will come back to school, rejoining his original class, and he'll graduate next spring. He is a young man with purpose and self-esteem. Thank you Curtis, you can sit down." There was scattered applause for the boy. "Earl did all this when he was too ill to work.

"In the audience, I see Governor Lock, governor of the State of Washington. Earl was appointed to the State of Washington Human Rights Commission. He had also served on the State Board of Realtors. I suspect that, since he came all the way up here from Olympia, the governor has a great respect for what Earl did for his commissions." The governor sat, arms crossed, nodding his head.

"Also in the audience are two young men from Redmond. They are business associates of Linda and Earl Campbell. They have asked me to announce that there will be a scholarship fund set up in his name. This fund will guarantee three scholarships each year to students from North Bend. The top qualifier will receive five thousand dollars toward his college education. The second qualifier will receive three thousand dollars and the third qualifier will receive two thousand dollars. Earl would have been proud to know he had something to do with helping young people prepare for the future. This scholarship fund will be administered by the North Bend School Board." A huge round of applause erupted. The two computer executives seemed pleased by Jodi's explanation of this fund. He had made it sound like it was meant, not as an advertisement, but as an unselfish donation to the children of North Bend in the name of Earl Campbell.

"Seven years ago, tragedy struck our little town. Five of our children were murdered. One of those children was the son of Linda and Earl Campbell. The only bitterness Earl ever harbored was against the person who killed his son. After the death of their son, Darren, Linda took the reins of the family business. She finished the raising of their remaining son, Matthew. Earl became too distraught to work, though he still organized and directed community tasks from his home.

"In the years since the murders, Gil Stevens and his wife have moved away and since divorced. Ben Wilson and his wife lost their home and moved to Oregon. John and Ruth Ng were particularly tragic. Their daughter was the third victim of this killer. John moved with his wife to California. She is frail and in poor health. John works as a farm hand in the Sacramento Valley. Earl's son was victim number four. Number five and the final one, was Bobby Carstairs. His mother was struggling with life before his death and lost the battle six years ago. Mona Carstairs committed suicide, despondent over the death of her son.

"Many of you may know that Earl found the person responsible for these deaths. He tracked the killer down and extracted his pound of flesh. He was responsible for the death of the killer of these children. By law he was wrong. We cannot justify vigilantism within our society. Earl came home, satisfied his life was now complete. He confessed to his crime and passed away.

"I will not judge Earl. That is the domain of a higher power. We may have different religions, but each of us believes in a just and merciful God. It is up to Him now. For my part, I will remember all the good he has done for our town. I will remember the people he has helped to a better life. I will remember his untiring efforts for the children of this community.

"I have special, personal memories of Earl Campbell. Those are the memories I will keep. It is with great respect that I say to my neighbors and to Earl's family, Linda and Matthew, I am proud to say that Earl Campbell was my friend." Jodi was having trouble holding back the tears. He picked up the stack of cards, returning them to his suit coat pocket.

"We will sing a final hymn and the pastor will give a final prayer. Thank you all for coming."

The reverend returned to the podium for the final words. Jodi had returned to his seat. He looked across the aisle at Eileen and Linda. They were both crying. Linda saw him and gave him a thankful nod and a pained smile. Her face was streaked with tears.

The minister directed the throng to file down the outside aisles to the casket and leave by way of the center aisle, waiting outside until the family was loaded into the limousine. He came down from the stage to say some quiet words to Linda and her son.

The line moved quickly and in a matter of minutes the hall was empty except for the pallbearers. The six men rolled the casket to the front door and helped Harry Makin load it into the hearse.

Jodi met his family at the car. He turned on his headlights and followed the hearse to Fall City road and on to the cemetery where a site had been prepared. The sun was bright and the crowd large. Eileen and the boys joined Linda and Matthew in seats near the grave. Jodi and the others carried the bronze-colored casket to its final resting place, next to Darren Campbell.

The final readings were done and the final prayers offered. Linda lingered at the gravesite for several minutes. Harry Makin told her he thought it was time to go; the crew needed time to cover the grave.

It surprised Linda to see how many people returned to the gymnasium. It especially surprised her to see that the governor and his aides had come to say a private word to the widow and her son. Linda's notable business partners appeared at the reception with the same purpose. None of the celebrities stayed long, but each had kind words for the family. Bill Gates looked for and found Jodi. He expressed his appreciation for the way he handled the eulogy, especially the statements about the scholarship. They shook his hand and left he school in a private limousine.

As the crowd began to thin, Harry Makin offered an escape for the widow and her son. The Eagle family followed a short time later. Assistants had taken some of the flowers to the Campbell home. Some were delivered to the office, too. Cards, guest books and other memorabilia were gathered to be taken to Linda tomorrow. There would be a lot of thank-you cards to be written.

Back at home Eileen made coffee. Jodi sat in the coolness of his living room, thinking about Earl, when he heard a faint knocking on the front door. Standing on the front porch was Mike Masters.

"Mike," Jodi greeted, "this is a real surprise. What are you doing here?"

"I had talked with your office the other day and they told me about you and Earl Campbell. I didn't know you two were so close. I'm sorry things turned out this way. I just wanted to come down and pay my respects to you and your friend's family."

"Come in, Mike. I want you to meet my wife and sons."

The Alaska State Trooper followed Jodi to the kitchen where Eileen was pouring coffee. The boys had come to see who the visitor was and joined them all at the kitchen table. Jodi introduced Mike to his family and the group began to swap stories. The boys were especially interested in learning about Alaska, the Great Land.

A room was prepared for the guest. Eileen called Linda and invited her and Matthew to join them for breakfast in the morning. Linda accepted.

Mike gave Jodi a thumbnail version of the final outcome of the Dava Bennett case. He thanked the deputy for his assistance in bringing the case to an end. Jodi talked with Mike about the offer he had received from Pete Kaufman. The two men discussed the pros and cons of accepting the offer.

"How long can you stay?" Jodi asked.

"I'll have to go home tomorrow night. I thought I might go over this paperwork with you in your office tomorrow. Will you have time for that?"

"Yes, of course." Jodi answered. "I'll take you downtown and introduce you to Pete and the sheriff. It'll give you a chance to see the big city."

It was late when the men turned out the lights. They climbed the stairs, said good night and disappeared into their separate rooms.

Jodi was tired. He showered, found clean pajamas and fell into bed beside his wife. It was the best night's sleep he had in years.

CPSIA information can be obtained
at www.ICGtesting.com
Printed in the USA
BVHW030616180922
647215BV00023B/560